Bam
I hope you
enjoy read
this as muc
I loved wr
K F

Winter Roses

By

K.F. Coffman

This book is a work of fiction. Places, events, and situations in this story are purely fictional. Any resemblance to actual persons, living or dead, is coincidental.

ISBN: 0-9766-2600-4 (Paperback)
ISBN: 0-9766-2601-2 (Hard Cover)

Library of Congress Control Number: 2005901595

This book is printed on acid free paper.

Printed in the United States of America
Carter Lake, IA

Cover drawing by Artist Keith A. Goc
Brother-In-Law of Author.

K.F. Coffman Publishing - rev. 01/26/05

Dedication

To My Children

To my first born, my daughter Randi, Daddy's Little Girl.
You show me a new way to love each and every day.
I am so very proud of you in ways words could not express.
To Kelly Jr. my little clown, you make me laugh and light up my life
in ways words could never say. You make me complete.
To my baby boy Carl, what can I say that could begin to express my
love and pride in you, you are my hero now and always.
Without the three of you in my life there would be
a void that could never be filled.
I love you all with all my heart, my soul, my very being.

Also in Memory of my late Father, Dale Coffman
He didn't live long enough to see my first book
published, let alone a second. Even though he
couldn't read or write, he still understood
the concept and would have been proud.

Special thanks to my Brother-In-Law Keith Goc
for his unbelievable artistic ability. You took
an idea from my minds eye and the final result
was this remarkable cover drawing.
I love you and thank you Keith.

Chapter 1

She lazily rolled and stretched, almost catlike, desperately trying to shake off the slumber of the night before. She shook her head gently from side to side trying to clear her thoughts and focus on the clock beside her bed. Like trying to find your way through a thick and murky fog, it was difficult to say the least, to focus and find her way to the reality of a new morning.

As her eyes slowly focused to see the time on her clock, she sat straight up in bed as though an unseen force had just poked her with a sharp object. "Oh my" she shrieked as she sprang from the bed with a newfound life and energy. She had overslept, or so she thought, and grabbed her robe as she dashed madly for the door.

She took the steps two at a time as she headed straight for the kitchen to start a pot of fresh coffee. "How could she sleep in like this" she thought as she hurriedly prepared coffee and headed for the refrigerator? She flung open the door and grabbed bacon, eggs, and whatever else she could bundle into her arms and went to the counter to unload her haul.

Pans banged, bacon sizzled, coffee was brewing, orange juice poured and on the table. The toaster sitting patiently on the counter waiting to play its role in this morning ritual, she sat and listened for the shower upstairs. She strained to hear, but only silence and the ticking of the kitchen clock filled the air. She was sure by now that her husband was done with his shower and busily getting dressed, ready to face yet another hectic day at work.

She quickly went to the stove and removed the bacon sizzling and popping in the pan, drained the grease and cracked a couple of eggs into it. She reached over and pushed the toaster down with one hand as the other was preparing her husbands eggs. At times like this she wished she had two or three more hands, but, she didn't oversleep very often and was sure that she could have everything ready and on the table before he reached the kitchen doorway.

She removed the eggs just as toast popped up from the toaster. She quickly buttered it and placed it on the plate with the eggs and bacon and sat it on the table by his orange juice and morning paper. Just as she was ready to breathe a sigh of relief, she heard the coffee pot gurgling. It's way of letting her know that the morning shot of caffeine she so desperately needed this morning was ready.

She poured two cups and placed his on the table by the rest of his meal and sat down to ingest her first cup of "morning wake me up" and wait for her husband to enter. She slyly smiled and was actually quite proud of herself. She did it and he will never know that she overslept and raced around like a madwoman trying frantically to play catch up this morning.

She looked at the clock and sipped her coffee, wondering what in the world could be keeping him. He was always very punctual, reality once again came crashing down upon her like a ton of bricks. "Why did she keep doing this" she asked herself, "how many more mornings would she keep doing this" she silently thought to herself? The harsh and cold reality was her husband would not be coming down for breakfast, not this morning nor any other morning for that matter.

It had been just over a year since he announced that he was leaving and she had to endure his "it isn't you, it's me" speech. He had assured her that it wasn't anything she had done nor was there anything she could do to make things better. It was just something he had decided he had to do and knew that it would be hard on her but he had faith that she would recover and be able to go on with her life.

She wondered in silence as the tears once again welled up in her eyes, "was this his idea of recovering and going on with her life?" She knew that she had to stop putting herself through this. Something she had caught herself doing less and less lately, nonetheless, something she still did.

She still found herself looking for his laundry, cooking his breakfast, waiting for him to walk through the door at the end of the day. Things that had become so routine for her over the years were now the very things that continually tore her heart out again and again every time she caught herself doing them.

"This must be his idea of getting over it and going on with her life" she thought in silence as tears streamed down her cheeks and dropped onto the sleeve of her robe. She quickly cleared her head and busily went about the task of preparing another plate of food before the first plate got cold. She would have to get her children up soon anyway and no sense letting perfectly good food go to waste she thought.

As she went about preparing more food she faintly heard the stirring and clambering of footsteps upstairs. "Wow" she thought to herself, at least one of the heathens, I mean, little Angels are up on their own. She usually had to threaten them with garden hose and brass bands to get them up and moving in the morning. She wondered what could possibly be different this morning.

Now she could hear arguing coming from upstairs, she was sure they both were up and around and it was evident "they live" she thought to herself and smiled. It was her daughter that appeared first with her son following a close second. "Morning Mom" they chimed, almost as though they had rehearsed it.

"Sit down you two, breakfast is almost ready and I don't want to hear any excuses on why you can't eat or don't have time" she told them as she placed the second plate on the table. They knew better than to even consider arguing with her or trying to get out of it, they were going to have breakfast this morning even if it killed them.

Nothing out of the ordinary this morning, small talk, "how's school," and the occasional "pass the salt and pepper" were exchanged as the children ate. As she cleared the table and cleaned up, her daughter informed her that they would not be home for dinner tonight.

They explained that tonight was the first football game of the season and they would attend the pep rally right after school, get something to eat while they were out, and be straight home after the game.

"So that was it" she thought, "it wasn't my fantastic, irresistible cooking this morning that got them up and running." She listened to first her daughter then her son as they told her all about how good the team was this year and how they "could go all the way to state this year."

She simply smiled, nodded and turned her head to and fro as if watching a tennis match, thinking how very lucky she was to have them in her life. If it hadn't been for the kids, she didn't know how she could have gotten through the last year as well as she had, they were lifesavers for her.

As she put the morning dishes in the dishwasher and got her second cup of coffee, the kids went about gathering their books and necessities of the day. Preparing to leave her alone for yet another event-less day. The only difference between today and any other day she thought, would be that they would not be home shortly after school, making this an empty and lonely day for her.

She actually looked forward to the kids coming home from school, it filled the house with life and activity, something it lacked while they were gone. "Kisses, good-byes, thanks for breakfast, and Mom can I borrow a few dollars?" out of the way, they headed out the door and told her they would see her later tonight.

It was her daughter that hugged her and kissed her cheek and said "you did it again this morning didn't you" as she headed for the door. "You have to let go Mom, we have" her daughter told her. "Besides, it's his loss Mom, he screwed up, not us" she said to help comfort her mother before she headed out the door.

"I know honey" she told her daughter, "I am getting better though. At least it isn't every day anymore" she told her daughter and hugged her tight as she pushed them both toward the door and watched them as they pulled out of the driveway. She frantically waved and blew kisses until they were out of sight, then sat down at the table, sipped her coffee, and once again let the tears flow.

"How in the world had she gotten to this point in her life" she wondered as she sipped her coffee and listened to the silence that surrounded her. They had been married for almost 20 years, were high school sweethearts and always voted the couple most likely to be together forever.

Steve, her husband, or to be precise, her ex-husband, was on all the school sports teams it seemed. She was always there to cheer him on, she was his biggest and most devoted fan. Diane didn't know what it was like to not have him in her life, and, never thought she would find out either.

She couldn't remember a time in her life when he hadn't been a part of it in one way or another. They had known each other all their lives. He had always been the one that she just knew she would end up spending the rest of her life with. Nothing could change that, or so she thought, until he changed all that for her.

They had gone to school together since elementary school, all the way through high school. He had been her prom date, they were homecoming king and queen, prom king and queen, done everything together and always, and I mean always, were together.

You never saw one without the other being there, or close by. They were always inseparable. They had planned on attending college together and had sat on many a starlit night and planned each and every detail of their lives together. In such detail that anybody in the world that knew them couldn't see them making it happen.

They were the couple that love stories are written about, endlessly in love and unshakably devoted to each other. It was as though each and every breath they took was a shared breath. Their heart's beat as one, one mind, one soul, never to be separated.

People even made fun of them at times because they could finish each others sentences. It was as though they each knew what the other was thinking before they even thought it, it was uncanny. Steve's family were farmers, fourth generation to be exact, and Diane's father was a district manager for a chain of department stores. He was a typical country boy and she was a city girl all the way, yet they fit so perfectly together. One would think they had been separated at birth or something.

Steve had planned on attending college and getting a degree in agriculture and Diane was going to major in business. That was no surprise to anyone though. He always teased her that he could use a good business mind to help him on the farm. He said that maybe she could teach him a thing or two.

During his senior year though, his father had passed away suddenly and his dreams and hopes of college soon began to dissipate. Being the devoted and loving son he was, he concentrated on picking up where his Dad had left off, guaranteeing the farm would stay in the family. Even then, she supported him in every decision he made and followed him down every path he chose to take, never looking back or second guessing him.

After high school she decided to stand by him in all he did and every way she could. She attended the local community college instead of going away to school.

She just could not bear the thought of being separated from him and she just knew in her heart that he needed her love and support to help him through each and every day. She soon found out that she was right and was his salvation in some of the most uncertain times of his life. He couldn't even imagine his life without her in it.

Instead of business management she quickly became interested in architecture, she was a natural in drafting and several of her designs went on to win awards. He was so very proud of her in all she did and it seemed that the sky would be the limit with talent like hers. He couldn't have been happier for her.

Steve did feel a little guilty though, in the back of his mind he always felt as though he were holding her back in some way. He just knew that she could be a huge success if she were to move away and make a name for herself.

Something that she sensed and always told him, "don't even think about me moving away." She knew that she just couldn't bear to leave him and go out on her own.

They even talked several times about her opening her own business after she graduated from school. Something the small town they lived in could desperately use, and again, Steve was just sure that she would succeed in everything she did.

They married shortly after she graduated college and the event was one the whole town turned out for. It was everything she could have ever hoped for or dreamed of, and she just knew in her heart that this was the beginning of a brand-new life for both of them.

They of course lived on his family's farm in south central Iowa, and she adapted quite nicely to country living, he couldn't be prouder of her. The one thing that kept haunting Steve was the fact that he knew how truly talented she was and felt that he was keeping her from fulfilling her own dreams. Little did he know that in her heart and mind, he had already made her every dream come true.

Steve quickly found that his remarks about being able to use a good business mind on the farm were more fact than fiction. She was remarkable and helped him in ways that no one could ever imagine or guess. He gave her all the credit for turning his father's farm around and making it a very profitable and lucrative business and there seemed to be no end in sight to their success.

It wasn't long though before Steve's mother passed too and farming just didn't seem to be that important to him anymore. He even thought seriously about selling the operation and moving to the city where he knew she could pursue a career that he knew she was destined to excel in. Diane of course wouldn't hear of it and told him that under no circumstances would she consent to something that ridiculous.

Besides, she had a surprise for Steve, she had just received confirmation from the doctor that she was pregnant. She just couldn't wait for him to be done in the field that day so she could tell him. She was so intent on telling someone or she thought she would burst, so, she called her parents and told them they were about to become grandparents. Her mom shrieked so loud Diane swore she could hear her without the phone, her dad couldn't be happier.

Diane was an only child, as was Steve, and this would be their first grandchild. She just knew that they would spoil the poor child rotten. "Have you told Steve yet?" her mom asked, "no I'm waiting for him to come in from the field now" Diane told her. "Well, it will be our little secret that we knew first" her mom assured her before hanging up.

It was late afternoon when she heard the tractor rumbling in from the field, and she greeted him at the back porch with a huge glass of fresh iced tea. His favorite on a hot sweltering summer day like today.

She held the glass out to him then quickly pulled it back, just out of his reach. "What do you say" she asked before taunting him with the cold refreshment he wanted so badly? "Please" he said. "Nope, not even close" was her playful response.

"I give up then" he said as he reached quickly to grab the glass before she could once again pull it back. This time he was successful in his attempt and pulled her close and kissed her deeply. "I love you" he said as tea spilled over them both then quickly finished with "thank you."

They both laughed and she teased that now they both would need a shower, he quickly took her by the hand and led her upstairs to the bathroom. "After you" he said as he pulled the shower curtain aside. She quickly undressed and got in, he didn't waste any time in joining her.

They showered but one couldn't say they showered quickly, he loved it when she got into her playful moods and loved it even more when the end result was lovemaking in the shower.

It was always sensual and passionate and today was no different, although he did feel that something was different today. More like sensed it, she was absolutely glowing today. Sex between them had always been earth pounding but today it seemed to have something more involved, something more complete and special.

They toweled off and she went to the bedroom to dress, for the second time today. She was about to burst and just blurt out the news as he finished drying off. But, wanted to see the expression on his face when she told him, so, she decided to wait till dinner. She told him to hurry and get dressed because she needed help with dinner. "Yeah, yeah, you wash I'll dry" he jibbed as he quickly dressed and followed her down the stairs.

Preparing dinner seemed to go quickly and uneventful for the most part, small talk and playful slaps on her bottom was the norm around this kitchen and tonight was no different. As she set the table and started bringing in the food he quickly noticed that tonight was different, seriously different.

She had the linen tablecloth on, the good china and silver were laid out. Candles were placed all over and lit, "oh man" he thought, "I forgot something, but what is it?" He wracked his brain as she finished and sat down beside him at the table. "Ok, spill it, what did I forget?" he quickly stammered. "A birthday, an anniversary, what?"

She just couldn't keep it from him any longer and smiled a smile that lit up the entire world. "You didn't forget anything, honest Daddy" she said as she took her fork in her hand and started to eat. Steve dropped his fork, right into his mashed potatoes and dropped to his knees beside her. "What did you say?" he asked her over and over. "I said, you didn't forget anything," "not that part, what else did you say?"

"Oh, you mean the part about you being a Daddy?" she quickly asked as tears formed in her eyes. He hugged his wife, and, as tears flowed down his tanned face he asked, "are you sure?" "Yes, I got the call from the doctor today, the results were positive, we're having a baby" she said. That was one of the happiest nights of their lives, the other would be about two years later when she would tell him she was pregnant again

With the news of becoming new parents came new worries and responsibilities and he was great. He was attentive, loving, caring, a woman couldn't have asked for a better husband.

She just knew that he would be the best father ever, he was a natural. They talked in more detail this time about selling the farm and moving to town. He worried about her being in the house alone while he was in the field or working the livestock.

It was beginning to take a toll on him and was apparent to even her, no matter how much he tried to hide it. She sat while he worked during the day and tossed around some ideas. She made a few plans and even did some designs and drawings, she was finally ready to spring her idea on him.

As they ate that evening, she told him that instead of selling the farm and moving to the city, why not bring the city a little closer to them. They talked it over and she showed him her plans and drawings. It made perfect sense to him and they decided that instead of selling the farm they would sell parcels and develop a housing project.

It seemed to fit them perfectly, he could stop working from dawn to dusk waiting for good weather and market fluctuations to subside and do something he loved. He was always good with his hands and loved construction. He even worked for a local contractor during the winter to keep a steady income in the house and he always knew that she was a natural at drafting and architecture.

They decided to wait till spring of the next year, that way the harvest would be done and clearing of the land could begin. Besides, they would have to sell the livestock, farm equipment and start plotting out the site for new construction to begin. They were close enough to town that city water and sewer and natural gas lines could be brought in making it that much more attractive to prospective buyers.

The closest town was only 8 miles away and was experiencing

tremendous growth. The town was still a small town at heart. Complete with town square and courthouse that gave it that small town appeal yet was sprawling toward the outskirts giving it all the conveniences of big city living. They even had a good sized mall built not long ago.

They planned on dividing the land into acreage's, something that always seemed to appeal to future homeowners. It seemed like everyone wants to be in the country with all the luxuries of the city, this would be the best of both worlds. They even set aside land for commercial development. Maybe a convenience store, possibly a medical clinic, some retail shops, truly the best of both worlds indeed.

Spring came, everything was ready and their plan could finally be put into action, their dream was finally going to become a reality. They worked long and hard and before they knew it a new community in the country was taking on a new life of it's own. They couldn't believe how quickly things came together, even the weather cooperated.

South-central Iowa is usually known for it's harsh and somewhat severe winters complete with mounds of snow. Bitter icy winds that can cut right through one and ice covering everything. Mother Nature was on their side it seemed and her present to them was mild winters, construction went on year round the first two years as a result of it.

They were successful beyond even their wildest dreams and suddenly making ends meet seemed to be a thing of the past. She designed their new dream home and Steve built it with meticulous care and pride. "It was built with love" she always told him. Soon the dream that started as drawings in her pad were thriving family homes and successful businesses and it seemed that things could only get better for them.

As the demand for their homes became overwhelming and supply was running drastically low, they soon started buying land around them. Their tiny development was soon becoming more than they ever dreamed possible.

Steve was busy and happy doing something he loved and she was finally putting both her natural business sense and love to design to use. Something she never thought she would do. All the bills were paid in full, they had money in the bank, more than either of them could have dreamed possible, with no end in sight.

They finally had it all she thought, two wonderful children, a business that she was an equal part of and it was prospering beyond belief, and a beautiful new home. She only wished Steve's mom and dad could have lived long enough to see his success. She could remember them both saying they expected great things from him.

He was always the one to succeed in everything he did and was not good with defeat at any cost. They would have had a bit of a problem with his decision to divide the land and develop it, of this she was sure. She also was sure they would have come around and supported him in every way they could. It wouldn't have taken them long to "warm up" to the idea when they started seeing the end result.

His dad would have been particularly proud of Steve, he always had a love of working with his hands and was always doing some kind of home repair or remodeling project. He always told Diane how good it felt to know that he had made something with his own hands, and she was sure that Steve had inherited his father's love of building.

All in all their little project had outperformed anything they could have dreamed and soon was bigger than life itself. Diane was sure that his parents would have been as proud of him as her and the kids were. The only thing that could have made it any better would have been if his parents could have lived long enough to see their grandchildren. She was sure that the kids would have been as much the center of their world as they were to her parents.

Those were much happier times, a time that she could have never dreamed would come to an end. Yet here she was, just her and the children and Steve off doing God knows what, or who.

Suddenly she was snapped out of her daze and her walk through the past by the ringing of the phone. "Now who in the world could that be" she thought as she was brought back to earth and went to answer the phone.

Chapter 2

"Hello" she said as she picked up the phone, hoping it would be Steve telling her what a terrible mistake he had made. "Hi mom, can you bring our jackets to town if you come in today?" her daughter Debbie asked. She continued, "Mike and I walked off and forgot to grab our jackets this morning and it's supposed to be kind of cool tonight."

Diane assured her daughter that she would make the trip to town and leave the jackets in her car. "That way you two will have them when you need them" she told her daughter. "Thanks mom, you're the greatest" Debbie said as she hung up the phone.

"Well now, what to do, what to do, such a busy day ahead of me today" she thought as she walked up the stairs. Heading for her bedroom to get her shower and dressed for the day.

She looked at herself in the mirror as she headed toward the bathroom to shower. She was 42, about 5 foot 9 inches tall, was slender as she only weighed around 130 pounds and had the most beautiful red hair that fell down her back and cascaded to her butt.

"Damn, I have a nice butt" she said as she admired herself in the mirror. She had full and very firm breasts and looked more like her daughter's sister than her mother.

She got carded every time she bought wine. Although she had to admit that getting carded excited and flattered her, she really never thought of herself as anything more than average. Yet here was this beautiful, desirable, voluptuous woman staring back at her from the mirror. As she turned and checked herself out from every angle one thought kept coming to her mind. "If I am as good as I look, why did he leave?"

His "it's not you it's me" speech kept ringing in her ears, that had been a year ago and yet it was if she were hearing it again for the first time. She couldn't figure out what had went wrong, why he decided out of nowhere that he just had to leave. She could have at least understood if he had left her for another woman, but, that wasn't the case.

At least she didn't think it was the case, she had never heard anything in the year since he left that would suggest that he was being unfaithful to her. And, in a small town atmosphere like they lived in, everyone knew everything.

The rumors would have been running rampant if he had been sleeping around on her, she was sure that he wasn't. "Oh well" she thought as she headed for the shower, she had things to do today and had to get around and started or she knew that the whole day would be a total waste.

Shower done, make up applied and dressed in blue jean shorts and a white tank top she went down to look for the kids' jackets. She couldn't have the poor darlings getting a chill because she hadn't taken them their jackets. "Yeah right" she smiled to herself as she gathered the jackets, her purse, her cell phone and a cold soda from the refrigerator and headed out to her car.

She decided to pick up something fast and easy for dinner tonight as it would only be her anyway. As she started the car her mind was making a mental list of what she would do, where she would go and what she needed and didn't need to do while she was out.

If everything went well, she could get all her errands done, get home and put everything away and lay out by the pool for a while and soak up some sun. "Sounds like a plan to me" she thought to herself as she backed her car out of the drive.

She was snapped out of her mental inventory process by the honking of a horn, it was the man from down the road. She had backed right out in front of him without realizing she had done it.

"She quickly rolled down her window and said "I'm terribly sorry" over and over again. The man just waved and laughed and told her it was a good thing that one of them was paying attention or they both could have been in trouble. She laughed, apologized again and drove off ahead of him.

She caught herself looking in the rear-view mirror from time to time, catching glimpses of her neighbor. After all she thought, "I'm not dead ya know." He had been one of the last to buy land and build before Steve played his Houdini act and disappeared. He too was single, well divorced, his wife ran off with half his money and his business partner, she remembers feeling so bad for him when it all happened.

He told her it was the best thing to happen to him, he now owns all of the business and his profits have never been better. They still manage to laugh about that and it makes her smile to think of it, something she doesn't do on a regular basis anymore.

His name is Greg and he is tall, tanned and very well built. It is very obvious that he spends time at the gym and takes pride in how he looks. He has dark hair with grey highlights and the most beautiful blue eyes she had ever seen. "Damn" she thinks aloud as she steals another glimpse in the rear-view, "I can't believe that I'm still looking at him."

Several men had asked her out after the "respectable" waiting period, but she had turned them all down. She just didn't feel like getting on with her life just yet. Maybe she was being a fool and hanging on to hope that Steve would come back and tell her what a fool he had been and they would still live happily ever after.

In her heart she knew that the odds of that happening were astronomical, yet she couldn't help but hang on to hope. And she knew that Steve was now seeing someone new, he either kept it quiet for a while so people wouldn't talk or had just met her and started seeing her. Either way she knew that Steve was involved and she was fairly certain that getting back together with her was not on his agenda.

Maybe she should start to date she thought as she drove along. Her daughter Debbie was always telling her that she could "hook her up" with one of her friends' single dads or something. Just then something caught her eye, as she looked in the rear-view she noticed that Greg had his signal on and was turning. She waved as he turned and saw that he waved back as he sped out of sight.

Greg had come over several times to check on her and make sure she was all right, especially right after Steve left. She wasn't sure if he was doing it to be a real friend or doing it as more a favor to Steve. She was sure it wasn't the latter as it upset Greg when Steve did move out. He just couldn't understand how Steve could do that to her, so, she was fairly sure that she had a good friend in him.

Before she knew it she was pulling into the parking lot of the school and was driving up and down row after row of cars to find her daughter's car. She found it, found her spare set of keys to the car and put their jackets inside. As she drove off, she once again was searching that mental database of hers to see what came next.

She decided to make the bank her next stop and just use the drive through to take out enough cash for the weekend. She knew that once she got home she wouldn't feel like going back to town again.

The supermarket was her next stop, groceries and supplies for the monsters, I mean little Angels, she thought as she grabbed a cart and started up and down the aisles. She found something interesting for dinner for one and supplies to keep the troops fed for a while. Now, back home and sunning by the pool she thought as she loaded up her groceries.

The drive home was quick and hot as the summer sun was bright and unforgiving today, it was going to be humid and very miserable today, you could just feel it in the air. As she carried bags into the house, she heard a car that sounded like it had pulled into her drive. She looked out and saw Greg reaching into her car and grabbing bags of groceries and heading toward the house.

"Thanks" she said, as she greeted him at the door with a smile and held the door open for him. "I just thought that if I stopped and helped it would keep you off the road until I go home" he said as he placed the bags on the counter.

"Gee thanks" she said as she laughed and asked if he was going to hold her trying to run him over this morning against her now.

"Naw" he told her with a smile, "I know you were only funnin' me this morning ma'am" he teasingly said.

They laughed and she asked him if he would like something cold to drink. He told her that he would have to take a rain check as he forgot some papers he needed this morning and had to run home, grab them and get back to work.

She told him that if it wasn't too late when he was done for the day maybe he could stop for dinner as she had to fend for herself tonight. "Kids deserted you didn't they?" he asked as he headed toward the door. "Of course, a silly old football game is more important than mom, you should know that" she said as she opened the door to see him out. He told her that if it isn't too late he might stop and have dinner, at the least he could stop by to say hi and be company.

Diane thanked him again for the help as he started toward his car, he waved and said "anytime" as he got in and backed out of the drive. Now what would she do. She thought, the interesting little thing she found for dinner at the supermarket was clearly enough for one, not two.

Maybe she would just save that for another day, she was sure that this wouldn't be the last time that she would be having dinner alone. It was only the beginning of football season she thought and smiled as she finished putting away her groceries.

She couldn't believe that Debbie was already 18 and a senior in high school, let alone that Mike was 16 and a sophomore. She was sure that Debbie would be off to college soon and that made her feel even more alone and empty and she hasn't even graduated high school yet. She filled a large glass with ice and fresh iced tea and headed for the stairs and back to her bedroom again.

She sat down her tea and opened a drawer of her dresser. Should she be conservative this afternoon and wear a one piece or daring and wear her skimpy two-piece that barely covered anything. "Decisions, decisions" she thought as she pondered her mood at the moment.

Definitely the skimpy two piece mood this afternoon she thought as she laid it on the bed and started to undress. She slipped on her tiny teal colored two piece and looked in the mirror as she made all the final adjustments. "Damn I have a nice butt" she thought to herself again as she grabbed her tea and headed down the stairs.

The back yard, if that's what you would call it, was huge and very private. She and Steve designed it that way for a reason. They loved being daring and making love by the pool when they first built the house. They also loved to entertain and the privacy and vastness of the yard seemed to fit the purpose perfectly.

She pulled a chaise lounge over to the edge of the pool and slipped her foot in to test the temperature. It was warm and felt good on this hot and sticky afternoon. She slipped off her slippers, sat her tea on the table next to her chaise, took a deep breath and dove in.

The warm water felt great, very refreshing, and she felt like she could just float there and get lost in forever without a care in the world. It was times like this that she could almost, key word here almost, forget her cares and worries and feel like a normal person again. She swam a couple of laps and swam to the side and got out. Deciding to let the hot afternoon sun dry her, she laid in her chaise and sipped slowly on her tea.

She went and found her radio and turned on an oldie's station she liked to listen to and laid back in her lounge again, letting herself get lost in the music softly playing. This felt so good she thought, she didn't pamper herself that often.

Most days she could be found cleaning the house or rearranging this or that, anything to keep her mind off Steve and stay busy. Today she decided that she was going to do whatever she wanted. And, what she wanted right now was to do absolutely nothing but bask in the warm glow of the afternoon sun.

She knew that all her cares and worries would once again come rushing in as soon as she let them. For now though, she was keeping them as far from her mind as she could. She turned from front to back and back to front several times.

Never staying on one side or the other long enough to burn. She burned easily as her skin was fair and somewhat delicate. As she noticed the sun getting lower and lower on the horizon she just knew the day was getting away from her and soon would give way to night.

She turned off her radio, picked up her empty glass and headed back to the house. As she started through the kitchen, she heard a soft knock on the back door. Without thinking anything about it, or about how she was dressed at the moment, she went to the door and opened it. There was Greg, his mouth dropped open and he caught himself staring at her. He couldn't take his eyes off her, she was beautiful and had a flawless body.

He had never seen her in anything so revealing. Shorts and tank tops were about as daring as he had ever seen her dress and it was clear that he was taken aback. It was Diane that gathered her wits first and snapped back into reality. Greg did manage to ask if he was early or interrupting anything without making a total fool of himself.

She assured him that he hadn't and asked if he wanted to go home and get something to swim in and they could have dinner by the pool. He could only manage to shake his head yes, turn and started toward his car.

As he reached to open his car door, he assured her that he wouldn't be long. She told him to just come out back when he got back and she would be there.

She turned and shook her head and wondered why she hadn't covered herself up with something and ran off in total embarrassment when she saw Greg at the door.

Tonight for some reason she just didn't seem to care. They were both adults, they were friends and she was sure that she wasn't the first woman that Greg had ever seen in a skimpy bikini before.

She took a couple of steaks from the freezer, grabbed a couple of potatoes and headed for the grill out back. She started the grill, put on the potatoes and went back in to start making salads and getting seasonings and other items she needed.

She placed everything on a tray and headed back out to the grill. Greg appeared from around the side of the garage and announced this time that he was there. She laughed and told him to come in and join her.

He thought to himself as he walked toward her that it was good to hear her laugh, better to see her smile and better yet to see her let her hair down and enjoy herself if even for one evening. Greg had been so upset when Steve did what he did by leaving her and the kids. He could never understand how or why Steve could do anything like that, especially to someone as sweet and loving as Diane.

He tried desperately to be a friend to both of them during the time after the split as he himself knew what they both were going through. He had run through the emotional gamut shortly after his wife had run off with his friend and business partner. So, he could kind of understand both points of view and the feelings they both were feeling.

At first Greg came around more as a favor to Steve. He wanted someone that Diane and the kids knew and trusted to check in from time to time and make sure they were as well as could be expected. Then as time went by and he became more familiar with Diane and the kids, he did it because he had become friends with Diane more so than Steve.

Steve for the most part quit coming around all together. He stopped checking in with Greg and just seemed to care less and less as weeks turned into months. Again, this was something that Greg could neither understand nor accept and he drifted further and further from Steve as time went by.

"Hi there" Greg said as he got closer to the grill, "anything I can do to help" he asked as he held a chilled bottle of wine out to

Diane. “Thank you, that was so sweet, you didn’t have to” she said as she opened the wine and went to the house to retrieve glasses. She appeared shortly with the wine in a bucket on ice and two glasses. She handed the glasses to Greg and sat the bucket on the table.

Greg poured himself a glass and asked if he could pour her one also, she nodded yes, thanked him and finished the salads. They sat and talked only being interrupted by her moving the potatoes to a higher rack on the grill and putting on the steaks.

She put on a pan of vegetables on the side burner and seasoned the steaks and asked, “how do you like your steak?” as she turned them. “Medium is fine if it’s no trouble” he told her and she assured him it wasn’t. “I like mine well done and I mean well done” she told him as she checked them again.

Greg’s steak was about done, the potatoes were done, and the rest of the meal would be ready soon. It felt good to her to be cooking for someone other than herself and the kids. As she placed his steak and potato on a plate he asked if there was anything he could do to help?

She told him the only thing he could do was eat before it got cold. As she finished her own plate and joined him, Greg thought how nice this was, he was learning things about her that he never knew before.

He had known Steve and Diane both for about two years but became a good friend to Diane over the last year since Steve had left. He knows now that she likes her steaks well done. He learned that she likes French dressing on her salad. He learned that beneath those shorts and tank tops was a beautiful, desirable woman.

He always knew that she was attractive but tonight was different. It was as though she were letting him see a side to her that few ever get the opportunity to see and it felt good. He was glad that she felt comfortable enough around him to let her hair down and have a good time and be herself.

They ate and talked, shared a laugh or two, then went to the pool and sat and just enjoyed the evening. Without even thinking Diane walked past Greg and shoved, pushing him into the pool.

He splashed and couldn't believe that she had done that to him. Soon he was grabbing for her and trying to pull her in as well. They swam and laughed and it made him feel good that he could be a part of her having a good time.

It was getting late and the night air was soon taking on a chill as they decided to call it a night. They toweled off and he helped her take the dishes and things inside. When they were done he thanked her for a perfect evening and started toward the door.

She told him that it was her that needed to thank him for a perfect evening, something she hadn't let herself do in a long time, enjoy herself. Goodnights' were exchanged and soon Greg was backing out of the drive and heading toward home. She went upstairs and slipped into her pajamas just as the kids came crashing through the door hooping and hollering.

As she rushed into the kitchen to see what all the commotion was about, she saw her children giving each other high fives. "I take it you won" she said as she pulled a chair from the table and sat down.

"Of course" Debbie told her Mom, "did you expect anything less Mom" she asked as she pulled a chair out and sat down beside her mother. "It was awesome mom" Mike chimed in as he too pulled out a chair and sat down to tell his mother all about it.

They sat and talked and she fixed them a snack as she was sure that all they had eaten for dinner was junk food or hot dogs and nachos at the game. It was her daughter that noticed something seemed to be different with her mom tonight. She didn't seem to be so down and lost tonight for some reason.

After their snack and putting the dishes in the sink, she told her children it was getting late and they needed to start heading off to bed. Mike kissed his mom on the cheek, gave her a big hug and said goodnight.

Debbie lagged behind purposely and asked her mom, "what is

going on, you are in much too good of a mood?" Diane told her daughter about her day and having Greg over for dinner and how good it felt to just be herself again.

Her daughter was ecstatic, she couldn't remember the last time she saw her mom smile and feel good about herself. "You need to do things like that more often mom" she said as she too started toward the stairs and her bedroom.

"You know the funny thing about it Deb, I don't feel guilty or feel like I did anything wrong either" she told her daughter. "That's because you didn't do anything wrong mom." You deserve to have a good time too" her daughter reassured her as she kissed her mom on the cheek and said goodnight.

Diane sat and sipped a glass of wine and thought about her evening, thought about why she felt so comfortable being herself and liked the way she was feeling. Tonight for some reason she didn't feel all alone and empty and betrayed, she felt like a person again.

She liked the feeling and thought to herself that this would definitely not be the last time she let herself have a good time. Maybe her daughter was right, maybe she does deserve to have a good time and feel good about herself, no she thought, she knew her daughter was right.

Maybe her daughter was also right about her taking a few chances and saying yes when asked on a date. After all it had been a year now and it was pretty obvious that Steve wasn't coming back or joining any monasteries himself. "Why not" she thought as she made sure the doors were locked and all the lights were off before heading to bed herself, "why not indeed."

Chapter 3

The bright morning sun of a new day flooding her bedroom woke Diane to the songs of birds chirping outside her window. She lazily rolled and stretched and glanced at the clock beside her bed. Quickly realizing it was Saturday, she rolled back over and pulled her pillow over her head. Debbie entered her mothers' room carrying a tray complete with fresh orange juice, coffee, and toast with fresh strawberry jam on it.

"Ok, what have you done with my daughter?" she sleepily asked as her daughter sat the tray on the bed beside her mom. "Hey, I can't do something nice for my mom?" she asked.

"What do you want and how much will it cost me?" Diane asked as she sat up in bed and reached first for her coffee. "How could you ask such a thing?" she asked her mom, "can't I just be nice for once?" she continued. "I can ask that because I know you my love" Diane told her daughter as she sipped her coffee.

"Ok, you got me, I want something" her daughter confessed. "I knew it" Diane said as she laughed, hugged and thanked her daughter for breakfast in bed. "Now spill it, what do you want and how much is it going to cost me?" her mom asked once again. Debbie laughed and told her mother that she needed to take her car into the shop to be serviced and wondered if Diane could follow her to town and bring her back home.

"Sounds innocent so far" she told her daughter, "now tell me the rest of it" she said. "How do you always know there is more?" her daughter asked her. "I gave birth to you my dear, I know you better than anyone" Diane told her. Debbie admitted that there was more and told her mom that after they got back home, Debbie wanted to take Diane's car to town to meet some friends for lunch at the mall.

"Oh sure, strand me here with no car and your brother, what did I do to you?" she asked her daughter. They both laughed and Debbie told her mom that Mike was going with her as he wanted to see friends in town too. She told her mom that if it was all right with her, Mike could drive Diane's car home after she picked hers up from the shop.

Diane was proud of the fact that both of her kids were responsible and very careful drivers. "I guess that would be ok" she told her daughter as she pushed her toward the door. "Let me shower and get dressed and I'll be down in a bit" she said as she closed the door behind her.

Her shower done, hair combed and an old pair of cut off shorts and baggy tee shirt on, she headed downstairs and into the kitchen where her daughter waited patiently for her. "You're going to town looking like that?" Debbie asked her mom when she appeared through the doorway of the kitchen. "What?" was Diane's response as she looked herself up and down, "what's wrong with it?" she asked again.

Debbie just shook her head and told her mom that she would be waiting for her at the shop and headed for her car. Diane grabbed a cup of coffee to go as she needed more caffeine this morning. As she was backing out of the drive, Mike came out half dressed and hopping on one foot trying his best to put his shoe on. "I thought I was going too" he shouted out to his mom as he hopped toward the car.

All Diane could do was laugh hysterically and shake her head at the sight of her son. "I'm meeting her in town and bringing her back home, you two are taking my car to town when we get back" she quickly explained.

"Oh" was all he could manage to say and hopped back to the house and waved as she backed out of the drive. "If nothing else, he was good for a laugh this morning" she thought to herself as she laughed and drove into town.

She found her daughter waiting at the shop when she arrived and asked if she was ready to go. Debbie quickly got in the car and told her mom to go before anyone saw how terrible she looked this morning. "You don't look terrible honey, I think you look just fine this morning" her mother fired back at her. "I was talking about you" Debbie volleyed back to her mom.

They laughed and drove toward home and talked about what her and her brother were doing today and what time they would be home. She was making sure that they would be there for dinner or if her little meal for one would come into play tonight. Debbie told her mom that they would probably miss dinner as she thought they were meeting friends and taking in a movie later.

She assured her mom that she would make it a point to make sure Mike was careful with her car and asked if that would be ok with her. Diane nodded yes and told her daughter that she would be fine. She would eat dinner early and watch a movie or something, she would be fine she said.

"Are you sure you don't mind us going mom? Her daughter asked. Diane told her again that it would be fine. She might pop some popcorn and curl up with a good book instead, either way she would be fine.

Debbie felt better as she really hated to leave her mom alone for very long. She knew that all her mom would do would be to wallow in her own pity and beat herself up about their dad leaving. She hated it when her mom did that to herself and her brother liked it even less. They love their mom and only want to see her happy, they just wish she would let herself be.

They pulled in the drive and Debbie laid her hand on top of her mom's, "tomorrow we do breakfast in bed together. Complete with some girl talk, sound good to you?" she asked her mom. Diane smiled a smile that could have lit up the night and told her daughter that she would be looking forward to it. As they entered the kitchen Mike was just finishing breakfast, cereal and Pepsi, she swore that boy could eat tin cans and think they were good.

Diane turned to Debbie and busted out laughing, remembering what her pathetic son looked like as she was leaving. As she told her daughter about the incident Mike just kept telling her that he didn't want to hear it. "His hair was a mess, he wasn't dressed and was hopping on one foot, one shoe on and trying to put the other one on" she told her daughter.

They laughed and hugged him as he put his dishes in the sink and flicked water at them from his fingertips. "Very funny you two" he kept telling them as he went upstairs to get his things and get ready to go.

"We thought it was" they chimed in unison as he went upstairs and they laughed at the thought of the sleepy boy hopping around on one foot. "There's times I don't claim him, you do know that right?" Debbie asked her mom. "There's times that I don't claim either one of you, you do know that right?" her mom said back to her then laughed.

Diane was glad that she had always had a good relationship with her children, she cherished the closeness they always seem to have. She knew that she was lucky as some parents don't have that, some don't act like they want it.

She has always been a very big part of their lives. She was always there for everything, good or bad and the children knew it and never forgot to tell her just how much they loved and respected their mother.

With Mike finally ready and everything already taken to the car, Debbie told her mom that they were finally ready to go. With hugs and kisses and good-byes out of the way, she asked if they needed any money or anything before they left. They assured her that they were fine. Both children felt a bit guilty for leaving her alone for a second night in a row, they knew all she would do would be to reminisce about happier times and what went wrong.

As the kids backed out of the drive, she went to the freezer and took out the "interesting" little dinner for one that she had intentions of having last night. She found a station on the stereo that she liked to listen to and went about doing dishes from last night and this morning. This would give her a chance to do some cleaning and laundry she thought as she went from room to room looking for dirty dishes and clothes.

She looked out and noticed that it would once again be hot and sticky this afternoon as the sun was blinding, not a cloud in the sky. So was the norm this time of year, cool mornings with just a hint of dew, hot, sticky, humid afternoons and clear and chilly evenings. It was early September and it warmed up rather quickly yet cooled off even quicker when the sun was riding the horizon before ducking out of sight for another day.

She loved this time of year, flowers were still in abundant bloom, you could still wear shorts and sleeveless shirts during the day and jeans and sweaters were just right at night. It was as if mother nature were giving you a taste of fall, thoughts of springtime past and letting you know that summer would soon fade all together.

The leaves on the trees were still green for the most part, although some are starting to turn shades of a warm gold and soft hues of red, it was just beautiful she thought as she wandered out into the yard.

She walked the backyard first, checking her flowerbeds and pulling an occasional weed or two here and there. She made sure that she had turned off the gas to the grill from the night before and checked the pool. She finally made her way around the house and into the front yard, admiring the interesting colors of her mums.

She thought to herself that she would have an abundance of them this year, as all her mums were hearty and healthy and full of buds. As she walked the yard, she heard a car pulled up and honk, as she turned around she noticed it was Greg.

"Morning" he greeted her, "I see it's safe to pass your drive this morning without fear of being ran over" he continued with a hearty laugh and a bright smile. "I just knew that you weren't going to let me live that down" she said back with a smile of her own. "I promise, not another word about it" he told her as he started to roll the window back up.

About halfway up he stopped and rolled it back down, stuck his head back out and asked if she was busy tonight. She told him that she had been abandoned once again by her children and would be all alone tonight as well. "Would you like to come up to my place for dinner" he asked her, "it's the least I could do to repay you for such a wonderful evening last night" he said?

She told him to let her know when he got home today and she would make sure that nothing unexpected had come up, if not, she would be happy to join him for dinner. "Great" he said, "I'll call as soon as I'm done with my errands and see if it still looks good for tonight." She nodded yes and waved as he drove on down the road and out of sight.

Now she was second-guessing herself, why had she said yes, why didn't she just say no thanks and tell him she had a great time last night but would pass. Why didn't she just tell him that she had already made plans or something, then she remembered how good it felt last night to be herself and allow herself to have a fun evening with a good friend?

She wasn't going to feel guilty, there was nothing to feel guilty about and even if there was, she was over 21 and single now. She had a right to move on with her life, maybe last night with Greg convinced her that now is the right time to do exactly that. She knew that Steve was not coming back, she knew that being miserable was taking a toll on her and the kids, and she knew that last night felt good.

She allowed herself to have a good time and didn't allow herself to feel guilty or ashamed of herself for anything. She hadn't done anything wrong. As she walked to the house she immediately started thinking of what she would wear and put that poor little dinner for one back in the freezer. Now for that she felt a little guilty.

She went about doing laundry and finishing the dishes, went on to her dusting and vacuuming, and finished with a sandwich and salad for lunch. She caught herself dancing to the music softly playing on the radio.

Something she hadn't let herself do since before Steve had left.

She realized that her mood was definitely a light and airy one today and it felt good, it felt right to her. She hadn't felt this good for so long she thought that she had forgotten how to do it, but was sure glad that she hadn't.

Her daughter Debbie's words kept coming back to her, telling her that she deserved to have a good time. Telling her that she hadn't done anything wrong, and her daughter was right. She had never been unfaithful while they were married.

She didn't flirt and carry on with people. She was always the perfect wife and mother, at least she can say that she always gave her all to be. As a matter of fact, she hadn't even been with a man since Steve left, it had been over a year since she even had any activity that could be remotely described as sex.

"I've heard of dry spells, but man, this is ridiculous" she thought to herself as she cleared her lunch dishes and put them in the sink. She busted out laughing at her last thought, she just couldn't help herself.

Then she smiled an evil little smile and thought to herself, "I haven't even had sex with ME in over a year, now that's really pathetic" she thought and laughed that much harder.

She silently thought that maybe it was time to put on some dark sunglasses, put on an old trench-coat, find the dumbest looking hat she could find and slip unnoticed in the back door of an adult bookstore and break down and buy herself a "friend."

Now she was almost rolling on the floor at the mental image of herself looking like a really bad spy, slipping into an adult bookstore to buy herself a "marital aide" as they so politely call them.

She could just picture herself asking the poor guy behind the counter which one was the best, like he would know anyway she thought and laughed until she almost wet her pants. "Oh my God, I have to stop this" she thought aloud as she tried to gather some sort of composure.

The thought and mental image she had were almost hilarious to say the least, but, it did make her do some real soul searching. She hadn't had sex in over a year. She hadn't even given herself any relief and hadn't let herself really give it any thought, until now. Why shouldn't she think about it, it was a natural function, something we all think about and some of us even participate in from time to time.

She was almost positive that Steve wouldn't be able to say that it had been over a year since he had partaken in any kind of sexual activity. She always knew that the thought was in the back of her mind, her and Steve were always very sexually active and had a very good sex life.

She knew that one day the thought of it would hit her like a truck speeding out of control down the side of a mountain, she just didn't realize it would be today. Had one decent evening with Greg brought it to the forefront and uncovered those buried and forgotten thoughts and desires she had been suppressing all this time, she thought.

She had never thought of Greg as anything more than just a friend, a very good friend at that. He had helped her put a lot of little pieces of her life back together after Steve had left, by just being there to talk.

She had leaned on him mainly because he understood what it felt like to lose someone you thought you would be together with forever. His wife had done something similar to him. She poured a fresh glass of tea and wandered out into the back, toward the pool and was lost in thought.

She had a great time last night and felt very comfortable and at ease with Greg. She hadn't been shy or withdrawn, even by him seeing her in her bikini that barely covered anything.

She hadn't let it even cross her mind when she playfully pushed him into the pool and joined him as they laughed and had such a good time. It was as if she had done it a thousand times before and it was almost natural, but she knew that it wasn't natural, not to her anyway.

"Oh well" she thought, it wasn't something that she was going to let eat at her or sit and try to analyze it or pick it apart until her brain screamed for relief. All she knew was last night she had a good time and for some unknown reason, she knew she was looking forward to having dinner with him again tonight.

She was brought back to reality by the phone ringing, it was Greg letting her know that he was home early and finished his errands quicker than he thought. She was glad to hear his voice, even happier to know that dinner was still on and told him that she would come up around six that evening.

As she hung up the phone her thoughts went to what she would wear, should she consider this a date and try to dress somewhat nice or a causal get together between friends.

Nice clingy mini dress that showed a lot of leg or her usual shorts and tank tops? Should she go all out and do full makeup and hair or minimal makeup and hair nicely brushed? She hadn't felt this giddy and uncertain since her and Steve had been dating and she always did her best to look just perfect for him.

That was ages and eons ago she thought as she sipped her tea and looked at her watch. One o'clock now, five hours to decide and get ready, even she could pull that off she thought and smiled. She picked up her glass and headed for the house, "might as well see what's in the old closet" she thought as she started up the stairs toward her room.

Once in her room she opened her closet door and stepped inside, looking through this and that, never really finding anything that "jumped out" at her. She decided to play it safe and consider this a friendly get together between friends, on a date, if that made any sense. She chose a short, clingy little summer dress that was practically see through and short enough to make her pay attention to how she sat.

It was emerald green and a perfect color for her, it accentuated her flowing red hair quite nicely she thought as she held it in front of her and looked in the mirror. She was very pleased with what she saw. She always knew that she was an attractive lady, that was something that she had always prided herself in. She tried to always stay in shape, even after having the kids she worked hard to get her figure back and keep it, if not for Steve, for herself.

Now for what to wear under this flirty little number she thought as she started opening this drawer and that drawer. She wanted to find something that would flatter her figure and make her feel good about herself yet not scream out, "take me I'm yours." She decided to be conservative and wear something flattering yet sensible and laid everything out for later.

With clothes laid out and her plans for the evening made, she went about finishing things around the house. She once again caught herself dancing to the radio and humming to one of the songs. She was undeniably in a great mood and liked very much how it felt. She decided that she had spent much too much time weeping and mourning something that she neither had any control over or any fault in.

Steve had made the decision for her, he was the one that acted on his decision. She had no say so in it nor any course of action to take, he made up his mind and acted. Diane had laid awake many a night wondering if there had been anything she could have done to change his mind.

Maybe counseling, maybe giving him some time to himself, anything. She soon came to the harsh reality that nothing she did, thought or said was going to change things. Steve was going to leave come hell or high water.

How ironic it was she thought, a man had broken her heart and left her life in shambles, and it was a man that finally made her wake up and face the fact that she is still alive and should act like it. She was lucky to have a friend like Greg she thought, and she was glad she finally woke up and realized it before she had alienated everyone in her life including her kids and a friend like Greg.

It was time she thought, time to put Steve where he belonged, in the past. It was time to move on with her life and live for her and the kids. Not for what once was or could have been had things been different. She decided right then and there that she would start going out. Why should she let life pass her by while she sat around and cried over things that aren't.

She would start saying yes when a man asked her out. She would stop making a million excuses why she couldn't or shouldn't. The main one hanging onto something that just wasn't going to happen. She would stop getting up in the morning and rushing around like a mad woman making him breakfast.

Stop looking for his dirty laundry, waiting up late at night for him to walk through the door only to wake in the morning still on the couch alone. Today things were going to change, she would not go back to the way they were.

She wasn't fooling herself into some false sense of security or anything. She knew that she wasn't ready to make any commitments or be involved in any kind of serious relationship. But, she knew that she was ready for a change in her life. A change that was desperately needed and deserved. A change that she was sure her children would approve of and support her in.

The phone once again brought her back to reality, it was Debbie telling her mom that the movie they were going to see was sold out until the later show. "Is it all right if we go to the later show mom?" she asked. She explained that they had both her car from the shop as well as Diane's and Debbie guaranteed her mom that they would come straight home after the movie and she would follow Mike all the way.

Diane quickly agreed and told her daughter that it would be fine, she told them to have a good time and to be careful on the way home. "I'm going to hold you to the girl talk tomorrow too" she told her daughter before she hung up the phone. "It's a date mom" Debbie told her, "I can't wait." Realizing that time was fast getting away from her, she headed for the shower. Next step makeup and hair she thought as she toweled off and turned on her curling iron.

She decided that tonight she was going to look good, no, she was going to look damn good and feel good about it too. Hair done, shower finished, makeup applied, now it was time to dress and head up to Greg's house. She wondered what he would think when he opened the door and saw her like this as she turned and looked at herself in the mirror. She had succeeded, and she looked good, no, damn good. She grabbed her bag and headed out the door toward Greg's.

Chapter 4

The doorbell rang and Greg opened the door, he literally dropped the pan he was holding and his mouth dropped to the floor, at least it felt like it did. "Come in" was about all he could manage to spit out without looking like a complete and utter fool. "You look fantastic if you don't mind me saying so" he managed to say. Hoping it didn't sound lame or come off like one of the most stupid pick up lines he had.

"I'm glad you think so" she said, "or all that time I spent doing this would have been a complete waste" she continued as she stepped into the room. "Oh, believe me, it was no waste, you look fantastic." "Or did I already say that, I can't remember" he said as he picked up the pan from the floor. She giggled and told him he had but she didn't mind hearing it again. He invited her in and asked if he could get her a glass of wine, explaining that dinner wasn't quite ready yet.

She gladly accepted and asked if there was anything she could do to help. "I think I've heard that line before" he told her as he smiled and disappeared into the kitchen. She could hear pots and pans banging in the kitchen and could swear that she heard something drop.

Wondering if he really did need help she started cautiously toward the kitchen. As she entered the doorway to the kitchen, she saw what she thought was a battle zone and caught her breath before she realized she had done it. "Oh my goodness, what happened in here?" she teasingly asked and busted out laughing despite her best attempt to hold it in.

There was Greg standing in the middle of the room with what looked like every pot, pan and dish he owned strewn about looking lost. "I guess it isn't too late to order pizza is it?" he asked. Then joined her in laughing so hard he dropped the rest of the pans he was holding in the middle of the room.

After catching his breath from laughing so hard his sides felt like they would split, he asked if she would mind if he showered quickly and they went to town to eat. She assured him it would be fine with her. Actually she didn't have the heart to tell him that she was deathly afraid to eat anything that he might actually cook. "I'll only be a few minutes" he assured her as he dashed up the stairs and disappeared into his room.

Diane thought it would be safer if she waited in the living room, the kitchen was definitely a disaster area. She sat on the couch and sipped her wine as she waited patiently for him to finish his shower and dress.

Her thoughts started wandering wildly, should she go to town with him for dinner, what if someone saw them, would people talk, her mind was reeling. Suddenly as if someone had just slapped her and brought her back to earth she realized something. She was single, she was an adult and she could have dinner with anyone she chose to.

She heard what sounded like a herd of wild buffalo coming down the stairs and wondered if she should go make sure he was all right. Thinking it wiser to let him come into the room on his own accord, she sat and waited and listened for cries of help or the final thud as he hit the bottom of the stairs.

To her surprise, he walked into the room unscathed and no more worse for wear. Looks like he made it after all she thought as she got up and walked toward him. "Anywhere in particular you would like to go?" he asked as he opened and held the front door for her. She told him that anywhere would be fine with her and left it up to him to decide. Besides she thought, if the night was a total disaster he would have no one to blame but himself this way.

She smiled, she was proud of herself, this dating thing isn't that hard after all she thought as they walked to the car. He opened her door and she thought silently that it felt good to be treated like a lady for a change, she liked it a lot. As they pulled out of the drive Greg turned on the radio and they talked. Nothing complicated, just light and cheerful conversation as they drove toward town.

He asked if the steak house in town would be all right with her and she quickly approved of his choice. She hadn't been out to eat other than fast food and food court meals at the mall with the kids since before Steve had left. She was long overdue for a nice quiet evening out with good food, good company and even better conversation. She longed for a conversation that didn't start with "mom."

They laughed and talked all the way into town and before they realized it, they were pulling into the parking lot of the eatery. It wasn't anything fancy by any stretch of the imagination, but it was good food and a pleasant atmosphere and Diane had missed coming here.

As they circled the parking lot, looking for an empty stall, Diane noticed a vehicle that was all too familiar to her, Steve was there. Greg spotted it almost at the same time and stopped and turned to her. "I'm so sorry Diane, I had no idea he would be here tonight" he said with a very real concern for her in his voice.

"It's fine" she quickly told him, "I have to stop closing myself in that house, stop being afraid to go out for fear that I might run into him" she told her friend. "Besides, it was bound to happen sometime Greg, it has been over a year you know" she continued. She assured her friend that it would be fine and told him to park and they would go inside and enjoy themselves.

"I can't let him and the memory of him keep ruining my life" she said as Greg found a spot and pulled in. "I know Diane, but it is going to be hard, I'm sure he isn't here alone" he told her as he opened her door and helped her out. "I know, and I'm ready to do this" she told him as they walked toward the door of the restaurant.

Luckily when they entered there was not a long line waiting to be seated. Although it was a local spot it got very busy. Especially on the weekends, and Greg fully intended on a long wait when they arrived. They were seated rather quickly and as luck would have it were on opposite sides of the room from her ex.

She sat down with her back toward the side of the room where he and his date were seated. She figured that if she weren't seeing them every time she looked about the room she would have a better chance of getting through this evening.

She had a newfound determination tonight it seemed, one she wasn't quite sure where it came from. She was determined to have a good night and not let Steve or his being there with his new girlfriend spoil her evening or put Greg in an awkward position. After all, he was just trying to be a friend and get her out of that house and bring her out of her shell.

They sat and before long a waitress appeared, took their orders for drinks and dinner and left to fetch their drinks. They sat and talked and Greg was feeling a bit less uneasy. She seemed to be handling the situation like a pro, something he wasn't sure he could do if he were in her shoes.

He was rapidly realizing that this lady had more class and composure than he had ever known. This was a side of her that he had never had the good fortune of seeing, but then again, he had never seen her in this kind of situation before either.

Their drinks came and as she sipped her wine and chatted with Greg it seemed that she was becoming more and more comfortable. Greg could see that this was genuine, she was not putting up a brave front. He was so very proud of her, it was as if the butterfly had emerged from the cocoon tonight and he was glad he was there to see it and share this moment with her.

As they talked and patiently waited for their food to arrive at the table Greg noticed something out of the corner of his eye. As he looked up he saw Steve had recognized him and was making his way to their table. "Oh no, I was afraid that this was going to happen" he said as Steve got even closer to the table.

"You might want to brace yourself for this" he told Diane as Steve was almost upon them, "he's coming over and he's practically right behind you" he warned. She smiled the most evil smile he had ever seen and softly said it would be fine, then winked and assured him she was all right.

"Hello stranger" Steve said as he reached the table, "I haven't seen you in a long time" he continued as if they were long lost friends. Diane was silently thanking her lucky stars that she had decided to put on her makeup, fix her hair and dress to kill tonight. She almost had thought better of it.

Steve reached out to shake Greg's hand and without hesitation looked to see who the mystery woman was with him. Diane smiled the most beautiful smile and tilted her head just slightly as she said "how are you tonight Steve?".

It was visibly apparent that this took him by surprise and he was undeniably taken back by it. It almost appeared as if someone had just punched her ex in the gut and he looked like he was about to double over.

"Oh God this feels so good" she thought silently as she awaited a response from him. All he could muster was a pleasant "how are you Diane." He quickly excused him self and said he would talk to them later and headed rather quickly toward the mens room. She almost blurted out a loud and full laugh but contained herself quite nicely instead.

With her ex purposely trying to avoid them and him having to go on the defensive, Diane was really beginning to enjoy herself and her evening out. She had an easiness about her that Greg had never seen before, she almost appeared to be glowing. "I didn't realize this could be so much fun" she told him as their plates were sat before them.

"What's that?" Greg managed to ask back. "I thought that I would be putty in his hands. I thought I would become a gibbering idiot the minute he said hello. I wasn't and I didn't" she said. "He was the one that became uneasy. He was the one that got flustered and is now avoiding us on purpose, and I have to admit I couldn't be happier. This is fun and I want to thank you Greg for not letting me make up some lame excuse to stay locked in that house and not come tonight" she said.

Greg could only smile and told her that he was glad that he

could help. “Maybe the healing can start now” he told her. “I think you’re right, I think it already has” she told him as they settled down to eat. The meal was good, the wine was great and the company and conversation were the best. She couldn’t remember when she had let herself have this much fun. One thing she was certain of, it would not be the last time, not even close.

They finished their meal and were sipping an after dinner glass of wine as Steve and his date left. She made it a point to wave enthusiastically and say a hearty “good-bye” as they paid the check. She could see his date keep looking back and was sure that she was full of questions. Probably “who was that?” was at the top of that list she thought, and smiled that wicked little smile again.

About then she was thinking how rewarding it would be to be a tiny fly in the backseat of the car and hear that whole conversation. The very thought made her smile again. As they paid the check and exited the eatery Greg asked if she felt like a walk around the town square before heading back to their respective homes. She was feeling good tonight, she was feeling good about herself tonight and didn’t want the evening to end just yet so she gladly accepted the offer.

As they walked along the square of town looking in the store windows and laughing, Greg thought to himself that he was glad the evening had turned out as well as it had. He never would have thought that after spotting Steve’s car in the lot of the restaurant when they first arrived. He had fully expected her to be a mess and figured he would have to rush her home and try to put together the pieces again after her seeing her ex.

He was so very proud of her tonight. He had been there since Steve made the announcement that he was leaving. He had witnessed first hand this vibrant woman reach a low point in her life that he wasn’t sure she would recover from. He wasn’t sure that she had the will or the fortitude to start her life over and carry on. He even had his doubts that her kids could help bring her around, but they had.

Those kids had been her lifeline and her reason for going on. If it hadn't been for them he just knew she would have given up. Tonight though she had shown a side he wasn't aware existed. She had been great and honestly seemed to be enjoying herself, he was glad. He couldn't help but admit silently to himself though, he is cautiously waiting for the reality of what had happened tonight to fully hit her and he is ready to pick up the pieces once again.

They walked the entire square of town. Looking in the windows and pointing out new things that she noticed since the last time she had spent any time in town. She had to admit that usually she only went to the stores she needed to visit and went straight home. She hadn't taken the time to walk the square and window shop in a long time, it felt good.

As they made their way back to Greg's car, Diane told him that she had to confess something. She told him that when she first saw Steve standing behind her in the restaurant, she thought he would have to put her in a straight jacket and dump her in her front yard. She fully expected to be a total basket case. But she continued, it was the genuine concern on his face that helped her get through what would have been an otherwise disastrous evening.

Greg was happy to see her have a good time and even happier that she had allowed him the last two evenings with her. It truly gave him an insight to her that he had never seen before. She was a much stronger woman than she ever gave herself credit for. He had seen that first hand tonight.

He opened the car door for her and let her in, "don't shut me in the door for putting you through this tonight" she teased as he closed the door. "The thought never crossed my mind" he said with a sly little smile as he too got in the car and headed it toward their homes.

They once again listened to the radio and made small talk on the way back to his house. Laughing at the situation they had encountered earlier. "Did you see the look on his face when he realized it was me with you tonight?" she asked as they drove along.

"I thought he was going to choke or pass out or something" she continued and they both broke out laughing hysterically. "I thought the poor guy was going to drop his drink" Greg added and they laughed even harder.

"And his date, the poor guy will be explaining for a week to her exactly who I was" she went on. "Did you see them as they left?" she added. "I can only imagine what she was saying to him" Greg said as they neared their homes. "Do you want me to just drop you off at your house?" he asked as her house came into sight. "No, if you don't mind I feel like I could use the company for a little longer" she told him.

He assured her that it would be his pleasure and drove on to his house and pulled in the drive. As they entered the house she went into the living room and asked if he would mind if she turned on the radio. He told her that it was fine with him as there wasn't ever anything good on television anymore anyway.

"Would you care for a glass of wine" he asked from the kitchen, she gladly accepted and found a station on the radio that suited her. She slowly danced and closed her eyes, trying to put the thought of seeing Steve out of her mind. She thought that the first time she actually saw him with another woman would be the end of the world for her, she found that she handled it far better than she ever expected to.

She was proud of herself and for good reason, she could have made a terrible scene tonight and probably got the sympathy of nearly everyone in the restaurant. It wasn't like people didn't know the situation, it was a small town and gossip runs rampant. They had both grown up there and everyone knew them and what had happened.

Steve nearly got ran out of town for what he did in the beginning. So, sympathy would have come easy to her tonight had she decided to explode instead of keeping her composure. "Besides" she thought, "it was by far more fun seeing him squirm and sweat." She knew he fully expected and was bracing for the worst when he first noticed it was her seated with Greg, you could see it on his face.

Greg stopped in the doorway and just watched her in silence for a bit. He was so glad that she had handled the situation as well as she had. He knew that she had already been through so much at the hand of her ex and wasn't ready to see her go through anymore tonight.

He was ready and more than willing to get up and leave with her to avoid the situation. He would have taken her for a pizza before he would purposely put her through hell all over again.

It was plain to see that she had overcome her first run in with him. Especially with another woman, he was sure that would have just killed her inside. He was so very proud of her, she had really came a long way since she had first been told that he was leaving.

As he entered the room with their wine she was brought back to reality. She smiled and graciously said "thank you" as she took her glass from him. "You're very welcome" he told her as they walked to the sofa and sat down. They talked and laughed and sipped their wine, Greg made it a point not to relive the experience earlier.

She had handled it like a pro, but, he was sure that if he allowed her to keep going over it again and again, the other shoe would drop, so to speak. He wasn't going to let an otherwise perfect evening end on a note like that. She was much too good a friend to allow that to happen he thought.

To his surprise she started a conversation that he had never had with her before. Not because he hadn't wanted to, more because it had never come up.

She asked him how he had felt when his wife had left and how he got through it so well. He told her that a lot of credit would have to go to good friends like her and Steve for helping him through what he was sure would be the lowest part of his life. They talked about how he felt and how he hid it so well.

He always seemed to act like it hadn't taken any permanent toll on him. She always suspected that it had but didn't have the nerve to ask him to relive something so terrible in his life. Tonight for some reason it almost seemed right for her to ask him about it and share something so personal. Something that somehow they seemed to share and have in common.

They talked and sipped more wine and Greg for the first time noticed that he had far more in common with this woman than he had ever thought before. He hadn't opened up and talked about all of this in so long he thought he had buried it deep in the past. Yet here was his friend bringing it out like it all had happened yesterday.

Somehow talking about it with her, someone that had gone through something very similar, helped in more ways than he could have ever imagined. It was almost therapeutic he thought, he wished now that he had opened up to her long before now.

Greg noticed that she was getting very tipsy from the wine. He lost count but knew they each had drank several glasses and he knew that he was feeling a bit warm himself. He didn't want to put her off by asking a stupid question but was concerned about her walking home by herself by now. "Would you like me to drive you back to your house before neither of us is in any condition to drive?" he asked her.

She only smiled and hiccupped and swayed a little from side to side. He could tell it was definitely time to cut her off and start thinking seriously about how he was going to get her home.

It was then that she did the unexpected and Greg thought he would die right then and there. She leaned over and kissed him. Not a friendly little peck on the cheek or a thank you for a nice night kiss. Before he realized what was happening she was kissing him passionately and deeply, and to his surprise he was kissing her back.

His thoughts were reeling now, all of a sudden nothing was clear or certain anymore. He knew that what they were doing was the after effect of too much wine and didn't want to take advantage of a situation like this.

He wasn't dead either, he had on more than one occasion thought about what it would be like to spend just one evening of passion with this beautiful, desirable woman. Just not like this though, not from too much wine and other factors that he was sure were at play here tonight.

He desperately wanted to give in to the moment and throw caution to the wind, and, he knew that he would hate himself in the morning no matter what his next move would be. If he pushed her away and took her home, he would kick himself in the morning. Yet, if he took advantage of the situation and went through with this, he would never be able to face himself again, let alone face Diane again.

He was torn, his thoughts were racing a thousand miles an hour. What should he do, what shouldn't he do, he kept asking himself over and over. All the time Diane was kissing him and starting to remove her dress, that finally snapped him back to reality, he knew what he had to do.

He gently pushed her away and helped her to her feet. He gathered her shoes and belongings and led her to his car. He helped her in and quickly drove her home. Knowing that if he allowed himself even a second to think about it again, he would turn around and drive back to his house and give in to the feeling. Pulling into her drive he noticed that they had beat the kids home, so, he quickly helped her up to her room and slid her into bed, clothes and all and covered her up.

He turned and left without a second thought and drove straight back to his house and went directly to bed himself. He knew that he would have to explain to her tomorrow what had happened, or what had nearly happened. And, he was sure that she would respect him more for doing what he did instead of doing what he was thinking of doing. At least he hoped she would he thought as he closed his eyes and drifted off to sleep.

Chapter 5

As the morning sun came beaming through the blinds Diane slowly stirred and tried to clear the leftover haze in her mind. Wondering how she got home, how she got to bed, who helped her and better yet, what had she done, or not done last night. Her mouth was dry and felt like the Sahara desert. She desperately needed coffee this morning, and lots of it, quick.

She kicked off the blankets and noticed that she was still dressed. "That could be a good thing, or not" she thought as she slowly sat up in bed. For the most part last night was pretty much a blur. For the moment anyway, she was almost certain though that she would start recalling the evening and not really sure that she wanted to.

She managed to get to her feet and stand up without falling over in a crumpled heap on her bedroom floor. "This is a good thing" she thought as she lightly swayed a bit. Her head felt like someone was inside it, beating their way out, and she knew she needed that coffee fast.

She decided to change first. What if the kids were up and she had to start explaining why she was dressed like this. Or better yet, why she was still dressed like this.

She undressed and showered and put on her old familiar shorts and tank top and headed for the kitchen. That coffee pot was calling her name this morning she thought as she quickly made a fresh pot.

"Good, the kids are still asleep" she thought as she got her cup from the cupboard and poured her first cup of the morning. As she sat and sipped her coffee her thoughts slowly started to focus on last night and what exactly had happened, or hadn't happened.

She thought back and could remember going to the restaurant with Greg. She now remembered seeing Steve there, that made her smile that evil smile again just thinking about that. She remembered walking the square in town with Greg and faintly remembered going back to his house. Anything after that was so fuzzy she just drew a complete blank.

She could only hope that she hadn't said or done anything to embarrass either of them or put either of them in an awkward situation. She never had been very good at holding her wine and was almost sure that last night she had allowed herself to indulge way too much.

She just hoped that Greg would still speak to her after last night, whatever had or had not happened. She hoped she had not made a complete fool of herself.

Sounds of someone coming down the stairs brought her back to today. Slowly, very slowly, but nonetheless brought her back. "Good morning mom" Debbie said as she headed to the refrigerator and grabbed the orange juice. "I don't know yet if it's a good morning but it is morning" she told her daughter as her daughter poured a glass of juice and joined her mom at the table. "We noticed that you were already in bed by the time we got home so we let you sleep" she told her mom.

"Thank God, I was home before they got here" she thought. Not wanting to tell her daughter details of last night, since she wasn't clear on them herself. "Did you two have a good time?" she managed to ask as she continued to sip her coffee.

Not wanting her daughter to know that she was fighting a slight hangover this morning. Her daughter told her all about the movie they saw and friends they met up with and what they ate and on and on. It was more than her poor brain could process this morning.

She could only smile and nod, hoping that her daughter would take that as acknowledgment that she was listening. After rambling on for what seemed like an hour her daughter stopped and said, "I thought we were doing breakfast in bed and girl talk this morning."

"I'm sorry honey, I completely forgot about that" she said in her best mom voice. Wishing she could just drink her coffee and go back to bed for about a week and start all over again. She just continued to smile and nod.

This morning it was the best she could muster and hoped her daughter didn't start asking a lot of questions about what she had done last night. Just then the phone rang, "saved by the bell" Diane thought as she answered in the most cheerful voice she could manage this morning. It was Greg. "Are you all right this morning?" he asked with a noticeable tone of concern in his voice.

She assured him that she was fine but almost in a whisper asked if he would mind if she came up and talked to him about last night. He assured her that it was fine with him and told her that he had fresh coffee on. "Just come on up" he said as she told him good-bye.

She told her daughter that she was going up to have coffee with Greg and would be back soon, first asking Debbie if she wanted some breakfast. Debbie assured her mom that it was fine and told her to go and have a good time.

"Tell Greg I said hi" she said as Diane picked up her cup and headed for the door. "I will honey" she told her daughter as she closed the door and started toward Greg's.

Greg answered the door with coffee pot in hand and asked if she needed a refill yet. She was more than happy to accept and told him yes. They went to the patio where he had been sitting and sipped their coffee, in silence at first.

It was Diane that spoke first. "I have to ask something" she started. "How did I get home last night and did I do anything that I need to apologize for first?" It was clear to Greg that she didn't remember anything past dinner and thought it best to leave it that way.

"We came back here after dinner, we had another glass of wine and while I tidied up, you fell asleep on the sofa" he told her. "I took you home, noticed the kids weren't there yet so I decided to tuck you in as is and locked up as I left" he finished.

"So I didn't make a complete and total ass of myself in any way last night?" she cautiously asked. He assured her that she had been a lady all evening and simply fell asleep and that is when he decided to take her home and tuck her in safe and sound.

He told her that he almost let her sleep on his couch but thought better of it as he knew the kids would be beside themselves if she didn't come home at all. He just didn't have the heart to tell her what had almost happened last night, but it was clear that it was already haunting her.

He again made it clear that she was a total lady and nothing out of the ordinary had happened. She remembered dinner and seeing Steve, and he left it at that.

She didn't need to start beating herself up for letting a little too much wine get the best of her. And him for that matter, and almost making a terrible mistake. Not that he thought it a mistake to make love to a drop dead gorgeous woman like this.

A man would have to be certifiable to think that. But Greg knew her, she would never let herself think for a minute that it was anything but a mistake. And, that she was a horrible person for letting it happen, that was just her.

That was one of the things he liked so much about her. She always went out of her way to do the right thing and would make herself go through hell if she thought for one minute that she hadn't succeeded in the attempt. He was not about to let her think that last night was anything more than good friends enjoying a night out and each others company.

As they talked, he could see that she was feeling better about herself and for allowing herself have a good time. He wasn't about to do or say anything to ruin that, she deserved that and so much more.

She never gets out of the house, has devoted her entire life to her kids since Steve left, and deserves to go out and enjoy herself from time to time. Even though she was the only one stopping herself from doing just that. They sat and talked and before long it seemed like old times and she was definitely at ease and comfortable with last night.

They laughed again about seeing Steve and how he had reacted, it seemed to make her feel even better. Before they realized it morning had slipped away and she was saying good-bye to head for home.

She had to at the very least start planning dinner, even if she let the kids fend for themselves for lunch as she was sure they had for breakfast. If they were both even up, she had the funniest feeling that her daughter had headed straight back to bed and her son didn't even know it was morning yet.

As she entered the back door she found the house exactly as she suspected she would, dead silent. She was sure that Debbie had went back to bed and even more certain that Mike hadn't even woke up yet. Now that her head was much clearer and her worries about something terrible happening last night put to rest, she set about straightening up the house and setting out something for dinner.

Before long her two sleepy children stumbled down the stairs and looked as if they were lost. She told them to sit down and she would make a late breakfast as she too could eat. She quickly prepared scrambled eggs and bacon, toast, juice and was joining them at the table.

They ate and she heard about last night all over again from both her daughter and son, again just nodding and smiling. "I wonder if they actually know that I'm not listening" she thought to herself and just smiled that much more and finished her breakfast.

The children quickly finished their meal and darted up to change, they were headed for the pool. They both loved the water and wanted to get as much swim time in as they could before the weather would no longer allow it.

After dishes were done and the rest of the house cleaned she went out to the pool and joined them. The early afternoon was already quite hot and sticky and a few laps in the pool were starting to sound good about now.

She joined them in the pool and before long her and Debbie were splashing and ganging up on Mike. Poor guy she thought, he has to deal with his sister and mom. They laughed and had a good time and before she realized it, it was fast approaching time to start dinner.

As she busily prepared dinner, Debbie pitched in and helped with anything she could and Mike sat the table. She considered her self lucky, she really had two great kids. They seldom ever whined or moaned if she asked for help.

They loved and respected her more than words could say. And, would never even think of disrespecting her or telling her no if she asked for help, she seldom asked them for anything anyway.

They chose their friends wisely and Diane knew about every one of them and their parents. Things like drugs, alcohol or smoking were completely out of the question. They both had assured her that she had nothing to worry about on that front.

She was a very active part of her children's lives and was so very proud of them. Never having to worry about the decisions they made or having to second-guess them. They always got good grades, loved school, were active in sports and other activities at school and gave her no reason to be anything but proud of them.

They were genuinely glad to include her in their plans and asked for her opinion often. Something a lot of kids today don't do. She was so very happy that they loved, respected and trusted her enough to make her such a huge part of their lives.

Debbie was a bit shorter than her mo. Slim build and long auburn hair that flowed to her waist, she could almost sit on it. She was picture perfect, not because she was Diane's daughter. She had those looks that always made people say "she should be a model."

She looked like she should be on the cover of every teen magazine, was not impressed easily with material possessions, and could care less about status symbols. She was a down to earth, well-rounded girl that had the IQ of Einstein. Mike was tall for 16, already 6 foot 3 and was big built. He tipped the scales at around 275 pounds and you couldn't find an ounce of fat on that boy anywhere, except maybe between his ears.

He had short blonde hair and a baby face that made him look almost sissyish, but looks were definitely deceiving in this case. He would fight a grizzly bear with his bare hands just for exercise and come back for more.

He didn't seem to be afraid of anything yet had a heart as big as the world. He would go out of his way to help someone and was loyal to the very end to his friends and family. "Yes" she thought and smiled to herself, she was very lucky indeed to have two of the greatest kids in the world.

She was just putting the finishing touches on dinner and about ready to set it on the table. She called the kids and told them that it was ready. They sat and talked and Mike asked if he could borrow the car after dinner to go into town.

He told his Mom that he was to meet friends in town and just hang out for a while if she didn't mind. "Don't want to spend another night strapped to your sister huh?" she asked him and smiled.

"I love her to death mom, I just need some time with the guys. That or I have her take me to town and I ditch her" he said teasingly. "You couldn't ditch me if you tried and you know it" Debbie fired back.

They teased and taunted each other almost constantly. Like brothers and sisters do, but Diane couldn't remember the last time that she had seen them actually fight. It was apparent that they loved and respected each other and would fight to the death for each other.

"Yes you can borrow the car, and don't forget what a gas station is" Diane told him as he finished his meal and cleared his dishes. "I know what they are mom, I just don't always remember to stop at one" he teased as he put his dishes in the sink. "Yeah, I know" she told her son. "I'm the one that always gets the reminder when I get in my car and it's nearly on empty" she continued. "So like I said, don't forget where the gas station is before you come home mister."

He crossed his heart and promised to put gas in the car before he came home and assured her that he would be home early as tomorrow was school. He bent down, kissed her cheek and said "you're the greatest mom" as he headed toward the door.

"Would you still say that if I didn't have a car?" she asked as he reached for the door knob. "Wow mom, tough question" he said with a smile as big as he was. "Have a good time and be careful" she said as he closed the door.

"And what is on your agenda tonight my darling daughter?" she asked Debbie as they cleared the rest of the dishes and placed them in the sink. "Well, I was thinking you, me, popcorn, TV and girl talk" her daughter told her as she placed the last of the dinner dishes in the sink. "Sounds like a date" Diane said as they entered the living room arm in arm.

Debbie turned on the television and started to flip through the channels, trying to find something that caught her attention. "There has to be something besides sports and infomercial's on" she told her mom as she continued to flip from channel to channel.

Suddenly she found a movie. It was one of her and Diane's favorites. "Hey look, we love this one" she told her mom as she settled on the couch next to Diane. "Good, it's just starting too" Diane said as she went to the kitchen and started a big bowl of popcorn.

Debbie joined her mom in the kitchen and got glasses and started getting their drinks as her mom finished the popcorn. They headed back to the living room, Diane with a big bowl of popcorn, Debbie with a glass in each hand.

They sat on the couch and rapidly got lost in the movie. Diane spoke first, thinking it best to tell her daughter about seeing her dad last night. She didn't want Debbie to hear it from Steve as he might try to make a federal case out of it and she wanted her daughter to hear it first hand.

"I went to dinner last night with Greg" she started. "Cool, it's about time you get out of this house and do something" was her daughter's response. "We went to the steak house in town" Diane continued, "and someone we both know was there, with his new girlfriend."

"Oh my God, don't tell me dad was there" Debbie shrieked in disbelief. "Yes he was, with his new girlfriend, and he came over to the table to say hi to Greg" Diane said.

"Did he see you mom, of course he did, he had to have seen you, right?" her curious daughter asked.

"Oh yes, he saw me and he almost fainted" Diane went on. "He looked like he had just seen a ghost and almost ran back to his table, it was so funny." "I wish I could have seen that" Debbie said with an ear to ear grin. "Actually it was pretty funny and I didn't help the situation any. I even waved and said good-bye as they were leaving" she said.

Debbie almost spit her drink all over the living room. She was laughing so hard and rolling on the floor, grabbing her sides and tears were streaming down her cheeks. It was quite a sight and soon Diane was rolling on the floor with her.

Laughing so hard at this point they both were in tears. As soon as they caught their breath and composed themselves a bit Diane told her about the rest of the evening as she remembered it or as Greg had told her.

"He was a perfect gentleman Deb, he even brought me home and tucked me in to bed, clothes and all" she said. "I think he was too shy to try and find anything that resembled pajama's so he left me in my clothes and just covered me up" she told her daughter.

They looked at each other, got the same mental image of Greg looking like a deer caught in headlights and rolled on the floor laughing hysterically, tears streaming again.

"That poor guy mom, I can just imagine him looking around and finally saying to heck with it and tossing the covers over you" Debbie said and they laughed that much harder. They laughed so hard they both thought they would pee their pants. Neither of them could remember how long it had been since they had laughed that hard.

As Diane picked up the mess her and Debbie had made in the living room she breathed a sigh of relief. She was glad her daughter had heard all of this from her instead of anyone else.

She also had to admit that something Debbie had said was right, very right. It was about time that she started getting out of the house and having a good time. She had locked herself up in that house long enough. The mourning period was definitely over and it was time that Diane started thinking of moving forward with her life.

Before she knew it both Debbie and Mike would be off to college and she would be all alone in the house. Something she thought about often but wasn't looking forward to. "Maybe it is time I start thinking about my future and what makes me happy" Diane thought to herself as she finished picking up.

It had been enough thus far that she had the kids and her parents to fall back on for support, and Greg had been the best friend she could have ever wished for. But she knew that before she realized it, she would be all alone and the harsh reality of that was almost more than she could even bear to think about.

Everyone had been telling her, especially in the last couple of months, that it was time to start thinking of herself. Even Mike and Debbie were always trying to get her involved in their activities just to get her out of the house and meet some new people.

Being with Greg the last couple of days and being herself felt good to her and she couldn't remember the last time she felt good about herself. She only knew that it had been before Steve had left and that was over a year ago. Much too long to live in her shell and shut out the whole world.

It was time she thought, time to get out and start accepting some of the offers she had dismissed so quickly. She was still clinging to some false hope that Steve would come back to her and beg her to take him back. She was more sure now than ever before that her chances of that happening where slim, very slim. As the old saying goes, “the writing on the wall is clear” and it was time she started reading that writing on the proverbial wall and let herself start living again.

She would have to thank Greg the next chance she got for helping her wake up and see things clearer than she had seen them in a long, long time. She was sure he would be genuinely happy for her and would approve of her newest decision to join the real world once again.

She could almost hear him saying over and over again, “I told ya so, I told ya so.” She knew that she would have to let him have his glory and admit defeat. He had told her so and continued to tell her so every chance he got she thought and smiled.

As she sat there in the silence, her mind was soon filled with thoughts she hadn’t allowed herself to think in a very long time, thoughts about sex.

She was a normal, healthy woman with the same urges and needs that all people have. She though, had suppressed hers for what seemed like an eternity now. She wasn’t some naive, sheltered little creature that had grown up locked away from such things. She had always had a very healthy sexual appetite and her and Steve had always had a fantastic sex life.

She just hadn’t let herself dwell on the fact that she hadn’t been active sexually. Or that the thoughts of it were even in the most remote recesses of her mind. Until the last couple of evenings. She had to admit that on more than one occasion this weekend she had stolen glances at Greg and had wondered what he would be like in bed.

Just the thought made her blush, even that felt good to her. Nonetheless, it was true, she had found herself thinking more and more about it the last couple of days. And, found herself wondering if the thought had crossed Greg’s mind at all.

She was sure it had, after all, he was only human and she was almost certain that her tiny bikini the other evening had brought more than a smile to him. "Would it be wrong or out of line for her to talk to Greg about this?" she asked herself.

"Would it ruin a perfectly good friendship if she was so forward about something so personal with him?" she pondered. Maybe she could just drop some subtle hints and see if he picked up on them. But then again, what if he didn't.

She just knew that she would feel like a total fool if she threw herself at him and he ran the other way screaming. Then again, she didn't have to throw herself at him now did she? They both are adults and have been through similar situations.

They both had been without companionship sexually for a while, maybe it would be just the thing they both needed. Some much needed and deserved release of what she was sure was pent up sexual tension that could be cut with a knife.

Maybe she would just get up the courage to talk to Greg and see what his thoughts might be on the whole thing. What would be the worst thing that could happen she thought to herself.

He could tell her that he isn't interested and thank her for even thinking about him. Or at worst, he might say that he thought it a bad idea and feared it might ruin their friendship. She could handle that and would just agree wholeheartedly with anything he thought best. At best, she might find out that she could be in for at least one night of much needed passion and release.

Either way she just knew that sex was at the top of her wish list the last couple of days. And since she had opened the flood gates and allowed herself to think about it, she knew now that she just had to do something to remedy the situation.

She decided that she would wait for the right moment and talk to Greg about it. She was sure he would understand and would let her down easy if he wasn't interested. That was it, she had made up her mind and would do it. She would sit Greg down and let him know what her thoughts were and hope for the best.

Something got her attention as she was just about to ascend the stairs for the night and head for her bedroom, it was the back door.

Mike was home and soon she found herself sitting with her youngest at the kitchen table, hearing all about what they had done tonight. "Did you remember to stop anywhere before you came home?" she asked her son.

"Now let me think" he teased back. "I can remember saying that I was going to stop somewhere but where was it?" he teased even more. "Do the words gas station ring any bells for you?" she playfully asked.

"Oh yeah, that was it, I was going to stop at the gas station before I came home" he said and laughed. "So did you stop?" she asked. "Yeah, I stopped, I got myself a cold soda and a snack because I was sure you would already be in bed. Then I came straight home" Mike told her.

"So that means I have a nearly empty gas tank right?" she asked. "Oh, that, no you have gas I filled it up while I ate my snack" he told her. Then quickly covered himself preparing for the playful slap he was certain he was about to receive.

Diane just got up, walked over and hugged him, and mussed his hair. "I told you I would stop and get gas before I came home, I even crossed my heart mom, remember?" he asked. "Yes I remember" she told her son. "I also know you are very forgetful and expected to have to do it myself tomorrow" she said as she laughed and mussed his hair again.

"Now would I do that to you mom?" he asked as he got an almost angelic look on his face. "Ya just gotta love the big dork" she thought to herself as she locked the back door and told him it was getting late and he needed to head off to bed.

They did a last pass of the house making sure everything was closed and locked for the night. He kissed her cheek, gave her a huge hug and told her, "good night mom, I love you." "I love you too honey and sleep tight" she said as she shushed him up the stairs and off to his room. She too went to her room and began to get ready to say good night to yet another day.

Chapter 6

Morning came much too soon. She quickly showered and dressed and knocked on her children's doors and told them it was time to get up before going downstairs to start coffee. She quickly started coffee for herself and poured fresh glasses of orange juice for each of her sleepy darlings that would soon be heard stumbling down the stairs.

She listened and heard first Debbie's voice then Mike's and knew that there would be no need to fetch the garden hose from the back yard to roust them this morning. She started toast and put the dishes from last night in the dishwasher as she awaited their appearance in the kitchen. She was certain they both would be half asleep and wouldn't have a clue that toast and juice were ready and on the table.

She would steer each of them to a chair and sit them down, she didn't want them hurting themselves after all. She turned just as they came into the room and had to laugh out loud. They both looked like they were half dressed and still sound asleep, like walking zombies. "What a sight you both are this morning" she said as she pulled chairs out for them. She wasn't sure if they had the energy this morning to pull them out on their own.

She sat their toast in front of them and told them to eat and finish getting ready for school. "But wake up first" she told them both. At times they came down bubbly and full of life. At times like this, one would think they had both been shot with tranquilizer darts. I can see this is going to be an interesting morning she told them as she went about laying out things she knew they would need to take with them.

They finished, put their dishes in the sink and managed to find their way back up to their rooms to finish getting ready for school. She had to once again laugh at the sight of them this morning.

It was times like this she wished they could have stayed little forever. She soon heard them laughing and teasing each other and before you knew it they were back in the kitchen grabbing this and looking for that as they prepared to leave.

"Looks like you two finally woke up" she said as she helped them find all their things and followed them toward the door. Good-byes said, hugs and kisses exchanged, they soon were on their way and she once again had the entire house to herself. Something she usually didn't look forward to but this morning for some unknown reason the thought didn't bother her. In fact she actually felt good about having time to herself this morning.

She sipped her coffee and walked from the back yard to the front, just enjoying the morning. She loved this time of year, the mornings were cool and crisp and full of the hints of fall. The days were still for the most part sunny, hot and humid. Summer wasn't quite ready to let go of her grip of the season yet fall was knocking loudly at the door.

Soon the leaves would turn to the most beautiful shades of red and orange and the days would soon become noticeably shorter and shorter. Before they knew it winter would be making its appearance and the entire countryside would soon be blanketed in white. As she stood there taking in the morning, she heard a familiar sound. Greg's car was coming past her house as it did almost every morning.

For the most part she never paid any attention to it. She knew he came and went daily but just never gave it a second thought. Today though she made it a point to look and wave, after her decision last night to speak to him about the apparent problem they both shared.

He stopped and said hi with a heart-warming smile. She made it a point to tell him that when he had time she wanted to talk to him, if that was all right with him. He assured her it would be fine with him and told her that maybe they could do it tomorrow evening as Mondays were always so hectic and busy for him.

She happily agreed and told him she would talk to him soon. She waved as he drove off and out of sight. "Well" she thought, "no turning back now, I've already told him I have something to talk to him about" she thought as she walked back to the house.

As she entered the house she turned on the radio and sang and danced to the music as she tidied up the house from the weekend. For some reason this morning she had a noticeable spring to her step and was in a light and airy mood.

Maybe it was just the thought of talking to an adult about adult things again that had her in such a good mood today she thought as she went about picking up this and straightening out that.

It had been over a year since she had any type of conversation that would even remotely suggest sex and today it was a subject that she just couldn't get out of her mind. Since Steve had left, it was a subject that she could never see herself even thinking about let alone thinking of acting on.

It was apparent to her that Steve was not lacking in sexual companionship, after seeing him at the restaurant this weekend with his new girlfriend. Why should she keep pushing those feelings and thoughts to the deepest, most remote part of her mind and fighting like hell to keep them suppressed? She had wants and needs just like he did and it was about time that she started acting on those impulses.

Before she realized it, the house was clean, the dishes done, something out for dinner and the rest of the day to herself. As if being led by some strange force that she could not overcome she found herself entering her room and running a nice warm bath. She went to the kitchen as she waited for the tub to fill and poured herself a glass of wine and went back to her room.

She had candles surrounding her tub although she never lit them, not since Steve had left anyway. They used to love to light the candles, sip a glass of wine and make love in the tub. She lit some candles, undressed and sat her glass of wine on the edge of the tub and got in. The warm water caressing her body gave her an unmistakable sense of security and awareness today.

She slid down in the tub, sipped her wine and let her mind

wander free and unbridled today. Soon she realized that she felt hands on her swollen and heaving breasts gently massaging and kneading them. Another hand slid down between her legs and before she could second-guess herself she was lost in passion. As if the hands belonged to another person, a person that was invisible to her, she let them continue until she was past the point of stopping.

She soon was overwhelmed with the fires of passion and release and fell over the edge with no regrets. The convulsions and spasms of her body ceased as the waves of sheer bliss passed, she was slowly coming back to reality. "Oh God I should have been doing this a long time ago" she thought as she stood up on shaky legs and gathered her composure enough to get out of the tub and reach for a towel.

She went into her room and collapsed on the bed, tiny aftershocks of passion still rocking her. Her mind was numb, her body still smoldering from the fiery waves of passion yet she felt good, she felt complete for the first time in a long time. She soon felt strong enough to stand and got dressed once again and went downstairs and out to the backyard. She found a chair by the pool and sat and sipped her wine, letting the warm afternoon sun warm her entire body.

The ringing of the phone snapped her out of her daze, she quickly ran to the house and answered it as she had forgotten to take the cordless phone out with her. It was her daughter asking if she needed anything from town before they came home. Diane told her that she couldn't think of anything they needed and would see them soon.

Now that she felt so much better and was standing without her legs shaking violently, she went about setting out things she thought she would need for dinner. She was putting the finishing touches on the salad as the kids came crashing through the door and dumped their things along the way to their rooms. "Hey you two, get back down here and pick your things up" she hollered up to them.

Soon they reappeared and were picking up the things they dropped along the way and asking her if she needed any help with dinner. She told them she had everything under control but would appreciate them straightening up their rooms before dinner was done.

Before long dinner was done, on the table and she was telling them to "come and get it." They sat and talked about how their day was, what classes had tests today and what the rest of the week had in store for them.

"I'm going to town tomorrow so if either of you needs anything, start a list" Diane told her children. She had decided that she would spend the biggest share of tomorrow in town getting groceries and running errands.

This time she would get enough groceries for the entire week, not just enough for a few days or enough to get them through the weekend. She really wasn't sure why she only picked up things that would last a few days instead of making weekly trips to town.

Maybe it was her subconscious way of getting herself out of the house. Tomorrow however she would make one trip, spend most of the day in town and get enough things to last a while.

It wasn't for lack of money, money woes would have been the last of her worries. Their housing development had made them more than enough money to last them two lifetimes. Actually it had made her and Steve very wealthy and she had tried to be more than fair during the divorce.

She was willing to split the money in half with Steve and remain partners with him in the development. He had other ideas however, he only wanted enough money to let him live very comfortably the rest of his life and gave the rest of the money and all of the development to Diane.

He had decided that a divorce was a permanent split and he didn't want to remain partners with her in the development. That would only add confusion and be bad for business Steve had thought. Diane agreed to the terms and took what was offered to her, at the very least she had enough money to last her and the kids forever and the development could be passed on to the children when she was gone. It seemed very fair she thought.

The breakup and divorce had been extremely hard on her but the kids were the ones she worried about the most. Thank goodness they were both old enough that they didn't have to go through that "I did something to cause this" phase.

They both understood that it was Steve's decision completely and that it wasn't anything that them or Diane had done to cause any of it. Debbie had a pretty tough time of it at first, she had always been a daddy's girl and that seemed to change dramatically once he left.

Diane had made it a point to let Debbie know that her dad still loved them both and would never shut them out of his life. Little did she know that Steve would distance himself from both her and the kids.

It seemed that once the divorce was final he put as much distance between both her and the kids as he could. He seemed to stop coming to see them or asking them to come stay with him and that just killed her inside. If he had suddenly just fallen out of love with her, that was fine.

She didn't understand it and it was hard for her to accept, but, she could at least deal with that. What he was doing to the kids though, that she could not understand or accept and she found that it wasn't something that she could deal with.

Mike was the first to distance himself from Steve. He couldn't understand how his dad could do something like this to his mom. He was her protector and would have fought tooth and nail to keep her safe from his dad. Yet he did everything he could to keep the bond between Debbie and their dad alive.

It seemed to be Debbie that saw through all the facades and saw him for what he had become, not for what he once was. She soon became bitter and distant herself and the wedge that Steve had drove between himself and his children only seemed to get worse with time.

Diane just couldn't understand why or how he could just turn his back on the kids like that. She had always seen the best in him, always known him for the loving, caring man he once was. What could have changed him so quickly and completely she often wondered.

How do people just wake up one day and decide that they aren't the person you have known your entire life? That was the real mystery to her, the kids, her parents and anyone and everyone that had ever known them.

Clinking of dishes brought her back to the moment at hand and soon they were all lost in conversation of who needed what, what food she just had to pick up and how much money they needed to get through another week.

Soon she was making a list and both her kids were frantically adding to it. From what she saw thus far it looked like tomorrow would be a rather full and busy day in town. It looked like she was going to have to make several stops and would be more than ready for the peace and quiet of the country before the day was done.

She loved the town and liked to shop and wander from store to store as much as any woman. But, she was one of these women that want to go, get what you need, and get out as soon as possible. She was definitely not what one would call a power shopper. She was much too organized for that and found it more a waste of time than anything. She could think of much better ways to spend her time.

List complete, dishes put away and the house straightened up, even their rooms, which was kind of a shock. They settled in for an evening together and television. Diane enjoyed their quiet evenings together and she also knew that before long it would be just her and Mike. That was what she had wanted to tell her daughter. She had received several letters from different colleges in the mail this morning.

Debbie had applied to several but was holding out hope that

UCLA would make her an offer. Debbie loved the thought of going to school in California. Even though she didn't look forward to being that far away from her mom and brother.

Debbie also knew that if UCLA offered her a scholarship she would jump at the chance so fast they wouldn't have time to change their minds. "You got several letters from schools today Deb" her mom told her, "they are on the counter" Diane continued.

Debbie raced into the kitchen and grabbed the stack off the counter and started shuffling through them. "Anything from UCLA?" Mike asked as he looked at his mom and crossed his fingers for her.

He didn't relish the thought of his sister that far away to go to school. He also knew it was her dream to go there, so he always held out hope for her.

"Oh my God" came the shriek from the kitchen. "Oh my God" again and again was all Mike and their mom heard. "What is it Deb?" Diane asked as her and Mike rushed into the kitchen. Debbie was jumping up and down and waving a letter in the air. "UCLA" Mike said to his mom. "It has to be" Diane said as she walked over and wrestled the letter away from her daughter.

Diane looked at the letter and tears started to form in her eyes. Mike just knew what it was, it had to be he thought. It was indeed a letter from UCLA, and they were offering her a full scholarship beginning with the fall semester next year.

Mike grabbed his sister in his big arms and lifted her off the floor and swung her around. "Way to go sis" he kept repeating as he spun her around like a rag doll. "I'm so very proud of you honey" Diane said as she told her son to put his sister down so she could hug her too.

"Thanks mom, I could never have done it without you, you know that" Debbie told her mom as they hugged each other tight. Now both women were in tears and Mike looked like he was about to join them. "Why the tears?" he asked.

"She made it, she made it" he kept saying over and over. "This calls for a celebration" Diane told her children. We have to do something special to celebrate this, "any suggestions?" she asked her children. "I think a new car is in order" Mike told his mom. "A new what?" she shrieked.

"Yeah, get Deb a new car and I get her old one, don't you think she deserves it?" Mike pleaded his case. "I was thinking more on the line of a special dinner or a party" Diane said.

"Whatever you decide will be great mom" Debbie added, not wanting to push her luck. Even though she really did like her brother's idea. "Oh well yeah, that too" Mike added, "but I still think a new car is in order mom" he continued to plead.

"You know something, you don't get brainstorms very often but this time you might be on to something" Diane told her son. "I am? I mean, yeah I am" he told his mom as he smiled a big smile. He was very proud of himself right now and really wasn't sure why or what he had done.

"A new car would sure make my life easier" she told her daughter. "What are you thinking mom?" Debbie quickly asked. As they pulled out chairs and settled around the table Diane explained her thinking to her daughter.

She explained that she would feel so much better knowing that Debbie had a new car that she could depend on. And, wouldn't have to worry about it breaking down on her so far away from home.

"See, I knew I had a good idea" Mike quickly added so very proud of himself for bringing it up in the first place. "Watch it genius, you'll give yourself a headache if you try to think very much more" Diane said. Then she looked at Debbie, and they both rolled their eyes and broke out laughing uncontrollably.

"What" Mike asked with the dumbest look on his face. This only made them laugh that much harder. "It's decided then, this week we go out shopping for a new car" Diane told her daughter.

The thought of Debbie going off to school was something she thought about often. Going to school halfway across the country was something she wasn't looking forward to.

She knew though that this had been a dream of her daughters for what seemed like a lifetime and she was not about to do or say anything that would put a damper on that dream. She was going to smile and be supportive even if it tore her heart out to do it. It was the least she could do for her daughter.

"Better call your grandparents and tell them you got in" Diane told her as she handed her daughter the phone. "You don't think it's too late?" she asked her mom. "It's only eight thirty Deb, they don't shut down and drop into a deep sleep when the sun goes down" Diane said with a big smile.

Actually Debbie couldn't wait to tell her grandparents. They had always been so supportive of her and had been her staunchest allies in her decision to try for the scholarship in the first place.

They had assured her that her mom and brother would be fine and they offered to check on them often to make sure for her. "Hi grandma, is grandpa there too?" she asked as her grandmother answered the phone. "Why yes he is dear, is there something wrong?" her grandmother quickly asked.

Debbie explained that she wanted him to get on the extension so she could tell them her news at the same time. He quickly got on the phone and she told them all about the letter she had received and how excited she was that she had made it. They talked for a bit and before good nights were exchanged they both told her how much they loved her and how very proud of her they were.

She told them that she would see them soon as she thought her mom was going to plan a party or special dinner out to celebrate. They told her they couldn't wait and asked to speak to Diane before she hung up.

Diane picked up the phone and talked for a while as Debbie and Mike went off to the living room to talk. "Are you going to be all right with this?" her dad asked. She assured them that she would be fine and told them of her plan to go car shopping. Her parents both agreed that it was a great idea.

They chatted for a while and her parents could both tell that she had an easiness about her tonight that they hadn't seen in such a long, long time. They couldn't be happier for their granddaughter for getting into the school of her dreams and were so very proud of their daughter and how well she seemed to be getting along all of a sudden. They soon said their good nights and Diane told them that she would let them know when they planned on the special dinner or party.

She went to join her children in the living room only to find them sprawled out in the middle of the floor. Debbie had every brochure she had ever got from UCLA spread out before them and was telling Mike all about the campus and what the dorms looked like and on and on. She had to smile, Debbie was so excited about this and she couldn't be happier for her daughter, or prouder of her.

She joined them on the floor and soon she too was lost in the excitement of seeing where her daughter would soon be off to. Off to start the beginning of a new life for herself.

Before they noticed it, time was passing swiftly and it was fast approaching time to get ready for bed. They gathered up the brochures and Debbie took them to her room as if they were her most prized possession. At this point in her life, they may very well be Diane thought.

They went through the house and made sure all the doors and windows were shut and locked and the house was secure for yet another night. Good nights, hugs, kisses and I love you's exchanged, they soon headed off to their rooms.

As she got undressed and was about to ready herself for bed, her thoughts wandered back to this afternoon and what she had allowed herself to do. Soon she found herself sliding under the covers nude and once again let her mind wander and her hands fulfill a void that she knew all too well had gone unfilled for much too long.

Before she realized it wave after delicious wave of molten passion was sweeping her over the edge and into a state of bliss she had yearned for all too much lately. She abandoned her inhibitions and let her body react in ways she thought she would never experience again. Her body convulsed violently and tightened as she left herself go completely. Soon she was drifting slowly back to reality and was succumbing to a very peaceful sleep.

Chapter 7

The sun beaming through her window awakened her to the welcoming of a new day with a verve and vigor she couldn't remember in years. She practically sprang from her bed, showered, dressed and bounded down the stairs.

This morning her daughter had her mothers' vigor as she too soon came practically skipping into the kitchen. They both soon were lost in preparation of breakfast as they talked and planned out Diane's day.

She would meet them after school and they would start car shopping right away. "The sooner we find what we are looking for the better" Diane told her daughter. She agreed with her mom wholeheartedly.

Although neither of the kids knew it, the idea of getting Debbie a new car and passing her old one down to Mike was one that Diane had been tossing around quite a bit lately. She knew that Mike was getting older and would soon want to go his own way with his own friends. Something rather hard to do when you have to rely on your older sister for transportation.

It was something she knew she would have to do anyway as Debbie would be graduating before she knew it. And, would go to school somewhere, even if it hadn't been California. It was time that Mike had a car of his own and this would give Debbie plenty of time to break in a new car.

Time to work out any bugs while still at home and Diane could get things fixed before she was over a thousand miles away. She was getting almost as excited as her daughter at the thought of shopping for a new car.

Soon Mike came bounding down the stairs, taking the steps two at a time. As he entered the kitchen and saw his mom and sister deep in conversation, he thought it best if he just sat back and listened for a change. So, he dug into his breakfast trying to catch as much as he could between the two of them. "Are you ok with the idea of getting Debbie's old car?" his mom asked him.

"I'm fine with it mom, it's a great car and I know it's mechanically sound. She takes good care of it" he told his mom. "Then it's settled, both of you meet me at the mall right after school today. We'll start looking for a new car for Debbie" she told them as they gathered their things to leave. "We'll see you after school then mom" they said as they headed out the door.

Diane gathered her things and headed out the door almost immediately after them. She wanted to get things done and out of the way so they wouldn't have any interruptions while car shopping.

Besides she thought this might give her time to do some scouting around and look without the two of them with her. Maybe she could find the best deals and steer Debbie away from something that might only give her headaches in the end. At least it would be worth a try she thought as she headed for her car.

She quickly buckled up and started to back out of the drive when she heard Greg's car coming down the street. This time she stopped and waited for him to pass before backing out. She didn't want him to think that she was trying to run him over again.

He stopped short of her drive and got out and came over to her car. As she rolled down the window he greeted her with a huge smile and a hearty good morning.

"You're off early this morning" he said as he reached the side of her car. "I know, errands, grocery shopping and I have to meet the kids after school" she told him. "We're going new car shopping for Debbie, she got her letter of acceptance for UCLA in the mail yesterday" she continued. "Tell her congratulations and I'm proud of her" Greg said with a big smile.

"I will, I promise" she said and told him that she would wait till he got past before she attempted to back out. "I don't want you thinking that I'm trying to run you over or anything" she said with a sly little grin. "What was it you wanted to talk to me about?" he asked before starting toward his car again. "Can we get together tomorrow night for dinner and talk then?" she asked him as she batted her eyes and smiled.

"How can I say no to a face like that?" he asked as he opened the door to his car and got in. "It's a date then, I'll call you tomorrow to make sure that everything is still on" she said. "Sounds like a plan to me" he said as he waved and started pulling away. She waved as he passed and he waved back.

She quickly backed out and followed him until he turned off. She had almost forgotten about telling him that she wanted to talk to him, it was apparent though that he hadn't.

The drive to town was uneventful and somewhat boring, then something dawned on her. She planned on going to the supermarket which would mean frozen items would be left in the car all day.

Deciding that was not a good idea, she quickly rethought her plans for the day and headed straight for the supermarket. She would get her grocery shopping out of the way first. Then she would return home, put away her things and come back to town.

She hated to make two trips to town but didn't really see any way around it. It would just have to be done she thought as she pulled into the parking lot of the market. She followed her list and kept away from impulse buying and items she knew they didn't need.

The faster she got done the faster she could get home put these things away and come back to town. She drove home and put the groceries away as quickly as she could. Soon she found herself once again on the road to town.

The trip back to town went quick and she was soon lost in the hustle and bustle of all her errands. She made the bank her last stop and went in this time to speak to the manager. Telling him about her plans to buy the new car and the need to stop back and pick up a check for it should they find one. He told her not to worry, if they found something they liked "just call from the dealership and I'll have a check ready before you get here."

They passed some time with small talk and before she realized it, it was time to meet the kids at the mall. She cheerfully said good-bye and assured her banker that they would call if they found something they agreed on.

She drove to the mall to meet the kids and spotted Debbie's car in the parking lot as she pulled in. She parked as close as she could and went in to find them.

It didn't take her long to find them, they were in the food court and of course Mike was stuffing his face with french fries. "You couldn't wait for dinner?" Diane asked as she approached their table.

"You should know him by now mom, he would eat all day and night if you would let him" Debbie said and smiled. "Hey, I'm a growing boy" he managed to say between bites. "Yeah we know" they said in unison and laughed until they thought they would cry. "Are you two ready to start looking at cars?" Diane asked. They said they were and Mike quickly grabbed his fries as they headed toward the parking lot.

They drove from dealer to dealer looking at first one car then another, none of them appealing to her or Debbie. Finally the last place they stopped had some models that Diane thought were practical and Debbie just thought they were "cool."

After test driving what Diane thought was every available model on the lot, they found one that they both just fell in love with. It was well equipped had a variety of options and was even in a color they both agreed on. Diane made the call to the bank and they informed her that a check was being prepared and could be picked up as soon as they got there.

Diane told Debbie to drive the new car to the bank and pick up the check and bring it back while she filled out all the paperwork. Mike asked if it would be ok for him to drive Debbie's old car home and wait for them to get there, Diane told him it would be fine.

She filled out the paperwork and warranty information while

waiting for Debbie to return with the check. Discussing dealerships in and around the area that Debbie would be attending school in.

She was quickly assured that the area Debbie would be in had a number of dealers and any of them could perform warranty work on her car at any time. That made Diane feel much better and a bit safer as well.

Just then Debbie walked in with an envelope in hand and placed it on the desk in front of her mom. Diane quickly opened it and withdrew the check and handed it to the salesman. He thanked them several times and told them both to keep track of the mileage and bring the car back for the scheduled checkups, they assured him they would. As they walked out to where their cars were parked Debbie stopped and hugged her mom tightly.

"I love you so very much mom, thank you for the new car and thank you for just being my mom" she said. Diane had tears forming and told her daughter once again how important a part of her life she was. "I'll follow you home" she said as they each got into their cars and headed toward home.

The first thing they noticed as they pulled into the drive was Mike cleaning and scrubbing Debbie's old car, now his new car. He had carefully taken all of Debbie's things out and placed them in a box to be put in her new car and was busily personalizing her old vehicle to say "I am Mike's."

As the kids soon became lost in fussing over Debbie's new car, Mike's new car, and putting things in one and taking them out of the other Diane slipped almost unnoticed into the house to start something quick and easy for dinner.

She decided it best to leave them alone at this point. They will sort everything out and before long they both will have those cars just as they want them. As she sorted through things in the freezer, left overs in the refrigerator and what could be prepared quickly with little or no effort, she came up with two choices for the menu tonight.

With the flip of a coin it was fate that decided dinner tonight, pizza. She tossed a couple of pizza's in the oven and looked out into the drive to see how they were doing. It looked as though they were done for the most part so she opened the door and announced that pizza was the menu item of the evening and it would soon be done.

They both smiled, said that's fine mom and went about the task of finishing the job at hand. She just smiled and shook her head, closed the door, and checked on dinner in the oven.

It would be done soon so she started setting the table and preparing drinks for all of them. Diane was just about to remove their evening cuisine from the oven when they both came dashing into the house arguing over whose car was the coolest now.

"You two go wash up before dinner" was all she could manage between the slaps and jibs. Soon they were all seated at the table and dinner went rather quickly tonight.

She told Debbie that she would call first thing in the morning and get the insurance straightened out on both cars and they both would need to stop and pick up their new insurance cards after school.

They both chimed almost in unison "thanks mom, you're the greatest" and went about eating. After dinner the kids gathered up the dinner dishes and put them in the dishwasher as Diane checked the answering machine for messages.

The only messages ever left were for the kids but tonight she found one for her, it was Greg. He just left a message saying he would be home all evening if she still wanted to stop up and talk. She glanced at the clock, it was still early, only going on seven and she didn't anticipate her talk with Greg would last long. So, she told the kids that she was going to run up to Greg's for a bit and would be back soon.

Diane decided to walk to Greg's, it was a rather warm evening and the walk tonight felt good. The entire way she kept going over in her mind just what she would say, how she would bring up a subject like sex with Greg. Wondering if she even had the courage to blurt out the words once she was face to face with the man. Or, would she freeze and chicken out and just talk to him about the weather.

She was about to find out as the walk seemed to go quicker than she realized and she was at his door. She slowly raised her shaking hand to press the doorbell. It was as if another person were pushing the button.

Like she was beside herself and before she could second-guess this decision the door was opening and Greg was inviting her inside. "Oh my God, now what do I do?" she was questioning herself as she smiled and walked inside.

"Can I get you something to drink?" he asked as they walked into the living room, moved to the sofa and took a seat. "I have wine or coffee, take your pick" he said as he stood and started toward the kitchen. Her mind was whirling about now, should she take the wine or coffee.

The wine would definitely help her relax and put her more at ease, "wine would be fine" she managed to spit out. "Coming right up" he said as he slipped out of sight and she heard glasses clinking in the kitchen. Not quite knowing how to even start a conversation about something so personal without sounding like a shameless tramp.

She wracked her brain trying out different opening lines and was coming up blank. "I can't just blurt it out and ask if he would like to have sex" she thought as he came back with two glasses of wine and placed hers on the table in front of her. "Thank you Greg, I really need this right now" she said as she downed the glass as if it were a shot.

"Would you like another?" he managed to ask in awe that she had just downed her first glass in a few gulps. She managed to say yes and thanked him for being so kind. Besides she thought, it would give her a few more minutes to come up with something to say. Greg quickly returned, this time he had her glass in one hand and the opened bottle of wine in his other. "Good call" she thought to herself and smiled.

As he sat beside her on the sofa he became aware that something was either wrong or bothering her and could see the difficulty she was having bringing herself to say anything.

As she sipped her second glass of wine, he was the one that broke the ice and got the conversation off to a rip-roaring start. "I have to be honest with you about something" he started. At first she thought that her libido had taken control of her mouth and she was just blurting out the words. She quickly realized it wasn't her words, but Greg's.

Greg thought it best to clear the air and be honest about what had happened. Or to be more exact, what had almost happened the other night. He was only hoping that she would respect him and be grateful to him for not taking advantage of a situation like that.

"Ok" she started, "don't tell me, you're actually a woman" she blurted out. They turned, looked at each other and laughed. "No, nothing so sinister" he continued, but, it is about the other night after we came back here after dinner.

"I knew it, I stripped and danced on the table didn't I?" she asked in shock. He told her the whole story, all about too much wine, the kisses, her starting to undress, and his role in her getting home unscathed.

Now that the proverbial ice had been broken, she found it easier to talk more openly about why she had came in the first place. She somehow found it easy to tell him what was on her mind and Greg was more than happy that she chose him to have this conversation with.

He told her that he had on more than one occasion thought about the two of them, alone, if for even one night of unbridled passion and bliss. As a matter of fact he told her that had he let the other night get the better of him, she would have been waking to breakfast in bed with him instead of a hazy uncertainty of what had transpired the evening before. They laughed and sipped their wine, both feeling so much better that they had cleared the air of this.

He put her fears to rest and assured her that should she get the urge, no, need to have some companionship of the sexual nature, all she had to do was call. And, he would be more than happy to lend a hand, and various other body parts for that matter.

They laughed and drank their wine and things between them seemed so much calmer and at ease now. Diane quickly added though that she was in no way looking for a serious relationship or commitment to become of anything like this, especially right now.

She explained that she just wasn't ready to take a step like again in her life. She was just starting to get used to the fact that Steve wasn't coming home and she was actually dealing with that better than she had expected.

He told her that he fully understood and could and would respect her decisions on anything such as relationships or commitments. To be honest, he wasn't sure that he was ready for another serious commitment in his life at this point. Like her, he was getting used to the fact that he was alone. His ex wasn't coming back, and he just had to move on with his life.

Before they noticed it the time was getting away from them and Diane said she needed to be going. He showed her to the door and told her that their talk tonight was safe and would be their little secret. She thanked him and as she turned to go out the door, Greg did the unexpected.

He turned her around, pulled her close to him and kissed her deep and long. She kissed him back and quickly said good-night. Knowing that if she allowed herself to stay, she wouldn't be able to stop herself, and tonight just wasn't the right time.

As she entered the back door she found Debbie and Mike on the sofa. Watching televison, talking cars, California, school in general and how much they would miss each other next fall when she went away to school.

She walked over to the sofa, hugged them both and told them how very peaceful and quiet it would be when she did leave for school. "Gee thanks mom, sounds like you're already thinking about renting out my room or something" Debbie said.

They laughed and Mike added that if she did rent out the room it had to be to a single girl around his age. "Like that would happen" both Debbie and Diane fired back at him. They discussed going away to school more in detail, would she live in the dorms or try to find an apartment off campus and find a roommate?

Diane assured her that it wasn't too early to start sorting things out now so she would be more prepared when the time did come to head west. Debbie told her mom that the first thing she had to do was accept the offer of the scholarship. Diane told her daughter that she was way ahead of her there, she had called UCLA earlier in the day and asked how to go about accepting.

She went on to tell Debbie that she had an acceptance letter already done, in the mail and they would soon get confirmation of her placement. "You are the best mom in the world" Debbie shrieked and jumped up and hugged Diane tight. "Yeah I know, I am kind of awesome, aren't I?" Diane asked teasingly. Mike started to cough and before he could get into full choke mode Diane asked if he remembered it was her that made it possible for him to be driving from now on instead of walking.

He quickly agreed that she was the most awesome mom in the world and would dare anyone to say differently. "It's so much easier when you either want something or just got something isn't it?"she asked her son.

All he could do was smile and nod. Diane and Debbie sat on the floor with brochures and literature strewn about the place and read anything and everything they could about her daughters upcoming trip to the west coast.

Diane knew they had more than enough time to make all the final decisions and arrangements. But, she also knew the time would fly by much quicker than she realized or wanted. They picked up the brochures and straightened up before going to their rooms. They gave Diane hugs, kisses and goodnights before heading up the stairs to their rooms. "Sleep tight you two" she said as they disappeared up the stairs.

As she sat in the middle of the floor in silence, she thought back and wondered where the time had went. It seemed like only yesterday Debbie was being brought home from the hospital and discovering her new life. Now here she was, all grown up, getting ready to graduate one school and preparing herself to go off to yet another, how had she grown up so fast.

Before long, Diane knew that she was going to have to face this scenario one more time when Mike prepared to leave for college. Now that she really wasn't ready for nor would she be able to take it as well, Mike after all is her baby.

They grow up so fast and before we know it they are adults with families of their own, how does the time pass so quickly. Yesterday she thought she would have them forever. Today she realizes that tomorrow is fast approaching and she will be saying good-bye to her oldest.

Its times like this that make one face their own mortality and realize the old saying that life is short is truer than one would like to admit. Not only is life short, but fast, Diane thought as she went through the house making sure that everything was secure and safe for the night. She poured herself a glass of wine and pulled out a chair at the table. Shifting her thinking now to Greg and the talk they had earlier this evening.

She was so very glad and respected him so much more now that he cleared the air about what had almost happened the other night. In the back of her mind she just knew that something had happened or almost happened. Part of her wished that he would have given in to temptation and taken her upstairs.

Part of her was glad that he hadn't. He was right, she would have blamed herself, would have never forgiven herself, and would have beat herself up over it forever had she woke up next to him the next morning.

She was so very glad he had the insight and restraint to control himself and make the right decision. God knows she didn't have the sense that night to make any decisions. In that moment she fully understood just how lucky she was to have a friend like Greg in her life.

He had seen her at her worst and hadn't run the other way. She was glad that he had stood beside her and been there to help her through some very rough times.

She finished her wine, put her glass in the sink and headed for bed herself. Tomorrow would be a busy day for her as she had to get the insurance straightened out on the cars and start checking into a trip to California during Christmas break.

She thought it would be best to go during the Christmas break, they would have time to tour the school, see the dorms and check out classes. Diane wanted to get things worked out ahead of time so when the time came for Debbie to leave, she wouldn't be overwhelmed by all the last minute details.

If they finalize a lot of the details now, it will make her transition to college life a lot easier Diane thought as she headed up to her room. As she closed the door, the thought crossed her mind, should she give herself that helping hand tonight as she had last night or just give in to the alluring effect the empty bed had on her tonight. She decided it best to give in to the bed and was asleep almost as soon as her head hit the pillow.

As she showered and dressed the next morning Diane fully expected to be the first up, as usual. Much to her surprise both Debbie and Mike were up, had coffee on and were at the table eating when she came down and into the kitchen.

"Who are you two and what have you done with my children?" she playfully asked. "I know you can't be them, I would still be trying to get them out of bed" she went on. Debbie and Mike just looked at each other, rolled their eyes and shook their heads.

Neither of them felt like sparring with her this morning. To be honest, neither of them felt they would win anyway. Diane got her coffee and joined them at the table. "I have an idea and want to see what you two think about it" she said. She told them about her plan to make the trip to California during their Christmas break so they could check out the school, check into classes and dorm space and have most of the details worked out before Debbie had to leave next year.

They both jumped up and hugged her and told her how excellent her idea was. They could hardly contain themselves at the thought. "I will take that as agreement on your parts" Diane said and smiled as she hugged them back.

"I'll start making arrangements today" she told them as they started gathering up their things for school. "Don't forget to stop and pick up your insurance cards after school you two" she said as they headed for the door. "We won't mom, we promise" they said as they each headed for their cars.

As she watched them back out of the drive and head off to school, she realized how strange it was to see Mike driving himself to school now. He had got his license right after his sixteenth birthday and was an excellent and cautious driver.

He just always rode with Debbie and it was strange to see him driving himself. "I guess this is just another step in his growing up" she thought to herself as she shut the door and picked up the breakfast dishes.

She quickly straightened up the house then sat down to make calls she before heading to town to check with the limited few travel agencies they had in town about travel plans for Christmas. She called the insurance company first and had things worked out before she knew it. Calls done, house picked up, something set out for dinner, she gathered her things and headed for her car. "Next stop town" she thought as she backed out of the drive and pointed the car toward town.

Chapter 8

The trip to town seemed to go quickly and before she knew it she was pulling into the mall parking lot. There were two travel agencies inside the mall and one in town on the square.

She thought it best to check out the mall first as she would be able to get some prices before moving onto the last agency. Besides she thought, this makes for only two stops instead of several and the thought of getting home with some spare time to herself kind of appealed to her today.

Maybe another candlelight bath, cold glass of wine and letting her hands have a mind of their own so to speak would be a rewarding way to end her busy day.

She soon found herself at the last travel agency and was finding the prices she was getting didn't vary much. Obtaining tickets and motel rooms close to the campus were proving to be quite easy as the school would be empty for the most part for their own Christmas break.

She decided to book the flight and rooms now as putting it off might prove to be a mistake should prices rise before they left. As she left the business she heard her name being called from across the street.

It was one of the salesmen from the car dealership where they had bought Debbie's car last night. As he crossed the street and approached her, she realized it was a man that she had went to school with.

She hadn't seen him in years and didn't recognize him last night at the car lot. He offered what she felt was a heartfelt "I'm sorry to hear about you and Steve" and was sincere in his intent she felt. He did however ask her if she might like to have dinner one evening and catch up on old times.

It would have been so easy for her to just say no as she always did, but, her own words came back to her. "It's time to move on and start living again." Instead of graciously turning down the offer, as she always did, she happily accepted.

He gave her one of his cards and told her to call and let him know what night would work best for her. She assured him that she would call soon and they exchanged pleasant good-byes as she headed for her car. With the trip planned and booked she returned home and called California.

She was assured that they would have staff available to process class information, dorm space availability and to give them a detailed tour of the campus and it's facilities. With all the finishing touches on their Christmas trip done, Diane poured herself a glass of wine and headed to draw herself a nice warm bath.

She soon was lost in thought as the warm water lapped her skin and she once again pleasured herself to total release. Her thoughts this time wandered to what it would feel like to have Greg's hands in place of her own. Bath finished and dressed again, she went down to start preparing dinner so it would be ready when the children got home.

Salads done and in the refrigerator she moved onto the main course. As she finished dinner and was about to set it on the table the kids came crashing through the door laughing hysterically. "What is so funny you two?" she asked as they hugged her and pulled out their chairs for dinner. "I got hit on today while we were going to pick up those insurance cards" Mike exclaimed.

"You what?" Diane asked. Debbie explained that one of the guys at school that has been trying to get her to go out with him forever thought it was her driving the car and screamed out "go out with me" as they drove by. "So Mike, are you going to go out with this young man?" Diane laughed.

"At the very least make him take you somewhere nice for dinner" she teased him. By this time Debbie and her both were laughing so hard they felt like they would fall out of their chairs, and almost did. "Very funny you two" was all Mike could manage before even he busted out laughing.

They laughed and ate and Diane told them about her day and

getting all the arrangements made for their trip during their Christmas break. The time would pass quickly and before they knew it they would be getting on a plane and trading the icy winds, cold and blowing snow for the sun and sand of California.

"I'll bet it will be kind of weird to decorate a palm tree instead of a Christmas tree this year" she told them as they finished eating and started to clear the dishes.

They laughed that night and looked online for places of interest around the area they would be visiting. She decided to make this not only a fact-finding trip but a much needed and deserved vacation for both her and the kids.

She even called and told Greg of their plans. He offered to drive them to the airport, drop them off and pick them up when they returned. It was so very sweet of him and would be appreciated more than he could know.

She really didn't know whom else she would ask to take them and pick them up other than her parents and she really didn't want them driving anymore than they had to in the winter. She feared for their safety anytime she knew they were driving in conditions like that and they knew it.

Diane was glad that Greg would be the one taking them and picking them up. She even told him of the offer she got earlier that day. He was happy that she allowed herself to say yes. "It might be good for you to go out and have a good time with someone other than friends or family" he told her.

She knew that he was right, she also knew it would be awkward and take some getting used to. He told her that she would be fine, as he had faith in her. It was early and she asked if she could stop up for a while.

She told him that she needed that helping hand, and various other body parts he had so generously offered the other night, and she needed it tonight. He almost yelled "yes come on up" so loud she was sure the kids heard him without the phone. She told him that she would be up in a while as she wanted to do something special before she came up.

She told the children that she was going to go up to Greg's and give him all the information on departure dates and arrival dates. Since he had volunteered to drive them to, and pick them up from, the airport when they leave. She couldn't very well say "I'm going up to Greg's to have casual sex because I'm tired of being without" now could she?

She went to her room and put on some lingerie that she had put away shortly after Steve had left. She didn't think she would ever have any use for it after that and it excited her to think that she had found reason to wear it now.

She quickly freshened up, put on the teal bustier complete with teal stockings held in place with garter straps hanging from the bottom. It accentuated every curve and complimented her breasts quite nicely.

She was extremely pleased at what she saw in the mirror as she turned to and fro. She was even more sure that Greg would approve. She quickly dressed and said "I'll be back in a little while" as she headed for the back door. "Tell Greg thanks for us" Debbie said, "I will" Diane said as she closed the door and started toward Greg's.

He met her at the door, she didn't even have to ring the bell. As soon as she had stepped inside he bent down, picked her up in his arms and headed straight for the stairs that led to his room.

Outside his bedroom door he looked deep into her eyes and said, "if you're going to change your mind about this, now is the time." She kissed him deeply and whispered in his ear, "I'm not going to change my mind, I want you, and I want you now." He entered the room with her in his arms and put her down at the edge of the bed.

As she stood there before him they kissed again, so deep and passionately they felt as though their entire bodies where on fire. He slowly started to undress her, and gasped at the sight of this beautiful woman before him. "Do you like it?" she asked as he undressed and took her in his arms once again and kissed her so hard she felt it to the depths of her very soul. “I’ll take that as a yes” she said as they slid into the bed and under the covers.

They kissed, they touched, they explored every inch of each others bodies and melded into one that night. He made love to her so passionately and completely she was sure that she would not be able to walk for hours.

Her body trembled at his touch and every time he kissed her she felt the fires of passion ignite all over again. She couldn’t remember anyone ever making love to her like this, she didn’t know that it could feel like this.

Greg took her to heights she only imagined existed. As soon as she floated slowly back to reality, he would lift her to the heavens again and again. It seemed as though the waves of passion would never end and to be honest, she didn’t want them to end.

They lay there entwined in each others arms slowly drifting back to reality, not wanting this moment to ever end. She couldn’t remember the last time she felt so satisfied and complete. She hated to admit it, but, she couldn’t ever remember feeling like this with Steve, ever.

She was glad she had decided to follow her urges and make this night happen. It was something she felt they both wanted and needed and she would have no regrets. They laid together for what seemed an eternity. She knew that she would have to leave and return home soon, she also knew that she didn’t want to. Finally able to move and function again, they got up, got dressed and went back downstairs.

Diane thought that now is when the reality sinks in as to what just happened and they both would feel that awkward silence envelope them and they would regret forever the actions of the evening. She was wrong, it didn’t change a thing between them. Instead, they sat on the sofa and talked about their upcoming trip and how excited Debbie was to make it.

Soon any discomfort they may have momentarily felt was

nothing more than a fleeting thought and they were deep in conversation about Debbie's new car, her acceptance to UCLA and the trip she was looking forward to taking with her children in a couple of months.

Before she knew it they were laughing and talking about accepting the date offered her earlier and where she thought they would go. She told Greg that she fully expected it to be a total disaster but would go just the same. Before long she noticed the time and said she had better get back home before the children thought she was lost.

He walked her to the door, kissed her goodnight and told her they did nothing to feel sorry for. She quickly told him that the only thing she felt sorry for was having to leave and go home, if it weren't for that I would stay, all night.

Greg understood and told her that maybe they could work it out before she left on her trip to spend an entire day together. "I would like that Greg, I would like that a lot" she said and kissed him good night and started toward home.

Diane quietly slipped in the back door, noticed the kids on the sofa engrossed in a movie and swiftly went straight to her room and changed into her old familiar pajamas. As she entered the living room, Debbie was the first to notice her mom.

"I didn't even hear you come home" she told Diane. Actually Diane was grateful for that, she wasn't in the mood tonight to answer a lot of questions and didn't want to start making up stories to cover her visit with Greg.

"I saw you two were so interested in your movie I went up and did some things and got ready for bed" she told her children. "We're sorry mom, you should have told us you were home" Debbie said.

They quickly changed the subject to Greg dropping them off and picking them up from their upcoming trip and how she had given him all the details. Debbie told her mom how glad she was they had a good friend like Greg around willing to help. She really didn't want any of their cars sitting at the airport while they were gone.

Diane quickly and wholeheartedly agreed with her daughter. She didn't relish the thought of any of their vehicles sitting basically unguarded and unwatched while they were having fun in the sun.

Diane went to the kitchen and quickly prepared a big bowl of popcorn and joined her kids on the sofa. Before long she was lost in the movie with her children and the thought of what had happened this evening with Greg pushed to the back of her mind, for now anyway.

The movie over, they picked up their mess and went about locking up and securing the house for yet another evening. Soon hugs, kisses and goodnights were being exchanged and they were all heading to their rooms to settle in for a good night sleep.

As she closed her bedroom door the thoughts and images of her and Greg came flooding back to the forefront of her mind. Suddenly it was all she could think about. She smiled a sly little smile at the thoughts going through her mind at the moment.

"Anyone that says that a woman can take care of things better than a man because she knows her own body never spent any time with a man like Greg" she mumbled under her breath.

"Oh my God he is fantastic" she thought to herself and felt tiny aftershocks of passion and bliss sweep over her for a moment. He had made her feel like she had never felt before, she always thought that sex with Steve was the best in the world. Of course, she had only been with Steve and didn't know what it was like to be with another man.

Now that she knew what it could be like, she decided right then and there that this would not be a one time thing. Sex was an important part of her life, after all, she was human and had needs too.

She wasn't by any means easy or a tramp just out looking for a good time, but, she also knew that she would stop suppressing these feelings and trying to ignore them. All that seemed to accomplish was to make things worse anyway.

She thought back to her chance meeting with the car salesman and how she had told him she would be happy to go out. Maybe that was a mistake she thought to herself.

His name is Tom, she had gone to school with him and he had made so many attempts to ask her out she lost count years ago. He had been one of the many that had waited for what some call "the respectable amount of time to pass" to ask her out.

She had always told him no of course, but, she could tell by his actions earlier that he wasn't about to give up just yet. She would be polite and courteous and endure what she was already deeming a total disaster of an evening.

She would gently let him down and avoid him like the plague from now on she thought to herself and smiled that wicked little smile again as she slid into the sheets and slowly started to drift off to sleep.

Several days had past and the phone call she was inevitably putting off couldn't be put off any longer. The weekend was fast approaching and she knew the kids would be off to football games and gatherings with their friends, leaving her alone for yet another weekend.

Not particularly looking forward to that, she decided to make the call and tell Tom she would go out with him. "Might as well get this over with" she silently thought as she dialed the phone.

They talked and finalized the plans on where to go, what night they would go, and what time she would meet him in town and where. She thought it best to meet him as she really didn't want him to come to her house and was even less enthused about the thought of having to depend on him for transportation and getting stuck at his place. "Like that is going to happen" she thought to herself as she said good-bye and hung up the phone.

Saturday evening she would meet him at the mall and they would go to a neighboring town about 20 miles away. They had a great place to eat, complete with lounge, live music and dancing.

She thought that even if the company was lame, the atmosphere could be quite inviting. At least the evening wouldn't be a total waste that way. She enjoyed listening to the jazz band that was playing this weekend and loved to dance, so, it might wind up being a wash she thought.

Terrible company, nice surroundings, really good food, fantastic music and a little enjoyment dancing and having fun. Then back to town to dump Tom, a quick goodnight and race back to her house to lock the doors and hide. Sounds like a plan she thought as she went about tidying up the house. But, she thought, what if Tom is a really nice guy and she has a really enjoyable evening?

Oh well, either way she was determined to make the best of the situation. After all, she had accepted his date and wasn't about to be fickle and cancel at the last moment.

With the house done for the most part she thought it best to pay some much needed attention to her yard today. The sun was bright, and it was already getting quite warm out and looked like a perfect day to work in the yard. She quickly put on some old ragged shorts and T-shirt and sauntered out to the backyard.

Pulling weeds in the flower beds, trimming, picking up fallen twigs and things that blew in with the wind done, she now went to the garage to start the mower.

She mounted the riding mower, started it and busily went about the task of mowing first the front then the backyard. With her work now done, she stood and admired how nice the yard looked. She always tried to let it reflect the pride she had in her home and she had succeeded wonderfully today.

Now time for a cold glass of tea and a shower. She was sweaty, had tiny bits of grass clippings all over her and knew she was a sight. She went to the house and poured herself a glass of fresh tea and headed toward her room to start the shower.

As she passed the mirror in her room the image looking back at her almost scared her to death. "Oh my goodness, what a sight" she thought as she undressed and jumped in the shower.

The next couple of days passed quickly and for the most part uneventful. Nothing out of the ordinary happening, phone calls from her parents, a couple of calls from Greg and one from Tom making sure the date was still on. Here it was, Saturday afternoon already and just as she had suspected it would be.

The kids already up, dressed, fed and gone, she knew that she wouldn't see much of either of them until Sunday as this was homecoming weekend and the activities were plentiful.

Pep rallies, bon fire, parades, carnival at the school, and homecoming dance would take up their entire Saturday evening and part of the night she thought as she busily laid out what she would wear tonight and went over last minute details.

She would definitely dress very conservative tonight. Dress at a respectable length, nothing flirty or sexy yet not looking like she was ready to attend a funeral either. She found a nice dress she hadn't wore in forever that would be perfect for the occasion.

Not too short, yet not formal gown length either. It was cute and covered everything nicely yet gave just a hint of her figure. After all, she wasn't going to church, she was going out for dinner, drinks and dancing.

"This will be just perfect" she thought as she held it up to herself and looked in the mirror. She quickly showered and dressed, now for the hair and makeup she thought as she looked approvingly in the mirror. She would definitely apply makeup sparingly tonight she thought as she set about the task of doing it.

Her hair too would be conservative yet nicely arranged, she was going for the respectable look tonight. Maybe that way Tom wouldn't get any funny ideas as the evening progressed she thought as she put the finishing touches on everything. She looked good, meet the parents and make a good impression good, but nonetheless, she looked fine.

Her look subtly said I'm out for a nice quiet evening with a friend. Not screaming I'm easy, I want you, take me now, she was pleased. The drive to town went quick and as she pulled into the parking lot of the mall she noticed Tom was already there, patiently waiting.

She pulled in next to him and got out, he approached her and tried to kiss her. She turned allowing only a gentle peck on the cheek. "If this is a preview of what's to come tonight, I'm not buying" she thought as he opened the door and let her in.

"You look very nice tonight" he said as she got in. "Thank you Tom" was all she could manage. He was more than perceptive and could tell that she was definitely uneasy.

The drive went fast and conversation was kept light and impersonal. Mostly centering on Debbie's new car and how much she liked it. It looked as if they were early and beat the crowd for the most part as the parking lot wasn't full or crowded, she was thankful for that.

Diane really wasn't looking forward to a long wait to be seated. She thought that would only open opportunity for him to order drink after drink while they waited.

She was not going to let herself be caught off-guard tonight by indulging in way too much wine, she would stand firm on that decision. She wasn't about to put herself in a situation that she would most certainly regret with this guy. He might have high hopes for the evening but she would deal with that when and if the time came.

They were seated rather quickly and ordered drinks first. She ordered a glass of wine and he ordered a beer. When the waitress arrived at the table with their drinks, they were ready to order dinner and gave her their selections.

They chatted and sipped their drinks as they waited for their meal to arrive at the table. He seemed for the most part to be a perfect gentleman to this point.

She only hoped he would remain such throughout the entire evening. Diane could actually see herself having an enjoyable evening if he behaved and didn't try some fast moves or lame pick up lines on her. Their meal was sat before them and they ate for the most part in silence. The occasional pass this please, and thank you, was the gist of their conversation. After their meal Tom asked if she would like to go into the lounge and listen to the band for a while. She gladly accepted and they moved into the other room.

The band was just as she had remembered, quite good, and they were playing a song she simply loved. They found a table close to the stage and sat down. A waitress quickly approached and asked if they would like a drink. Diane said she would like another glass of wine and Tom only ordered coffee.

Not sure if he was trying to be responsible and keep his wits about him for the drive back or trying to impress her. Whatever the reason she was thankful that he wasn't downing beer after beer.

As the drinks arrived, he politely asked if she would like to dance. She accepted as she thought he would never ask. She almost had him pegged as one of those "I like to listen but don't dance" kind of guys. She was pleasantly surprised to find out that she was wrong.

Much to her surprise, he was an excellent dancer and soon they were the envy of the entire lounge as they gracefully slid across the floor. She was not about to let her guard down at this point but she was more than ready to lower her defenses just a bit. Maybe she had been wrong and she would have a great time with Tom after all she thought as they danced the night away.

The drive back to pick up her car was airy and light. Much less tense and uneasy as the drove over had been. They shared a few laughs and before she knew it they were pulling into the mall parking lot and parking beside her car. "I had a great time tonight Tom" she said as she got out and opened her purse to retrieve the keys to her own car. "I did too Diane" he told her as he opened her door for her.

He leaned in again for a kiss, this time she allowed a goodnight kiss. Not a tongue twisting set your soul on fire kiss, but a nice "I had a good time" kiss. They said their goodnights and before she closed her door to leave he asked if she would like to do this again.

She told him that they would have to play it by ear.

She admitted she had a great time but he had to understand that this was all still new and unfamiliar to her. He quickly told her he fully understood and would wait to hear from again if she chose to make a second date. She thanked him again for a wonderful evening, closed her door and pulled away.

The drive home went quick and all she could think about was Greg and the earth shattering evening they had shared the other night. Jut before she reached her drive her cell phone rang. She almost expected it to be Greg checking to see if a rescue attempt might be in order. "Hi mom, I know it's late but Mike and I have a quick question for you" was what she heard instead.

"What is it honey?" she answered. Debbie wanted to know if it would be all right with her if they both stayed at a mutual friends house tonight and came home tomorrow afternoon. It appears their friend was having a party and their parents were going to be chaperons for the event.

After confirmation that the parents would be there, were aware of the party and it was ok for them to stay the night she told them it was fine with her. "Night mom, see you tomorrow" Debbie said as she hung up the phone.

Diane knew the parents of their friend well and knew the kids would be safe and have a good time at the party, so she could rest easy knowing they were ok. This is almost a blessing in disguise she thought to herself as she pulled in the drive and locked the car for the evening. Maybe Greg would like to come down for a nightcap and stay for breakfast she thought as she entered the house and turned on the lights.

She noticed a message on the machine and played it as soon as she had sat her things down. It was Greg, he said to call when she got home and he didn't care what time it was, he just wanted to know that she was all right.

It only took her a moment to decide if she wanted to invite him down to spend the night and she picked up the phone and started dialing his number. "Hi stranger" she said as he picked up the phone, "I didn't wake you did I?" she asked.

He assured her that she hadn't. Telling her that he was just watching a boring old movie that he was totally disinterested in and was just about to go for a walk past her house to see if she might be home yet. "Well have I got a deal for you" she said and laughed. She told him about the phone call she had received just as she was getting home and that she suddenly finds herself home all alone for the entire night.

Before she could even ask if he might be interested in coming down for the night she heard "I'll be right there" then a dial tone. She kicked off her shoes, grabbed a bottle of chilled wine from the fridge, and placed two glasses on the table. Before she could even give a thought to going up and changing into something a lot more comfortable and revealing, there was a knock on the door.

She opened the door and laughed, she couldn't help herself. There was Greg in shorts, T-shirt and running shoes looking like he had just run the Boston Marathon, huffing and puffing.

She invited him in and told him to sit down and pour their wine while she went up and changed into something more comfortable. "And for goodness sake, catch your breath and take it easy, we have all night you know" she said as she went upstairs to change.

Greg was just returning to his seat after lighting a few candles she had in the kitchen and turning on the radio. He looked up just as she entered the room. She was dressed in a black shelf bra, a black garter belt with black stockings and a floor length sheer, see through black robe. He literally missed his chair as he sat down and ended up on the floor.

She couldn't help but laugh and went to him quickly. "Are you ok?" she asked as she helped him to his chair and made sure he actually hit the chair this time. "My God, you are the most beautiful woman in the entire world" he managed to say as he composed himself after his tumble. "I'm glad you approve" she said as she sat down and picked up her glass of wine.

They sat and sipped their wine and before she knew it they were wrapped in each others arms dancing across the kitchen floor. They were lost in each others eyes and at this particular point in time they both could swear that the world stood still. He kissed her deeply and passionately and they felt as if their very souls had been set afire.

It didn't take long and she was soon taking him by the hand and leading him up to her room. Outside her room she turned and said, "if you have any second thoughts about this, now is the time to tell me."

He took her in his arms and kissed her again as he picked her up in his arms and carried her to the bed and laid her on it. "I'll take that as confirmation that you aren't going to change your mind" she said and pulled him down beside her on the bed.

They once again made love so completely and passionately that the world could have ended at that very moment and she would have left this world a happy and fulfilled woman. She arched her back and her entire body shook violently as wave after wave of passion shook her to her very core. They melded as one again and she was so very glad to know that their first night together had not been a fluke.

This time was different though, they had time to take time tonight. Time to enjoy each other completely and totally and though not a word was spoken between them, they both knew that they would not stop until they had both quenched their sexual thirst.

It was passionate and beautiful, it was complete and earth shattering, it was wild and uncontrollable yet as soft as a whisper. It was like nothing she had ever experienced in her life.

He made love to her over and over again, taking her to even newer heights than she had ever known before. She didn't want this moment to ever end and he was doing everything in his power to make it last forever.

It was apparent that he wasn't about to let her down and she wasn't about to disappoint him either. They gave of each other completely that night. As they slowly drifted back to earth and their senses took over and brought them back to reality, they lay wrapped in each others arms. Neither of them wanting this moment to end.

He touched her in ways that no man had ever touched her and she couldn't wait for his next touch. He didn't disappoint her either, after they lay and held each other and kissed so deeply and passionately that the fires of passion were once again ignited, he took her yet again. They made love half the night and only after they both were totally spent did they fall fast asleep in each others arms.

Chapter 9

Diane was the first to wake the next morning. She just propped herself up on her elbow and watched Greg sleep in silence. She could not believe this man had touched her in ways she never dreamed possible last night.

But, she was sure glad he had. She fully intended to awake this morning, find him sleeping next to her and be overwhelmed with remorse and regret for what she had allowed to happen last night.

Nothing could be further from that though she thought as she slid out of bed and grabbed her robe. She was glad she had woke up next to him. It felt good to have someone lying next to you in the morning she thought as she went down to start coffee and breakfast. She felt satisfied and fulfilled this morning. Not full of regrets and second-guessing herself or beating herself up for letting this happen.

Just as the familiar gurgling of the coffeepot warned her that it was ready with her first cup of the morning, Greg came stumbling into the kitchen. “Set down before you fall down, again” she laughed as she poured him a cup of coffee.

“Hey that was entirely your fault that I fell” he said and laughed as he remembered how silly he looked last night. Greg was dressed, well, as dressed as he had been when he appeared at her door last night. She thought it best if she too went up and dressed just in case the kids came home early. “I’ll be right back” she told him and kissed him as she walked by him on her way upstairs.

“I’ll be here” he told her as he sipped his coffee and let his mind wander back to last night. She quickly dressed and returned to the kitchen to start breakfast. He slapped her bottom playfully as she walked past. “What was that for?” she asked with a smile. “For making me fall and hurt myself last night” he told her with an ear to ear grin.

Soon he was helping with what he could in the preparation of breakfast. He got the orange juice and started toast as she finished the eggs and other items. They sat, ate and talked and she thought about how nice it felt to have someone to share her morning with other than the kids. She loved them with all her heart but it had been apparent to even her since Steve had left that there was an unmistakable void in her life.

This morning was especially nice to have that void filled, even if it was for one morning. They ate and laughed, Greg reminded her that before she knew it they would be on their way to California. He asked how she felt about the trip and if she was looking forward to it as much as Debbie was. She told him that actually she was pretty excited at the thought.

Morning was passing fast and Greg thought it best to head for home. Just glad they had found some time to be alone and enjoy each other before she had to leave. She told him that she was sure they would be able to steal another chance to be together before her trip and kissed him good-bye as he headed out the door and started toward his house.

She went about picking up the house and doing breakfast dishes, wanting to have everything done before the kids returned home. She put out something for dinner and took one last look around the house. Her work was done she thought as she poured a glass of tea and went out to the pool to just sit and enjoy the sun.

She heard the cars pulling in and knew that Mike and Debbie were home. She decided that they would find her easily enough and just sat and took in the day and enjoyed her tea. “Hi mom” they said as they both neared her by the pool.

“How was your date last night?” Debbie asked. Diane told her it was ok, he was a gentleman and had shown her an enjoyable evening but she didn’t think she would be going out with him again. They talked more about her night, their night and soon the afternoon was giving way to early evening and they all went in to start dinner.

They ate dinner, straightened up the house and made an early evening of it as they all seemed to be beat. Before she realized it days were soon becoming weeks and weeks were bringing new months. Halloween had come and past and Thanksgiving was fast approaching. They all were getting more and more excited as their trip got closer and closer.

Soon it was Diane, the kids and her parents for Thanksgiving. Debbie suggested inviting Greg and everyone agreed happily. Diane called and invited Greg to Thanksgiving dinner and he gladly accepted as the closest thing to a turkey dinner he had planned was the TV dinner he had bought.

Diane and Greg had managed to steal moments here and there and had made love on a somewhat regular basis. It was more than Diane could have hoped for. He was an excellent lover and had respected her wishes of not wanting to get seriously involved or making any commitments.

As the time passed though it was becoming more and more clear to her that a bond and closeness were forming. One that she couldn't ignore nor deny any longer and the thought of another man getting that close to her scared her more than words could explain.

She didn't think she could live through loving and losing someone that she gave herself to that completely again. It nearly killed her both emotionally and physically when Steve left her. She couldn't bear the thought of falling in love with Greg and having something happen to ruin that for either of them.

Before they all realized it they were packing and making final arrangements to leave on their trip. Debbie and Mike both were getting so excited. Things were working out magnificently for her and Greg too.

Debbie and Mike were invited to another party that would mean an overnight stay in town before their trip, and Diane quickly told them it was fine with her.

After all, this would give her and Greg another night together before she left. Another morning that she could wake up in his arms. A chance to say that she would miss him before she left and prove just how much. It was perfect and she took advantage of the opportunity quickly.

This night together was no different from any other nights and moments they had managed to be together. It was heaven and no other words could describe it nor do it justice. He made love to her completely.

He was gentle, caring, loving, totally aware of her needs and wants, and, fulfilled every one of them. He was fantastic as usual. It was as if every time they made love she gave another piece of herself to him. And, he gladly accepted it, cherished it and would protect it always.

Diane was so very glad that she had found the courage months ago to talk to Greg and tell him of her desires and wants. She was even more grateful that he had been so willing to give himself so completely and unselfishly to her. They both had been through a lot and seemed to respect each others feelings more than they respected and protected their own.

It was beautiful and she was so very happy to have that with Greg. The next morning they again shared breakfast and small talk and went over last minute details of the departure times as well as their return trip. As Greg kissed her and prepared to return to his own house he did something that he had never done before.

"Can I ask you a question?" he asked her this time. "You can ask me anything, you should know that by now" she told him. "I know that we agreed to respect your decision to not get involved emotionally or make any commitments and I will abide by and continue to respect your decisions. But, I have to ask Diane, when will you ever let yourself love again?"

She looked at Greg with tears in her eyes and said, "when roses bloom in winter I will allow myself to fall in love again, and we both know that will never happen around here Greg." All he could do was smile and kiss her once again before turning and going out the door. "Maybe this trip will give her some time to think" he said to himself as he walked to his car and got in.

Diane could only sit and think about what Greg had just asked her. She knew that it was getting harder for him to treat this as a casual thing. Hell, it was tearing her in two trying not to think of a future herself. She just wasn't at a point in her life where she felt she could commit to another person.

She didn't think she could be fair and open with her emotions. She was afraid that she couldn't give her heart to him completely. She knew that if there would ever be any chance of them being together, she would have to be able to give herself to him completely.

Heart, body, mind and soul. She also knew that she was nowhere near a point in her life emotionally or physically, to be able to make that kind of commitment. Not to Greg or anyone else for that matter.

At this point she was more than certain that she couldn't even say that she could give herself to Steve if he came back like she needed to. It was almost more than she could bear to think she had let herself become so cold and calloused with her emotions and feelings.

Steve had done that to her and she was the one that in the end would pay the ultimate price for letting it happen. Maybe someday she would let herself feel again, let herself love again, but, it wouldn't be anytime soon she thought as she went about her day.

It was almost like Christmas morning, you can't sleep and even after you do fall asleep you're up much too early and can't let anyone in the house sleep either. They were all up early, dressed, and last minute checks of the house done to make sure they hadn't forgotten anything.

The phone rang, it was Greg asking if they would be ready to leave soon. She assured him they would be ready when he came down. The big day was finally here and Diane and the kids would be in warm ocean breezes and walking on white sandy beaches by evening, they could hardly wait. Greg was knocking on the back door before they knew it and Debbie greeted him and let him in.

Mike helped him take their bags to the car and load them while

Diane did one last look around the house. Satisfied that all was well and everything secure, she too joined them in Greg's car.

"I guess we're as ready as we'll ever be" she said as she handed a key to Greg. He told them he would check on the house while they were gone and bring in the mail and newspapers. "We're off then" Greg said as they backed out of the drive and started the trip to the airport.

The closest airport with anything resembling a commercial flight was over an hour away so their trip started earlier than they would have liked it to.

The drive went by fast though and before they realized, they were close enough to see the planes landing and taking off on first one runway then the other.

They parked in front of the terminal and Greg and Mike went in and brought back a cart to load their things on. Mike pushed the loaded cart inside as Greg went to find a place to park.

He made it perfectly clear that he wasn't about to leave until he saw their flight in the air. Diane was glad for that, it would give her a bit more time with Greg. Even if it meant spending it with the kids and an airport full of people. She wouldn't see him for two whole weeks and oddly enough was already missing him, even though they hadn't actually left yet.

She too was becoming closer and found it harder to put her fears aside and keep him at arms length from her heart. He knew the combination that opened it and wasn't about to give up his attempts to do exactly that, of this she was sure.

The thought of being pursued had a strange and alluring effect on her. She had never been pursued before and it felt strange, but in a good way. They checked in at the counter, tickets checked, bags checked and carry ons in hand they only had to wait now for the announcement that their flight would be boarding soon.

Greg found them and joined them as they walked to the gate where they would be boarding. As they approached their gate Greg put his arm around Mike's shoulder, leaned in and whispered something in his ear.

They both smiled, looked at each other and then broke out laughing. "Ok you two, what was that all about?" Diane asked with an inquisitive look on her face. "Oh nothing mom, Greg just wants me to bring him something back from California" Mike said and busted out laughing again.

"Ok, spill it you two" Diane said in a stern voice. "I asked Mike to bring me back a string bikini" Greg said with a smile. Trying hard not to burst out laughing again. "Yeah but you said it would be even better if there was a cute woman wearing it when I bring it back to you" Mike said.

They laughed and teased about Greg's request and soon heard that their flight was boarding. "Looks like this is finally it guys" Diane said as they picked up their bags and headed to the door.

Mike and Debbie both gave Greg a hug and said good-bye, thanking him for being there to see them off. "It was my pleasure" he said. "Have a great time and I'll be here when you get back" he said as one by one they disappeared through the doorway.

Diane was the last to go and quickly stole one last kiss and told him that she would miss him and would call when they got there. "I'll be waiting to hear from you and will miss you more than you know" he said as she waved and walked out of sight.

They found their seats and quickly settled in for what they hoped would be an uneventful flight. Mike had the window seat, Diane somehow got stuck in the middle and Debbie got the aisle.

Debbie was already pulling out her brochures about the campus and pouring over them intently as the plane taxied down the runway and took off with an almost deafening roar. Now picking up speed and the nose pointing toward the heavens they could officially say they were on their way.

The flight would be a nonstop, of that Diane was grateful. She really wasn't looking forward to a lay over somewhere with nothing to do but sit and count the minutes until they once again boarded.

The flight would take just over two and a half hours. Mike was still amazed at the fact that they would land only a half hour after take off, time wise anyway. "Those pesky time zones" Diane told him. "They'll get ya every time" she told her son.

"That will be nice though" Debbie told her mom, "at least this way we will still have all day to take in the sights." She admitted that not landing in the middle of the night was one of the many appeals that helped her decide on an early flight out.

"This way we can get a taxi, find our motel, get settled in and call grandpa and grandma to let them know we made it safe and sound" Diane told them. "Then check out the beach" Mike said with a smile as big as he was.

"You just want to check out those bikinis' Greg asked you to look at for him" Diane said and squeezed his big hand. "Heck yeah" was his only come back.

Passing literature she had ordered on the motel, the area and attractions and the campus itself back and forth made the time seem to go by that much quicker. It seemed like they had only been in the air a short time and the Captain was coming over the intercom announcing that they would be landing soon.

He went on to tell them that it would be sunny, 82 degrees and the winds would be calm. A typical winter afternoon in California. "A far cry from ten below zero and eight inches of snow like we just left" Debbie said.

"And just think mom, I will have to get used to these kinds of winters, I'll be thinking about you and Mike shoveling all that snow" she continued and laughed.

"That's ok sis, you'll be home for Christmas and the snow will be there waiting for you" Mike said and laughed. Before they knew it the plane was making its descent and land was coming into view. Palm trees and sunshine, were all they could see so far.

The plane landed without incident and pulled up to the gate for unloading. Soon they were inside the terminal and were totally taken back by the vastness of it.

It was huge and they knew that they needed to stay together.

Getting separated would only lead to disaster and Diane joked that they would spend the entire two weeks just looking for each other. They went to the baggage check area and Mike quickly spotted their bags on the turnstile. Between Mike, Debbie and Diane they got everything on the first try.

Everyone there seemed to be pleasant and helpful and soon they found their way to the front of the airport and hailed a taxi. As the cabby loaded their bags Diane gave him the information on the motel they would be staying at. He told her that it wasn't far away. She was glad of that, as she wasn't in the mood for a long ride through miles and miles of bumper to bumper traffic just to get to their room.

They pulled up in front of the motel and were greeted by doormen helping with bags and opening doors for them. "This is nice mom" Debbie said as they entered the lobby. They quickly checked in and found their room to be more than Diane thought it would be. She had booked a 2-bedroom suite as Mike had told her that he would be more than comfortable taking the couch if they had one.

Debbie even offered to trade off, she could have one bedroom for half the trip and Mike could have it the last half. Diane said they would work it out. When they entered the room, it became evident that none of them would be uncomfortable or would feel slighted in any way. "I would even sleep out here" Diane said as she tipped the bellhop and closed the door.

The suite was luxurious in every way and left them to want for nothing. It was absolutely gorgeous complete with a balcony that overlooked the ocean and beach. "This is awesome mom, I can wake up to bikini clad babes bouncing up and down the beach every morning" Mike said as he wandered out onto the balcony and looked around the beach. Diane soon joined her son on the balcony and gasped, the sight was truly breathtaking.

Blue skies as far as the eye could see, not a cloud in sight. Palm trees swaying gently, a warm ocean breeze, and waves lapping the shore. The sand on the beach was almost as white as the fresh blanket of snow they had left this morning at home.

It was picturesque to say the least, sights like this are what postcards are made of she thought to herself. Debbie soon joined her mom and brother and was in total awe. She had never seen anything like it before, even the brochures and literature they had received hadn't done it justice.

They went inside and unpacked their bags and put everything away. Diane thought it best to do it now as she knew none of them would feel like doing anything later. She also knew the more time passed, the less likely they would be to want to do anything but take in the sights and have fun. With unpacking done and their bags stacked neatly away for the time being, Diane picked up the phone and called her parents.

She told them they had arrived safely and how beautiful it was when they got there. Debbie and Mike took turns talking to their grandparents and soon they were all saying their good-byes. Diane knew that she just had to make one more call but would rather make it with a certain amount of privacy.

She asked the kids to go to the lobby and get information on taxis or shuttle busses that could take them to their destinations. They almost raced each other out the door. Diane quickly took advantage of the privacy and called Greg. She told him they made it without incident and how gorgeous it was there.

He was glad they were safe and couldn't wait for them to return with pictures of their trip. He told Diane that although she had only been gone a few hours me missed her terribly already. She assured him the feeling was mutual as she already missed him too.

As she hung up the phone and thought for a minute she realized that feelings far greater than those of good friends, even if those good friends were sleeping together, were starting to emerge. "I have to be careful" 3he thought to herself. "I could fall for a guy like Greg" and that was the last thing she needed right now she thought.

Mike and Debbie burst through the door, out of breath and having difficulty speaking. She told them to settle down and try again. They told her that shuttles were available and one was leaving in twenty minutes.

It was going right past the campus, they could take it and check out the school first and decide where to go from there. They picked up things they thought they would need and headed out the door, locking it behind them.

"Did you get the camera mom?" Debbie asked as they entered the lobby. Diane assured her that she had the camera, extra rolls of film and they would be fine. Their wait was short and the driver friendly and more than helpful.

He helped Diane map out a route to take and told her the times he would be back to those spots for their return trip to the motel. She was so very glad that services like this were available.

She was not looking forward to renting a car just yet and did not even want to attempt traffic out here. From what little she had seen it was far more hectic and nerve wracking than anything she had ever seen before and wasn't her idea of anything she wanted to try soon.

They would be just fine for the time being with taxis and shuttles. Maybe before they left for home she would brave the conditions and rent a car, now was not the time though she thought.

They gathered their belongings and prepared for their stop. The driver told Diane again of the times and spots where they could catch the shuttle again and was off with a smile and a wave. They stood on the corner across the street from the main entrance of the school and just stared for a moment.

It was beautiful, huge, and looked like a place one could get lost in without trying. She was sure Debbie would soon get more than her share of asking directions. The thought made her smile and yet at the same time brought a tear to her eye. She wasn't ready for this, yet here it was upon her faster than she realized.

They crossed the street and entered the campus, looking here and there, asking the few people walking the paths' directions to the administration building. They soon found their way without much difficulty and entered the huge double doors.

They were greeted almost as soon as they entered. The friendly lady at the information desk asked if she could help. Debbie quickly explained why they were there and they were told what room to go to and to whom they needed to speak.

They spent the rest of that first day just touring some of the classrooms and campus. It was bigger than it looked from the outside. They were shown the dorm area and found the room to be very spacious and roomy.

It would be more than Debbie would need and rooms were available in either single person or she could choose to share a room. Their last stop was back where they had started, this time though it was Debbie that began making the decisions.

She signed up for the classes she wanted and was given a list of books and things she would need to make her first days enjoyable and easier. She next signed up for a dorm room, this time though she asked for moms' opinion.

Diane thought about it for a moment and decided that she would feel much better if Debbie had a room to herself. Debbie quickly agreed and they assigned her a room on the spot.

Diane asked if they might be making preparations further in advance than was needed. She was assured that now was the time to get all the details worked out as it would make the transition for Debbie that much easier next fall.

They were told that too many parents and students alike wait till the last minute to work these things out only to find that space is limited and classes are already full. Diane could see the reasoning behind the thinking and had to agree that now was a good time to finalize everything after all.

As they left the administration building, they were given a map of the campus to make their visit easier and more enjoyable. The next stop was the student bookstore. They found the bookstore easily and once inside it was apparent to Diane that everyone would be going home with UCLA T-shirts and sweatshirts. Debbie picked out shirts for her grandparents, some of her closest friends and even found a tiny, very revealing bikini that had UCLA printed on the butt.

"Look what I found mom" she yelled across the store. As Diane approached Debbie held it up and showed her mom. "Oh no you don't missy, over my dead body" was Diane's reaction to the skimpy little pieces of fabric her daughter was holding in her hand.

"No mom, think about it for a minute" Debbie said. Diane was now very confused and wracked her brain to see the reasoning behind her daughters' selection.

"Didn't Greg make a request to Mike this morning before we left?" she asked her mom. They both almost rolled on the floor laughing uncontrollably. Mike came over to see what all the commotion was about.

"Oh no, my sister isn't about to wear anything like that" he said as he approached them and saw what Debbie was holding. Diane and Debbie looked at each other, they both looked at Mike and laughed even harder. "No silly, here's the little string bikini Greg asked you to bring back for him" Debbie told him. Mike laughed so hard he practically roared.

"We have to mom" Mike added and she agreed. Greg would get his string bikini from California after all. After buying things for everyone they could think of, Diane even picked up a shirt for Steve, he was her father after all, they headed for the checkout.

They took their bags of newfound treasure and decided it was getting late and would head back to catch the shuttle. They all were getting hungry and thought it best to put their things in the room and find a restaurant before poor Mike starved.

"Hey. I'm a growing boy ya know" was all he could muster as the shuttle came into sight and they boarded. The return to the motel seemed to be even faster and they were soon in the room dropping things here and there. Diane noticed information on the desk that described nearby eateries and they picked one from the various menus and flyers. It was only down the street from their room and they all chose pizza tonight.

The pizzeria was close and quaint and they found seating at tables right on the beach. They quickly chose a table and before they decided who would sit where a waitress was upon them. They agreed quickly on what kind of pizza, drinks and appetizers, ordered and sat and took in the wonderful view before them.

Their appetizers and drinks came quickly and soon they were lost in conversation of what they had seen and what tomorrow would bring. They ate and enjoyed the beautiful sunset and walked along the beach on the return to their room.

It was like nothing any of them had ever experienced and Diane had to say that for a brief moment she envied her daughter. This would be a good experience for Debbie though she thought as they entered their room and turned on the television.

They found a movie on TV they had been wanting to see but for one reason or another just never got around to seeing. Diane went into the kitchen area of the suite and soon found a microwave and asked Mike to run down to the lobby and ask if there was anywhere close they could buy some popcorn. She gave him some money in case he found some.

He returned with popcorn and drinks and soon they were gathered together watching a movie and eating popcorn. It was just like home for the moment anyway she thought. Before long they were all turning in for the night. The activities of the day were catching up to them all. Hugs, kisses and goodnights said, they all were soon fast asleep.

Chapter 10

They awoke to the sounds of seagulls crying outside their windows and opened the blinds to the patio doors to see yet another picture perfect day greeting them. They showered and dressed quickly and went to a nearby restaurant they spotted on the way back to the room last night for breakfast. Diane suggested they spend the entire day at the beach doing absolutely nothing but relaxing, swimming, and resting.

They all agreed on the plan as a detectable weariness had caught up with them all and being close to the room today was something that appealed to them. They could start taking in the sights and visiting attractions they planned to see tomorrow.

Today they just wanted to take it easy and catch up on their rest. Jet lag seemed to have finally caught up with all three. They went back to the room and changed into beachwear, grabbed sun screen, towels and headed for the beach.

Diane was glad that it was only a short distance from the room and they could easily go in for naps, snacks and drinks when they felt the need to. Diane took pictures as Debbie and Mike splashed and chased each other in and out of the water, up and down the beach.

The kids were having the time of their lives and it warmed her heart to be able to share this time with them. She saw them go through hell as well after Steve left and last year they had a rough time around Christmas. She was glad that this year would not be a repeat of that.

The day passed quickly and after sand dollars, seashells, and other souvenirs they had gathered during their day at the beach were safely tucked away in the room they ordered room service for dinner this evening as none of them really felt like going out.

They ate in the room and after a little televison they turned in for the night one by one. Debbie was the first to give in, Diane was next and Mike was the last to give up the fight and surrender to sleep. The next morning they showered and dressed quickly, gathered their things and set out to find first breakfast then attractions they planned on seeing while there.

Two weeks seemed to go by fast and before they realized it they were packing to go home. They were lucky as they got to see everything they planned to see, left nothing out and even had time to see things that weren't on their agenda. They all had a great time, wouldn't have traded the trip for anything and were all more than anxious to get home.

They would leave the next morning and Diane told the kids she would call and remind Greg that they were coming home. "We don't want him to forget us now do we?" she asked as she scouted the room for anything that might still be in need of packing.

They went to an upscale restaurant close to the beach that night. Diane wanted their last meal in California together to be a special one. They ate and one last time walked the beach on their return to the room. Taking in the moonlight bouncing off the motionless water.

The stars were many and shone brilliantly tonight. Like millions of tiny diamonds spread generously over a luxurious blanket of black silk, it was breathtaking. They fell asleep fast that night, woke quickly the next morning and were once again on their way to the airport.

Diane checked the tickets as Mike and Debbie checked their bags. The gate they would board from was close-by, of that Diane was thankful. The wait was short as their flight boarded on time and the pilot said they would be leaving and arriving on time today.

Diane thought in silence how good it would be to see Greg. She also hoped that once home one of the kids' friends might have another all night party welcoming them home. She yearned for a night alone with Greg, and she would waste no time showing him just how very much she had missed him these two weeks.

This time away from everyone and everything had given her time to think and sort out some of the feelings she was wrestling and struggling with. She was still sure that she didn't want any kind of serious relationship or commitment. But, the time away from Greg was giving even her second thoughts to her thinking.

She knew that there was something there, some sort of feelings for Greg. She was also sure it had nothing to do with the fact that the sex between them was out of this world. This was something much more than that. Something much deeper and more meaningful, she just wasn't sure what it was exactly.

She was confused and bewildered, fighting desperately with herself. One thing she was more sure of than anything though, she did not want to think of her life without Greg in it in one way or another. That was the one thing she was more certain of than anything in this entire world right now. She just knew that Greg had to be a part of her life.

She was once again seated in the middle, this time Debbie had the window seat and Mike had the aisle. She looked to her left then right and found them both sound asleep as their big silver bird winged its way eastward.

She was glad that they had fallen asleep. She was glad they hadn't seen her so lost in thought. They both would have wanted to know what was bothering her and she wasn't really sure how much longer she could keep it from them about her and Greg.

She wasn't really sure if she wanted to keep it from them. She was certain they both would be more than happy for her, but for time being, she was going to keep it to herself. At least until she could sort out exactly how she felt and in what direction things were going. Right now she wasn't sure of either.

She was snapped out of her daze by the pilot on the intercom telling them they were descending and preparing to land. He continued by saying that it was a chilly sixteen degrees with two inches of fresh snow. She woke the kids and told them they would be landing soon. They rubbed their eyes and looked around as if they were lost.

They walked through the door leading to the terminal and

immediately spotted Greg. He was waving frantically with a huge smile on his face. He grabbed both Debbie and Mike and hugged them tight, "did you two have a good time?" he asked.

He hugged Diane and told her welcome home, then he whispered in her ear telling her how much he had missed her. That brought an instant smile to her face as they headed to the baggage check area to find their bags.

As they walked through the terminal Mike and Debbie had him surrounded and told him all about the trip, the school, the sights they had seen and the things they had done.

Diane was sure that by the time they got home Greg would either feel as though he had been there with them or sick of hearing about it. Knowing Greg, she was sure that he would feel like he made the trip with them. He was great with her kids and after Steve left he stepped in and has been a big part of their lives since.

That was one of the things she liked so much about Greg, he was genuine. He didn't put up false fronts or do and say things just to please you. If you didn't like what you saw, leave him alone because that was the real him.

They found their bags, loaded a cart and headed for the car. They loaded the car quickly and before they knew it, they were on their way home. The trip home was full of chatter and the kids both mobbed him with the sights and sounds of the beach.

"Yeah Greg, we even got something for you" Mike blurted out. "I can only imagine" Greg said and smiled. Diane and the kids all busted out laughing only telling him that he was in for a real surprise.

Soon they were pulling into the drive. Much to Diane's surprise it had been recently cleared. "Did you do this?" she asked Greg as they got out of the car.

"Well I couldn't very well have you guys come back and have to tromp through all this snow now could I?" he asked as they unloaded the bags. The kids invited Greg to stay for dinner and he told them if Diane didn't mind he would gladly accept.

Needless to say, he stayed for dinner. They unpacked and put things away then all pitched in to help Diane with dinner. They made something simple and fast and soon were sitting down to eat. More talk about the trip, the weather, the beach, the ocean, the palm trees, Mike and Debbie didn't leave out a thing.

He listened intently and before they were through could see how truly happy the trip had made them, he couldn't be happier for them. With dinner done, Diane told them all to go into the living room as she cleared the dishes, then said she would join them.

Debbie stayed behind to help her mom so they could all meet in the living room and show Greg things they had brought back and "give him his gift" Debbie reminded her mom.

"He is going to strangle both of you" Diane said and smiled as she could just imagine the look on Greg's face when he opened his package. They quickly straightened up the kitchen and Diane went to join Mike and Greg in the living room as Debbie ran up to get Greg's "gift."

As Debbie came in the room Diane made it a point to let Greg know that she was no part of all this. "It was these two and these two only" she warned as Debbie handed him the package. Greg shook it a bit and asked if it was alive.

Debbie and Mike both swore to him that it definitely wasn't a living thing then busted out laughing, rolling on the floor. "Now I am really afraid to open this" Greg said as he started to cautiously open the parcel.

Once the item was unwrapped and he held it up to get a full view of the contents, or lack of, Diane joined her children on the floor, laughing so hard their sides hurt. "I'm not sure it's my size" Greg teased as he held it up in front of himself. "Do you think it's my color?" he teasingly asked them.

"Oh yeah Greg, it's you" Mike said and laughed so hard he thought he would pass out. "You told me to bring you back a string bikini, so Debbie and I found you one" he continued.

At this point Diane was laughing so hard she had tears

streaming down her cheeks and Mike and Debbie were hugging each other and rolling on the floor. The sight itself was more than he could stand and soon he was joining them on the floor.

They all laughed until they cried. Greg couldn't remember the last time he had this much fun. He was sure it had been a while since Diane and the kids had let loose and had such a good time also.

The evening was getting away from them and before they knew it, it was fast approaching time to turn in for the night. Mike and Debbie hugged Greg and thanked him again for taking them and bringing them home.

"We hope you like your new bathing suit" Debbie teased as she gave him a kiss on the cheek and told him goodnight. "I'll make sure to call you both when I get ready to model it for the first time" he fired back at them. "Oh man, that's not a sight I want to see" Mike said as he hugged and thanked him and told him goodnight also.

Soon he and Diane were alone for a few moments in the kitchen as he readied himself to leave. "I missed you so much, I thought the last two weeks would never end" he told her as he pulled her to him and kissed her.

"I was counting the days too Greg" she told him. "If we're lucky maybe the kids will have another all night party to attend soon and I can show you just how much I missed you" she said.

He told her that he would be looking forward to it and kissed her one more time before heading toward his car. Diane watched as he got in his car and started to back out of the drive, waving until he was out of sight.

She made sure the house was locked for the night and went straight to her room. She was so tired she thought she could have slept standing up that night.

Morning seemed to come much too quickly. Diane struggled to wake and move at all, let alone try to function. The kids were still sound asleep and she was sure they would spend most of the morning right where they were, curled up under the covers. She made her way to the kitchen to start her much needed coffee and began to open drapes and blinds allowing the bright December sun to flood the house.

The morning sun was bright and almost blinding as it reflected off the fresh blanket of white covering the countryside. The sun dancing off the fresh blanket was sparkling like millions of tiny diamonds had been sprinkled over it.

The bare and lifeless trees and shrubs were covered with a fresh coating of frost. Making everything seem so white and pure, it was a beautiful morning. Diane loved winter, with its blanket of white and the frost that painted all the fences, houses, trees and everything it stuck too in an almost heavenly glow.

She made herself breakfast, deciding that if Debbie and Mike did get up she would deal with making more then. She was sure that this morning it would just be her and the ticking of the kitchen clock to reflect and ponder her life.

Still trying desperately to sort out her feelings for Greg and give them some sort of definition and clarity. She knew her feelings had progressed past any she would feel for a good friend. At this point she felt like that may be all she could offer Greg and could only hope that for now, it would be sufficient.

She also knew that he had became much closer to her than mere friendship. She could only hope that he would let her set the pace and take her time to see exactly where this journey might take them, if anywhere at all.

What Steve had done to her and the children still stuck in her mind like it had happened yesterday. She didn't want to open herself up to another occurrence like that. Not that she ever believed that Greg was capable of doing anything like that to her.

She was still being overly protective with her heart and feelings and was not about to let down her guard at this point. She could only hope and pray that Greg would understand and continue to respect her decision. No one could tell what might or might not happen in the future. If she could do that Steve would have never left, but he did and she can't.

As she went from room to room sipping her morning coffee and looking out at the undisturbed blanket of white everywhere she looked, she noticed something outside her front window.

It was the biggest snowman that she had ever seen, complete with top hat, scarf, button eyes, mittens and carrot nose holding a big sign saying, "welcome home, I missed you." She was dumbfounded and could only stare and smile as she knew exactly who had done it, Greg.

Just then she heard the distinct rumbling and grumbling of the weary travelers rising to meet the new day. "Well, the peace and quiet was good while it lasted" she thought to herself as she went to the kitchen to meet them. She quickly sat them down, before they fell down, and went about preparing them breakfast.

"Good morning you two" she said as she set glasses of fresh orange juice before them. "Is it really morning mom?" Debbie asked. Mike could only grunt.

She placed their plates before them and watched in silence as they at least made an attempt to eat without wearing most of their meal. She smiled and thought to herself that maybe she should have put bibs on both of them this morning as the sight before her was truly one to behold.

As they ate, began to function to some degree and seemed to be fully awake now, she told them they just had to see what was outside the front window. They squinted and tried to focus as the sun beaming through the window was more than these two had bargained for this morning.

Debbie seemed to get her wits about her first and busted out laughing. "Oh my God mom, look at that" she said as she glued herself to the window and peered out. "Wow, that's cool" was the best that Mike could manage this morning.

As if poked with a red-hot iron, Mike opened his eyes wide and said, "hey sis, I have an idea." "This could be interesting" Diane said and laughed. Mike's brilliant plan was for him and Debbie to sneak up to Greg's tonight after he went to bed and build him a snowman with a sign that said, "thanks, we missed you too." Debbie and Diane could only look at each other in awe. He had actually come up with a brilliant plan, and he had done it all on his own. They were both so proud of him.

They hugged him and told him that it was a great idea and Diane said she would help by making the sign. They got dressed and started planning out their strategy. Everyone went about their tasks of gathering everything they would need to complete the mission.

They all were in agreement that it would be a fitting thank you for all Greg had done, making their trip possible and more enjoyable. He had done much more than he realized by seeing them off and picking them up. Even though Diane knew that he would say it was nothing.

The rest of the day went by pretty much as normal as any other. Debbie and Mike busily calling their friends and telling them they were back and filling in all the details of their trip. Diane called her parents and decided that since they had missed Christmas, they would have dinner and exchange presents later that week.

They all pitched in and straightened up the house. It didn't need much straightening up as they had left the house spotless and no one had been there. Except Greg to occasionally check on things.

They voted and agreed on what to have for dinner and Diane set out everything she would need to prepare it. It was all in all a good day to just relax and catch up from all the traveling and constantly being on the go for the last two weeks. Relaxation and catching up was something they all agreed they needed today.

With all the supplies they needed to build Greg's snowman rounded up and put by the backdoor, they sat about the task of helping their mom with dinner, Mike set the table and Debbie made the salads. Debbie asked her mom if it would be ok with her if they went to town tomorrow night and spent the night with their friends. Explaining that they all wanted to see their pictures of the school, beach and all the sights they had visited.

This was just the break Diane was looking for and she agreed without hesitation. Even though both her children asked if she was sure about being alone right after their trip.

She assured them that she would be fine and would find something to do to keep herself occupied. She was trying hard to remain calm on the outside because she was jumping for joy on the inside. This had been just the chance she was looking for to show Greg how much she had missed him.

Now they could share another night together making love. Something she found that she missed more than she could realize while they were gone. With dinner over, they quickly cleaned up and went into the living room to watch some television. Diane told them that Greg would probably turn in early.

He had to open his shop the next day and they would want to make sure he was fast asleep before putting their plan into action. They waited till Diane was almost certain that he would be asleep and Debbie and Mike gathered all the things they needed to complete their task and were off.

Diane was sure he would be fast asleep as he would be off and going early to open his store in town. Greg owned a small print shop complete with copy and fax service. He worked long and hard to make his business a success and had been more than rewarded for all the effort and sacrifices he had made along the way.

He was a good man that worked hard to see his dream become a reality. And, even harder to grow and nurture that dream into a very successful and thriving business.

As she sat and let her thoughts wander to what tomorrow night might bring she was snapped back to the moment by her children running in the backdoor huffing and puffing.

Their faces were red and icy cold from the clear winter night and they were covered with snow from head to toe. "Did you actually leave enough snow on the ground to make a snowman with?" she asked them as she took their soaking wet clothes and headed for the laundry.

"It looks awesome mom, he will freak out when he sees it" Debbie said. "I had to fix it though, Mike tried to put boobs on it mom" she continued as Diane just looked at her son with mouth dropped open. "You didn't" she shrieked.

He assured her that his level-headed sister had made it a respectable snowman by removing his contributions and artistic expressions. They all laughed at the sheer thought of such a thing and Diane asked if they had placed it in a spot where he would notice it.

"Oh he'll notice it" Mike assured his mom. "We put it right next to the driveway, right outside the garage door." "When he backs his car out in the morning he can't help but see it" Mike went on. "I just hope it doesn't scare him into heart failure" Debbie chimed in and her and Mike laughed.

"Oh God no, please don't kill him" Diane said. "He was just trying to be nice with his gesture" she continued. "He'll be fine mom" Mike told her, "and he'll know exactly who did it too" he continued. "And you know this how?" his mother asked with a tone of curiosity in her voice.

"Well, Debbie and I added a little something to your sign" he said as he and Debbie looked at each other and laughed. "Ok you two, spill it, what did you do?" Diane asked. "We just signed all of our names to the sign mom" Debbie said.

"It was innocent, believe me." "I wasn't about to let the boy wonder here add anything on his own" she told her mom. That put Diane's mind at ease, well, as at ease as she could manage for the moment.

Diane quickly made the two fresh cups of hot chocolate and they sat and talked about the secret mission the two had just completed. It was plain to see that they were both pleased with themselves and quite proud of their accomplishment tonight.

She couldn't be more pleased with them. Before they realized it, it was getting later and bed was sounding better and more inviting to all. They locked up and did one last check of the house before heading to their rooms for another peaceful nights rest. They exchanged hugs, kisses and good nights and were soon off to their rooms for the night.

As Diane readied for bed she had a giddiness that could not be overlooked nor denied. She was already looking forward to telling Greg that they would have tomorrow night to themselves. She just hoped that he didn't have any plans that would change things. Soon she was snuggled deep beneath the covers and fast asleep.

She awoke first as usual, showered, dressed and went to the kitchen to start her morning ritual of coffee and breakfast. As she entered the kitchen she glanced at the clock, checking to see if it might yet be too early to call Greg and tell him of her plans for tonight.

"Well, at least some of the plans" she thought to herself and smiled. She had decided that tonight she would have a few tricks up her sleeve that she hadn't shown him before. And, was sure that he would like the surprises in store for him.

She started coffee and found that toast and coffee were all that appealed to her this morning. She was too excited and anxious to eat anything more. She picked up the phone and dialed Greg's number as the coffeepot gurgled and spat, telling her that it was ready if she was.

He sleepily answered and she asked if she woke him up. He told her no, he was always up this time of morning, then asked her what time is was anyway.

She laughed and told him that she would have waited but wanted to call before the kids got up and she couldn't speak freely. She told him all about their plans to spend the night in town, leaving her all alone in that big old house.

She asked if he had any suggestions that might help her get

through a night by herself. He assured her that he would stop later and tell her his suggestions in person as he had several things in mind that would pass the time productively.

She told him that she was almost sure that she had thought of the same things he had, but that she would be more than happy to listen to them anyway. He told her that he would call her later from work.

He couldn't see anything coming up that might change things but would wait till this afternoon to be ceratin. She told him she could barely wait and told him to get up and around so he wouldn't be late for work. "I might as well get up now, I am awake after all" he told her and laughed.

They agreed to talk later before hanging up and she went about getting her coffee and toast and planning out her day. She was awakened from her trance like state by a distinct knocking on the back door.

As she approached it she saw Greg standing there with a smile that could light up the day. As he stepped inside and quickly stole a kiss he asked her if her children might be up. Just then they heard distinct sounds coming from upstairs that would confirm that they had indeed woke and starting to stir at the very least.

Soon two sleepy teenagers rubbing their eyes, stretching and yawning stumbled into the kitchen. "Come here you two" Greg said and grabbed them both and hugged them tight. "I want to thank you both for the frosty friend that greeted me this morning and the heartfelt thank you note that was attached to him" he said. They all laughed and they too said thank you for the big thank you they found in their yard yesterday morning.

They laughed and chatted for a bit and as he prepared to leave. Debbie hugged him and whispered in his ear "we're going to stay in town tonight Greg, would you mind checking in on mom to see that she is all right, Mike and I would feel better if you did."

He just winked and whispered back "it will be my pleasure, don't give it another thought, you two go and have a good time."

He waved and said his goodbyes and headed toward his car to finish his trek to work. "And just what was that all about?" Diane asked her daughter. Debbie just smiled and told her that she thanked him for being such a good friend and for being there for them. Diane couldn't agree with her daughter more.

Chapter 11

Debbie and Mike left fairly early and left her to herself for the biggest part of the day. She took advantage of the situation by planning and plotting just what tonight would involve.

Greg had called and told her that he saw no reason to put off their plans as today would be a normal day and he would leave on time. With Greg confirming his attendance to tonight's festivities, she went about putting her plan into motion.

She had decided that tonight was going to be different. They usually sat and talked a bit then headed straight to her room and made wild passionate love.

While that was fine with her and more satisfying and fulfilling than anything she could even dream of, tonight she just wanted it to be different, wanted it to be perfect. She had no idea why, just that she was determined to make tonight something special for both of them.

She set about straightening up the house and getting things out for a nice quiet dinner for two. With everything as ready as she could have it for the moment she went to her room to lay out something sexy and very revealing.

As she sorted through what she had to choose from she decided against wearing anything at all. Tonight they would start with dinner, wine after dinner, a nice warm bubble bath for two and then on to the bedroom to make wild passionate love. Now that sounded like an evening to her and she shook with anticipation.

She strategically placed candles throughout the bathroom and bedroom. Everything was going to be perfect she thought as she stood back and examined the finished product.

She was more than pleased with herself and was certain that Greg would be too. She would shower before he arrived, the bubble bath would be just an alluring effect for lots and lots of hot foreplay before moving onto the bedroom.

She was so amazed at how easily and eagerly she looked

forward to casual sex with Greg lately. She never would have allowed herself even fleeting thoughts of anything like that a year ago.

There seemed to be a lot of things lately that she knew she would never have thought about a year ago, dating among the list of many. She looked around and was happy with her work and couldn't wait for Greg to see what she had in store for him tonight.

She quickly went back downstairs to start early preparations for dinner. She would make even dinner special and checked the wine chilling in the fridge. Everything was perfect she thought. With everything done that could be done in advance, she turned on the radio, danced and let herself be lost in thought and anticipation of what tonight would bring.

Her shower, makeup and hair done, she dressed in something that she could easily slip out of later. She smiled that wicked little smile when she turned and looked at herself in the mirror. She wasn't wearing anything under the flimsy little dress she had tossed on and suddenly felt very naughty.

She was so full of anticipation that she thought she could soar. This is something she needed and tonight she would not be denied. Tonight Greg would see just what she was capable of when it came to being herself and tossing her cares and inhibitions to the wind.

She was prepared to let him see yet another side to her tonight. One that until tonight he had never seen or suspected. She was like a lioness on the prey for food for her cubs, cunning and sly.

A sexual hunger in her had been awakened and tonight she would stop at nothing to satisfy it. She smiled as she took one last look in the mirror, "yes" she thought, "tonight Greg is in for the night of his life."

She went downstairs and went about the task of finishing dinner and having everything ready and perfect by the time Greg arrived. She knew he was already home as he had honked as he passed the house on his way to his. He had already called and said that he would be down as soon as he showered and dressed.

She almost told him not to bother, but decided it best to let him do what he felt he needed before coming down. She was definitely in a mood like she had not seen in herself before and could not explain why.

She was just setting dinner on the table when she heard his car pull in the drive. She met him at the door and took his coat. "Dinner is ready, sit and eat before it gets cold" she told him as she hung up his coat and joined him at the table.

They ate and exchanged small talk. It was evident that Greg had no clue as to what was in store for him this evening. And how could he, this would be new to even her tonight.

They finished dinner and cleared the dishes, Diane went to the refrigerator and pulled out the bottle of wine that she had been chilling all day. Greg saw her fetching the wine and quickly retrieved two glasses and poured it as she finished putting things away. She asked if he would like to go into the living room.

Little did he know that she already had music softly playing on the stereo, lights dimmed just right, and a fire crackling and popping in the fireplace. It was picture perfect and the minute he stepped in the room he could tell something different was going to happen tonight.

They sat on the floor in front of the fireplace on some gigantic throw pillows she kept there and sipped their wine. It was Diane that made the first move as she settled back against him and turned her head just right to kiss him deeply and passionately.

He thought twice and decided that he was not going to question why. He was just going to follow her lead and let this night take them wherever it would.

Diane excused herself for a moment and disappeared up the stairs toward her room. He had to admit this was a bit intimidating as he had never seen her act quite like this before.

She quickly reappeared and took her place next to him on the pillows in front of the fire and kissed him again. She then stood in front of him, took the flimsy fabric she called a dress and with one motion dropped it to the floor and stood before him naked.

He was mesmerized by the sight of this breathtaking woman before him. The light from the fire gave her skin a glow and he could not believe this was happening to him. He half expected to wake any moment. He didn't wake though, she took his hand and told him to follow her.

He gladly accepted and at this moment would have followed her to the ends of the earth. They went upstairs and she led him into the bathroom where he found a bath drawn, full of bubbles, and candles flickering all about the room.

Without saying a word she stepped in then told him to join her. It didn't take him long to comply. He wasn't about to deny this woman anything she desired tonight. She gently pushed him down into the tub, sat on his lap and kissed him so deep and hard he thought he would faint.

They kissed and his hands began to explore every inch of her body. She arched her back and a distinct moan escaped her lips. That night they took their time, they knew each others bodies better than they knew their own that night.

He became a part of her and her of him. They soared to heights neither of them dreamed possible to reach that night. It was more than words could describe and neither of them ever wanted this night to end, ever.

They went into her bedroom and for the first time he noticed the candles flickering. Softly illuminating the bed, she led him to the bed and they soon were one. Their hands entwined, their souls became one, neither of them knew that it could be like this, they soared to heaven and beyond this night.

As she drifted slowly back to reality and the waves of passion subsided, she lay there wrapped in Greg's arms staring at the ceiling. Diane caught herself before the words escaped her lips. She had just come dangerously close to saying the words, "I love you Greg."

She had no doubts in her mind that Greg would have responded with a similar response. She knew that he was becoming closer and having feelings that went much further than anything one would feel for a good friend and right now those three little words scared her to death.

She couldn't, no she wouldn't, allow herself to say those words. Not now or anytime in the near future. She just wanted tonight to last forever and wasn't going to do or say anything that would ruin or complicate tonight.

They had both just experienced something so pure, so right that she would do nothing to jeopardize that now. Before she realized it, they were fast asleep wrapped tightly in each others arms. It was as if neither of them was willing to let go tonight and she liked the feeling.

She rose earlier than usual the next morning so she could get Greg up and have breakfast ready before he had to leave. She nudged him gently and told him it was time to shower, she would be downstairs.

She went to the kitchen, started coffee and breakfast as he showered and dressed. They ate and talked about the weather, the kids, his business, any subject but last night. It was as if they wanted to keep it to themselves for fear of somehow ruining it or losing it forever.

It was something they wanted to cherish and keep forever fresh. And though not a word was spoken, it was as if they both knew that it would remain an unspoken subject. It would remain their little secret to be shared with no one.

He left almost as quickly as he had arrived last night, they shared a good-bye kiss and she waved until he was out of sight and on his way to work. She sat and thought about Greg, last night, her feelings or lack of.

What she had almost slipped and allowed herself to say last night, and tried to sort out her feelings. Was she actually falling in love with Greg or was it just fascination with him and the unbelievable sex they share? It was confusing and starting to cloud her judgement when it came to Greg.

As she went about cleaning the house and making a list of what she needed from town she saw something on the counter, it was a letter. She looked at it closely and saw that it had her name on it.

As she opened it she saw it was from Greg. Now she was worried, she was almost certain that she knew the contents and wasn't sure that she was ready to read it. As she sat back down, letter in hand, her mind got the best of her and she almost threw it away without even looking at it.

She could always tell him that she hadn't seen it and it had gotten picked up with something and thrown out. She knew in her heart though, that would not be fair to Greg. He had been through so much with her already. He had been the one to help her pick up the pieces of her life and go on.

As she read the letter her worst fears were confirmed. He told her in the letter that he could no longer deny his feelings for her nor could he keep quiet about them. He told her that he was falling in love with her and went on to say that he knew that was something she neither wanted nor needed right now.

He told her that maybe they should just go back to being friends, if that was possible, and leave personal feelings and contact out of the picture all together. She had been afraid that something like this might happen and it was the last thing in the world that she wanted.

She couldn't think of her life without Greg in it nor could she imagine how her life would be with him as nothing more than a distant friend. It was clear now that the time was fast approaching when she would have to face her feelings for him and deal with them.

She also knew that it wouldn't be now or today. She had things to do, and, only hoped they would be enough to keep her mind off this for now.

She gathered her things and headed for the car. As she backed out of the drive the snowman that Greg had made for her was staring at her as if to say, “why are you doing this to that poor guy?”

She shook her head to clear her thoughts and headed toward town. She could see right now that today was neither going to be ordinary nor easy for her. As she drove along the thoughts she was trying desperately to suppress came flooding in. Like a tidal wave, they couldn’t be stopped or controlled.

As she finished one errand and started another someone calling her name snapped her out of her daze, it was Tom. He approached her and asked how she had been. She told him that she was sorry that she hadn’t spoken to him but explained that her and the kids had just returned from two weeks in California.

They walked and chatted and the thing she feared the most right now happened, Tom asked her out again. She wanted more than anything in the world right now to tell him no and ask him to leave her alone, but, that just wasn’t in her.

She cheerfully agreed that she would call him later in the week and they would set a day and time to go out again. He told her that he would be looking forward to her call and waved as she walked away. Not really knowing why she had accepted his offer she went about finishing her errands as her parents would be there for dinner tonight.

She quickly finished her tasks and went straight home. She had more than enough on her mind to keep her busy for one day. She noticed the kids were home when she arrived and Mike soon appeared to help her carry in her bags.

Debbie asked if there was anything she could help with as they had both remembered that their grandparents would be there tonight, Diane was thankful for that. She was glad they had remembered as she almost let it slip her mind completely after reading Greg’s letter.

They quickly made things for dinner that could be made in advance and went to the living room to wrap gifts she had picked up in town today. The wrapping of gifts was truly the highlight of her day, Debbie and Mike soon made sure of that.

They taped each other, Mike tried to wrap his sister and they both ganged up on mom to get her into the fun. It was a pleasant and welcome distraction from her problems and feelings at the moment.

Diane heard the car pull into the drive and asked Mike to go out and see if any help was needed bringing things in the house. "Hi grandpa, hi grandma" he said as he lumbered out to meet them. "Do you need any help?" he asked and was soon loaded with packages.

They ate dinner and had a wonderful time, the kids helped clear the dishes and put things away and they all gathered in the living room. Diane had a nice warm crackling fire going in the fireplace and soon paper and ribbon was strewn about everywhere.

The kids brought out their pictures of their trip to share with their grandparents and soon they were all lost in thought. It was a good evening and before they knew it, was getting late. Her parents gave hugs and kisses all around and said their good-byes.

Diane decided tonight was going to be an early evening even if she had to ask Mike to knock her out to achieve it. They made sure the house was secure for the night and turned in early as all of them were spent. They exchanged their nightly hugs, kisses and goodnights and retired to their rooms, surprisingly enough Diane was soon fast asleep.

The days passed quickly and soon Debbie and Mike were heading off to school armed with pictures and stories of their trip to California. She once again had the whole house to herself. She actually looked forward to it for the first time since Steve had left. Her second date with Tom had come and went and would not be anything that appears in any diaries or anything.

He was once again a gentleman and nice guy. He had shown her a good time and not tried anything that she was certain he would attempt. She had spoken to Greg several times and not a word had been said by either of them about the letter.

All in all life was uneventful but she had to admit she missed her times with Greg. To compensate for her sudden lack of company, or to be more honest her lack of sex, she had become all too familiar with the act of pleasuring herself. It was empty and unsatisfying but at the moment it was the best she could deal with.

She knew that if she allowed herself to start anything with Greg, she might not be able to stop herself or control and hide her feelings for him any longer. She knew in her heart that she cared for Greg. She just wasn't sure that it could be defined as love and she knew that it wasn't fair to either of them to keep avoiding the issue.

She was more than certain that one day, and possibly one day soon, she would have to face reality and once and for all decide just exactly how she felt about him, it just wouldn't be today.

With time alone she found herself spending more time in town, she met new people and reaffirmed old friendships. She started having lunch with women she hadn't been close to since high school and found herself being asked out on a regular basis now.

Opportunities were opening up for her once she allowed herself to live again. She soon found that she was dating on a regular basis and both Mike and Debbie couldn't be happier for their mom. They were glad that she had finally came out of her shell and was allowing herself to have a good time with new people.

The days soon turned into weeks and the weeks were soon becoming months. Spring was upon them with just a hint of summer to come and before Diane could prepare for it, Debbie was graduating high school.

They threw a huge party at the house for family and all her friends and Diane couldn't be prouder or happier for her daughter. She was becoming quite a woman right before her eyes. Diane even broke down and invited Steve and his new girlfriend only to find that he had moved away during the winter and not said a word to anyone.

Just like he had left her and the kids going on two years ago, he had left his friends and the town he loved so much like a thief in the night. She heard rumors that he had taken his girlfriend and moved somewhere in either Tennessee or Kentucky, no one seemed to be sure which.

Right now Steve, his girlfriend and where they had or had not moved to, was the furthest thing from her mind. Debbie leaving for college soon and the lack of Greg in her life was much more important to her at the moment. Greg did however show up and for the most part acted like nothing was wrong, but, Diane knew that it was tearing him apart.

Summer was upon them before they realized it or were prepared for it. It was going to be hot and very sticky. Spring had been warmer than usual and that was only a sign of what was sure to come. Diane had been on several dates and much to her surprise had met a new man that she felt oddly drawn to, his name was Dan.

He was from Chicago originally and was a transplant to the area because of his job. He was a district manager for a manufacturing company, they had just opened new offices in and around the state of Iowa.

They met in town quite by accident, actually she almost backed over him too. She was backing out of a parking spot in town with much too much on her mind and stopped as she heard the horn.

"I have to stop trying to run over men in order to meet them" she remembers herself thinking as he approached the car and asked if she were all right. There seemed to be an immediate connection between them and they had been dating almost exclusively since. He seemed to be everything she wanted in a man and she slowly but surely started to let her guard down with him regarding her feelings.

It wasn't long before Greg was nothing more than an old friend and Dan was indeed the new man in her life. She didn't think it could get any better. The only thing lacking as far as she was concerned was he definitely did not measure up to Greg when it came to sex.

She wasn't really sure that anyone could but decided to

overlook Dan's shortcomings in the sex department as she wasn't really sure that you "could have it all" anyway. She was beginning to think that having it all was only a myth and something that she was determined not to spend her entire life chasing.

Summer was passing fast and Debbie was soon packing and busily getting everything ready to head west one more time. This time though would be the last trip for quite some time. Diane was becoming more and more comfortable with Dan and Debbie was happy that her mom might have found someone finally.

Mike on the other hand wasn't completely sure about Dan. There was just something about the guy that Mike wasn't sure that he completely trusted just yet. He could only hope that he was wrong and would never say anything to his mom or sister about his suspicions.

Mike and Greg on the other hand had become even closer and talked and hung out regularly lately. Greg was well aware of Mike's worries about Dan, as he too had his own suspicions. Mike and Greg had made a promise to just watch from the shadows and be there, ready to pick up the pieces again should this guy hurt her.

Greg was surrendering to the fact that anything that might have been between them was nothing more than a distant memory. After all, he knew that he couldn't force her to love him, and he wouldn't want to either.

If anything was to ever be between them he wanted it to be because they both shared the same feelings and desires to build a life together. Right now it was crystal clear that she had feelings for Dan and wasn't going to change her mind anytime soon. All he could do was be her friend and be ready to help her through the worst should she get her heart trampled on again. Just like he had when Steve left them.

Debbie was loading her car for a long and tedious trip ahead of her, and wanting to get an early start. She hugged Diane and Mike and told them both that they would have to make another trip out to see her, they assured her they would. Diane had the route mapped and planned for her daughter.

Motel reservations were made, and, she made sure Debbie had both her cell phone and plenty of money should something unexpected come up. They watched as Debbie's car drove out of sight and went into the house together and had a good cry.

Mike was going to miss his sister, she wasn't the typical sister. They never fought and were always close, now the big guy had a hole in his heart that would not soon be healed.

The house felt empty the night Debbie left and Diane decided it would be just her and Mike tonight. No Dan, no Greg, no anyone. They ate dinner, straightened up afterward and went in to watch some television, it just wasn't the same tonight.

They both knew that things would get better with time and before they knew it Mike too would be off on his own to start a new life. They talked and cried some more, hanging on desperately to each other and for the moment not wanting or needing any more change in their lives.

Just then the phone rang, it was Debbie letting her mom and brother know that she had made it safe and sound to the first stop of her trip. She told them that the motel was really nice and the trip had been a bit scary. As it was her first trip of any distance by herself, but had also been exciting.

They could understand both points of view and were just glad and relived to hear from her and know that she was fine and having fun so far. They all talked for a bit and soon said their goodnights and let Debbie go so she could get a good nights sleep and be on the road once again come morning.

Both Diane and Mike felt a bit better since hearing from her. It seemed to put their minds at ease knowing that she was safe for the night and had a fun trip thus far. Diane was so very worried that Debbie might feel overwhelmed with this trip. Might feel lost and confused and have more than a little difficulty in completing it.

She could now turn in for the night knowing that her daughter was safe and was having a good time on her first trip alone. As they made sure the house was locked for the evening Mike teased that he was kind of surprised that she hadn't waited till dark, snuck back in the drive and called from outside.

"She didn't, did she?" he asked as he turned on the outside lights and looked the driveway and grounds over. Almost expecting to find his sister sitting in her car outside. With a tone of disappointment in his voice he turned off the lights, shut and locked the door and said "no, she didn't." Diane made them a snack and they sat at the table and talked a while longer. Neither of them really wanting to go to bed just yet.

After a while they were much too tired to attempt staying awake any longer and succumbed to the alluring effect their beds seemed to have right then. They made a final pass of the house, exchanged hugs, kisses and goodnights and headed off to bed. After laying in bed and tossing for what seemed like hours, Diane got up, went to Debbie's room and opened the door. She couldn't believe what she found inside, Mike was sound asleep in his sisters' bed. She went over, kissed his cheek and made sure he was covered before returning to her own bed.

Chapter 12

As the summer sun came streaming through the blinds it woke Diane to find something she wasn't accustomed to. Mike was already up, had made her coffee and toast, picked her some fresh wildflower's from the yard and was entering her room with it all on a tray.

"Morning mom, are you awake yet?" he asked as he approached her bed with the tray. "Who are you and what have you done with my son?" she teasingly asked as she rubbed her eyes and stretched.

"Hey, can't a guy do something nice for his mom?" he asked as he sat beside her on the bed. "Only if he wants something, so what is it and how much is it going to cost me?" she playfully asked. He assured his mom that he neither wanted anything nor needed anything.

He was just trying to give something back to her after all she had done for both him and Debbie all these years. "You've always given to us, even if it meant going without for yourself mom, I just wanted to do something for you for a change" he said and hugged his mom.

Tears were soon forming in her eyes as she once again realized just how lucky she had been to have two wonderful children that loved and respected her. "I know honey and I appreciate it more than you know" she said as she hugged him back.

As he stood to leave the room he told her that he had plans today and wanted to know if she had anything planned that would interfere with his. She assured him that her only plans for the day involved a chaise lounge beside the pool.

He told her that he would be home in time for dinner and would see her later. He gave her a kiss and told her that he loved her before heading down the steps and out the backdoor. Just then the phone rang and she was sure it was Mike calling from his cell phone telling her he had either forgot something or needed something after all.

It was Dan, she was a bit surprised to hear his voice as he knew that the next few days might be difficult for her with Debbie leaving. He told her that he was only calling to see if she was ok or needed anything.

She told him of her plans to sun by the pool today and told him that if he found time he could stop by and spend some of the day with her. He told her that he would stop by as he really wanted to see her and wasn't sure he could wait a few more days.

He had to return to Chicago next week for several days. They agreed that he would stop by and might stay for dinner. She left that kind of open as she wasn't quite sure of Mike's plan just yet.

Her son was good at telling her that he would be home for dinner and more times than not, he found that his stomach wouldn't cooperate. He had on more than one occasion called his mom and told her that his plans had changed and he would eat in town and be home later.

So many times in fact that she almost counted on it now. She finished her breakfast and showered, deciding to just put her bikini on now instead of getting dressed and changing twice later. She went to the kitchen, got another cup of coffee and headed out to the pool.

She placed her lounge by the pool, turned on her radio and soon was lost in nothingness. Before long Dan showed up and they spent the biggest part of the day together both at the pool and in her bedroom. She still found herself longing for those nights with Greg. He was the best lover that she had ever had.

Dan on the other hand seemed to try but fell far short when it came to satisfying her or fulfilling her. The phone call she was expecting came sooner than she thought. It was Mike telling her that he had found some friends in town and they were all going to go out for pizza. He asked his mom if she would like to join them and she assured her son that she would pass this time but might take a rain check.

With plans now open for dinner she asked Dan if he would like to stay and she would make something nice for two, he quickly accepted. Diane decided that she could eat soon so she went to the kitchen and started fixing dinner.

She noticed that Dan was not in any hurry to volunteer to help in any way. He seemed much too content to let her do it all and be waited on. She wasn't sure that she liked that trait, but, knew that she would have to make some compromises if things were to work between them.

It seemed that the closer look she took at Dan the more she found that she either didn't like or would like to change about him. Could she be falling in love with this man or falling out of infatuation with him she asked herself as she set about making dinner. Another thing she had noticed lately since she had allowed herself to step back and pay attention, Mike didn't seem to be particularly fond of Dan.

He seemed distant and was always making excuses not to spend any time with Dan, always having something come up at the last minute. Maybe it was just her she thought, maybe she was over thinking things and seeing things that simply weren't there. She had a tendency to do that from time to time.

To be honest, she did it more than she should. Another thing she was beginning to notice, Dan sure was making a lot of trips back to Chicago lately. It almost seemed as though he was spending as much time there as he was here.

Then again, maybe she was making more of that than needed to be also. After all, the company he worked for was based in Chicago. It would only make sense that he would have to go there regularly. She decided that for now anyway she would give Dan the benefit of the doubt and not make a big thing of all the petty things she was suddenly becoming aware of.

After all, if she picked every little thing apart, she would spend the rest of her life alone. We all have things that annoy or cause suspicion in people, she knew that she was no different. It was her inability to admit her feelings or allow herself to be happy that had driven Greg away. She just now was beginning to realize that.

They ate by the pool and exchanged small talk. Dan did ask if she had heard from Debbie yet and she told him that she had called last night from the motel. They had an after dinner glass of wine and noticed that night was fast approaching. Dan said that he thought it best if he goes back to town as he had to start making plans to go back to Chicago and had a million things to do before he left.

She fully understood and told him that Mike would probably be home soon and Debbie would be calling from her second stop along the way. She walked him to the door and kissed him goodnight. He pulled her close and whispered in her ear, "I think I'm falling for you Diane" and kissed her again.

She couldn't respond to his comment as she had been totally caught off guard with it. They said their goodnights and she waved as he backed out of the drive and headed for town. Now this put a new light on things she thought as she went to her room and put her pajamas on.

She went back to the kitchen and straightened up as she waited for both Mike to come home and for Debbie to check in and let them know that she was fine. She didn't have to wait long for either. Mike came bounding through the door almost breathless asking if Debbie had called yet.

Diane told him that she hadn't and told him to catch his breath and settle down. She made them a snack and as she was putting it on the table the phone rang. Mike practically raced to the phone and answered it.

"Hi sis, how are things?" he asked with a huge smile. He talked for a while then handed the phone to Diane. Debbie was at the second motel and would only have one more stay ahead of her before completing her trip. She was so excited about all the beautiful things she had seen and how friendly and helpful the people she had met had been.

"Mom, you wouldn't believe how different it is by driving" she started. "I can only imagine Deb" she told her daughter, trying to imagine how much fun her daughter must be having. "I have tons of pictures and as soon as I get there and get my computer set up I'll send them to you guys" Debbie told her. Diane said she could hardly wait.

They talked for a while, Debbie telling her that the maps and directions she had were so accurate that she hadn't been lost once, yet. Diane told her not to get too confident as her trip wasn't over yet and she had faith in her daughter to get lost at least once along the way. They laughed and shared the experiences her daughter had been through this far into the trip.

She talked again to Mike and told him that she loved him, missed him and would call tomorrow night. It was then again Diane's turn to tell her daughter to be careful and how much she loved and missed her !lready. They told each other goodnight and hung up the phone. Diane felt better now knowing that her daughter was once again safe for the night on her trip.

Once again she joined her son at the table and heard all about his night out with the "boys" and of his plans to spend tomorrow with her, just the two of them. He told her that he would like to pack a picnic lunch and they could go to a nearby lake and enjoy the day. That sounded better than he could imagine. Diane loved to fish and hadn't been for what seemed like forever. A picnic lunch and fishing with her son sounded like her kind of fun. She was already looking forward to it.

They sat and planned out what poles they would take, what food she should pack and what bait to use and where they could pick some up. They went into the living room to watch the local news, paying special attention to the weather.

They didn't want to get rained out and soon found that the forecast was clear and hot for tomorrow. They would be set Mike told her as he went out to the garage to find their fishing tackle and rods. Checking them now so they would know if they needed tackle along with bait.

They were up late that night and Diane couldn't remember when she had looked forward to something so much. They soon were exhausted and both knew they were about to lose the fight with sleep. They exchanged hugs, kisses and goodnights like every night and headed off to bed.

Much to her surprise Mike was once again up before her the next morning. As she showered and dressed he started coffee for her. He quickly handed her a cup as she entered the kitchen and told her that he was going to go out and start loading the car.

She told him that she would fix breakfast then prepare and pack their lunch, and for him not to be long. They ate breakfast, cleared the dishes and started checking and double checking their mental list to make sure they had everything.

As she went out to put the lunch she had packed in the car she noticed Greg driving by. He stopped and asked how she was and if she had heard from Debbie. She quickly caught him up on all the goings on and told him of her date with her son today.

He could tell that she was excited and was glad that her and Mike were going to get some alone time, they needed it. Diane thought she noticed a distance to him today, maybe it was just her but it was just something she thought she noticed.

Mike approached and quickly started giving Greg a hard time and told him it was too bad that he had to work or he could join them. Greg would have jumped at the chance to spend the day with them but thought it best if he passes. Diane and Mike quickly stepped back, huddled together and began to plot. "Would you mind if Greg came along mom?" he asked her.

She assured her son that it was fine with her and they once again approached Greg's car. He wasn't quite sure if this was going to be a good thing or a bad thing with the look on Mike's face. They quickly invited him to spend the day with them and he asked if they were sure. Telling them that he fully understood them wanting to spend some quality time together.

They told him that it was fine with them both. Greg asked if they could give him a few minutes to go back home, call his shop and tell them that he wouldn't be in today after all and meet them back here. They told him to take his time as they were still loading the car and would stop and pick him up when they were done. He turned his car around and disappeared back up the road as fast as he had appeared. "Are you ok with Greg going today mom?" Mike asked again.

She was fine with it, as a matter of fact she had been trying to find a reason to include Greg in some of their plans so he didn't feel slighted. She didn't want him to think that she had closed him out of her life. That was the last thing she would ever do.

"I know that it was supposed to be just you and I but I thought maybe Greg could use a day off too" he continued. Diane couldn't agree more and they finished loading the car, did a final check of the house and headed for Greg's.

Mike was driving and pulled into Greg's drive and honked. Greg appeared right away with fishing pole in hand and a smile as big as he was. They loaded his gear and headed for the bait shop talking, and telling him of the adventures of Debbie. He was glad to hear that she was having a good time on her trip.

He too had been afraid that she would find it more than she could handle right now. Diane told him that she thought the very same thing but had been pleasantly surprised by her daughter. She was handling it as if she does it regularly she told him.

They made the stop at the bait shop a quick one and were soon on the way to the lake. Mike telling them that he was going to catch all the fish so they could just sit back and relax. The trip to the lake was short and fast and they were glad that they had picked a weekday to come.

They practically had the whole lake to themselves. They found a spot that Greg and Mike agreed looked like the perfect spot to catch that "big one" and unloaded their gear. Giving each other a hard time as to who would catch the most fish and the biggest. It was like listening to two five-year-olds arguing over whose toy was bigger and better.

She couldn't help but smile. Yet in the back of her mind, she couldn't help but wish that Mike would give Dan a chance and treat him as well as he does Greg, even if just once. She sat up the table with coolers of food and drinks and retrieved her pole from the car.

Deciding to let the "boys" fight over the best fishing spot she went down the bank a few yards and dropped her line in. Almost as fast as she could put her line in, she would pull it out with a fish attached. Greg and Mike just looked at each other in disbelief, mouths wide open.

They could only watch as she pulled fish after fish from the lake, and they weren't minnow sized fish either. These were some very impressive fish. "I guess we have dinner if we decide to stay that long" she said as she pulled yet another rather large fish into the bank. Mike and Greg could only look at one another and shake their heads.

"How is she doing it?" Mike finally asked. "I don't know but she is kicking our butts" Greg said. "We can't let her do this to us" Mike said, "what are we going to do about it Greg?" he asked. The two decided to go down the bank a good distance from her and try their luck. Unfortunately their luck there was about as good as it had been in their last spot.

Tired of pulling in fish after fish Diane decided to give herself a break and dig into the picnic basket she had brought. She luckily had loaded it with extra food. Knowing very well how her son could eat if given the chance, with Greg coming she was glad that she had. She was glad that Greg had came along. She was feeling a little ashamed of herself as she felt that she had been neglecting her friend.

That was one of the last things in the world that she wanted to do, make him feel that she was turning her back on him. She would never do that to him and she was almost sure that he knew it. It didn't help with her giving the appearance of avoiding him lately though and she knew this too.

Soon the two men came back to the table, with poles in hand and heads hung low. "Are you two hungry?" she asked as she started laying food out on the table. That seemed to lift their spirits a bit. They had fully expected to "have their noses rubbed it in" when they came back to where she was sitting. She sat and ate a snack and didn't say a word. Almost angelic in appearance, but both Mike and Greg knew better.

They both suspected to hear all about it before the day was done. And, thought it better to let her bask in her glory without antagonizing her in any way. They both knew that she could be down right vindictive if given the chance and neither of them felt like being squashed like tiny bugs by her today.

"Let's not say a word about fish or fishing right now, ok?" Mike whispered to Greg. He quickly and happily agreed that not a word would be spoken. They sat, ate, and laughed and Greg was filled in on where Debbie was, where she would stay tonight and when she should arrive at school.

He was genuinely interested in how she was doing and if she were enjoying her trip so far. After lunch Diane decided to take a blanket from the car and spread it near the bank and just take in some sun. Mike and Greg thought this to be a golden opportunity to redeem themselves and catch some fish.

"If she isn't fishing, maybe we can at least make a good showing" Mike said as they wandered off, poles in hand. The day went well and she was so very glad she had agreed to this outing, and even happier that Greg had joined them. This is just what they had been needing she thought. Just the three of them out doing nothing but having a good time.

Something they hadn't done since Diane had met Dan. She kind of surprised herself, that was one of the few times Dan had even entered her thoughts today and the world had not come to an end. Besides she thought, he seemed to be more and more scarce lately. She just couldn't figure out why. She wasn't about to let it bother her today. She was having a great time and wasn't going to let anything spoil it now.

As she lay on the bank sunning herself, she soon heard a distinct whistling getting closer and closer. She shaded her eyes with her hand and saw Mike and Greg coming toward her with a stringer full of fish. Mike held up their treasure as he got closer and said "look what we caught mom."

The two of them were gloating about their haul, so very proud of themselves. That is until she spoke. "You mean it took me to stop fishing all together in order for you two pathetic things to find fish" she fired as they just stood there before her. "I knew we overdid it" Greg said to Mike as they stood holding their catch.

They all laughed and decided to call it a day as she wanted to be home just in case Debbie called. They quickly loaded up the car and headed toward home. Arguing over who had caught more and whose fish was the biggest.

In the end Diane won hands down and the two men dubbed her Queen of the lake, for the day anyway. They dropped Greg off first and Diane told him to change and join them for dinner as she knew that Debbie would love to hear his voice when she called later. He told the two that he would see them shortly and disappeared into his garage.

As they pulled into their own drive Diane quickly told Mike that he had work to do as he had agreed before the outing that he would clean all the fish they caught. He could only manage a defeated "yes mom" as she started taking things into the house. "I'll unload the car, you clean fish" she told him as she returned for another load.

The car unloaded and everything put away she went about the task of showering first then dressed and started dinner. Just as she was putting the finishing touches on dinner Greg and Mike both came through the backdoor laughing and teasing each other about being beat by a girl today.

She told them the queen commands they both wash up and set

down before dinner started to get cold. She was just putting the last of the dishes in the dishwasher as the phone rang. Mike beat her to the draw again tonight. He quickly answered and his face lit up like a tot at Christmas, it had to be Debbie she thought.

Gathering bits and pieces of the conversation her suspicions were confirmed. It was in fact her daughter. Mike talked to her for a bit then handed the phone to his mom. Diane soon found out that the trip was going splendidly and nothing out of the ordinary had happened.

Debbie was more excited now than yesterday as she was nearing the end of her trip and tomorrow would be unpacking and putting things away in her new dorm room. Diane was glad that she was so enthusiastic about starting school and more excited for her daughter about starting a new chapter in her life.

Diane told her daughter that she had someone there that would like to talk to her for a bit and handed the phone to Greg. She could hear her daughter through the phone, clear across the room. "Poor guy, he's probably deaf now" she said as she looked at Mike and they both busted out laughing.

Greg spoke to her for a while and asked who got the phone next. Mike volunteered and told Debbie that she had ruined Greg's hearing with the scream heard around the world. They laughed and before long Diane heard the all too familiar "I love you too's" and knew that it was her turn to say goodbye to her daughter for another night.

As she hung up the phone Greg stood and thanked them both for one of the best days he could remember in a very long time. He told them how good it felt to hear Debbie again, he said his goodnights and said he should be getting back home.

As he headed out the door Mike stood and joined him saying he would walk Greg out to the drive as he had to make sure the garage was locked.

Just as Diane was about to head for her room and change into her pajamas the phone rang again. "What did you forget now?" she asked as she answered it, thinking it was Debbie and she had forgotten something. "I didn't forget anything" the voice on the other end said, she quickly realized it was Dan. He told her that he had tried several times that day to call but got no answer. She told him about her day at the lake with her son.

For some reason she caught herself purposely leaving out the fact that she had spent the day at the lake with her son, and Greg. She didn't even know why she had done it. Dan had never shown any jealousy or animosity toward Greg. As he didn't really know anything about what Diane and Greg had shared before she had met him.

It was a subject she just didn't speak of. She always felt that what had happened between her and Greg should stay between them. She had never even told her children of her brief relationship with Greg, if that's what one could even call it.

Dan told her that he was glad she had a good time and he knew how important it was for her to spend time with Mike, just the two of them. They talked and when Mike re-entered the house she quickly told him that Dan said hi, for the first time she watched Mike closely.

He just rolled his eyes and said "yeah, hi" and went upstairs. She could not figure out what it was about Dan that Mike disliked so much. Dan had never given him any reason to not like him that she was aware of. Tonight though it was clear to her that her son was not going to "warm up" to the idea of her and Dan. More precisely, the thought of Dan period.

She knew that she didn't want to put Mike on the spot or make him say something that he and she both might regret later. So, she thought it best for now to just leave it alone. After all, she wasn't even sure where if anywhere her and Dan were even going.

They talked a while and he told her of his plans to leave for Chicago in a couple of days. He asked if she would be interested in spending a day with him before he left. She told him that she would love to and asked what exactly he had in mind. He asked if it might be possible to spend the day with her at the house as he would be leaving day after tomorrow.

She asked him to hold on and went to ask Mike if he had any plans for tomorrow. He told her that he just spoke to one of his friends and they were going to meet in town in the morning and he would stay with his friend tomorrow night. Mike asked if that would be all right or if she had other plans.

She told him it would be fine and went back downstairs. She suspected that Mike already knew that Dan had asked to spend some time with her and just wanted to make himself scarce. She went back to the phone and told Dan that tomorrow would be fine and said she would see him when he got there. They said their goodnights and soon she hung up the phone.

She sat and sipped a glass of wine and was soon lost in thought. Trying desperately to figure out exactly why her son did not like Dan. She wracked her brain trying to remember every time Dan had ever been around her and Mike or Mike and Debbie for that matter. She couldn't think of a single time that Dan had ever been really alone with the kids.

So, she thought that the outside possibility of it being something he may have said could be ruled out. She couldn't remember anytime that Dan had ever been around when he hadn't treated both Mike and Debbie with respect, and her for that matter. He had always been a gentleman around her and the kids so she was pretty sure it wasn't anything that he could have done.

Maybe Mike was just going to have a hard time of it no matter whom she might be seeing. Maybe he wasn't comfortable with the thought of his mom dating anyone. She found that a bit odd though as he didn't seem to have any problems with her being around Greg or them both being around Greg for that matter.

Today had been a perfect example of that, after all it was Mike's idea to ask Greg to come with them in the first place. Then again, she had kept everything between her and Greg very secret and never gave him or Debbie the impression that her and Greg were anything more than friends. Maybe that was it after all, maybe he was going to have a hard time dealing with anyone that she might decide to see.

All she knew right now was that Dan seemed to make her happy and she had no intention of not seeing him just to please Mike. She would be more than happy to sit down and talk to Mike about it. She would work it out anyway she could short of not dating at all. After all, another couple of years and he too would be off to college and she would be left alone in this big old house. That was something she was not looking forward to.

Mike just had to start realizing that she was not about to live like some hermit and be alone just to please him or anyone else. She decided she would just have to deal with all this the best she could as the situation warranted. It was getting late and she was tired, she put her glass in the sink and went upstairs. She poked her head into Mike's room, he was on the phone but stopped long enough to give his mom her goodnight hug and kiss and to tell her that he loved her.

Chapter 13

Diane slept in the next morning as it was rather late when she finally drifted off to sleep. She tossed and turned for what felt like forever. She couldn't get it out of her mind that Mike might be having a hard time dealing with the thought of her seeing someone. She didn't want to hurt her son in anyway. She would die first, but, she also didn't want to start sneaking around and keeping it from him just so she could see someone either.

She got out of bed, stretched and headed straight for the shower. She quickly dressed and went to make coffee. She desperately needed some, she just had no get up and go this morning.

As she poured her first cup of the morning she looked out to see if maybe Mike had already left, his car was still in the drive. As she sat and sipped her morning pick me up, Mike came bounding down the stairs in a remarkably good mood.

"Morning mom" he said as he headed for the refrigerator and grabbed the orange juice. "Did you want a glass mom?" he asked as he poured himself a glass. She told him no thanks and asked if they could talk this morning.

She thought it best to get all this out into the open and clear the air so to speak. Before she had anymore sleepless nights. He joined his mom at the table and asked what was on her mind. She told him that she saw the way he acted last night when she told him it was Dan on the phone.

"I have to ask honey, do you have some kind of problem with Dan?" she asked. "Ok mom, I didn't want to upset you or hurt you by saying anything, but, I have to tell you, there's just something about the guy that I don't like and definitely don't trust" her son told her.

"It has nothing to do with you dating. I love the thought that you are finally trying to find someone new in your life. There's just something about that guy mom" he went on. She let her son continue as she was glad that he was opening up to her. She respected his opinion and was proud that both of her kids could talk to her, about anything.

"It hasn't been anything that he has done or said so don't think that mom, it isn't" he said. "I just don't like him or something about him and I don't trust him" Mike said. "If I'm wrong and he turns out to be the one for you, I will be the first to admit it and say I'm sorry mom" he went on.

"But until that day comes, I will be civil to him, I won't disrespect him and I won't antagonize him in any way. Then again I won't go out of my way to treat him like an old friend either mom, I just won't and can't, I hope you can respect that" he finished.

She told her son that she fully understood and respected his decision and perspective on the situation and would never put him in a situation where he would feel uncomfortable. "I would never openly treat him badly on purpose mom. You know that, but I'm not going to treat him like he's my buddy either" Mike told his mom as he hugged her and told her how much he loved her.

"I understand and now that I know how you feel I will not ask you to do anything you don't feel comfortable doing" she told him. "If I get to the point that I know in my heart that I was wrong and know that he's right for you, I will be the first to talk to him and apologize mom, you know me" he said. "That's all I can ask for honey" she told her son and thanked him for his honesty.

She quickly made breakfast for the two of them and felt so much better knowing they had talked this out. "So what's your plans for the day?" she asked as she sat his plate in front of him. "I am meeting some of the guys in town this morning and we are going to the mall to look for girls, what else?" he said with a smile.

"I should have known" she told him and mussed his hair and laughed. "Are you going to be ok today mom?" he asked as he gathered his things to go. She told him that she would be fine as she too had plans and she knew that he wouldn't want to be included in them.

He just rolled his eyes and said he understood. He gave her a big hug and kiss and told her to tell Debbie hi for him when she called tonight. She assured him that she would and waved until he backed out of the drive and was out of sight. Feeling better now that she had talked to her son, she went about clearing the dishes and straightening up the house.

The phone was the only thing that interrupted her and it was Dan saying that he would see her in about an hour. Today would be a perfect day to spend outside by the pool swimming and sunning she thought as she went up to put on her bikini.

She went out and set up chaises and turned the radio on before going back to the house to make fresh glasses of tea and take them outside. She knew that Dan would be there soon and wanted to have everything ready for him. She wanted to spend as much time as she could with him before he left tomorrow.

His trips seemed to get longer each time he took them and she knew it might be some time before she would see him again. Her words to Greg kept creeping into her mind, the ones she spoke when he asked when she would allow herself to love again.

She remembered herself telling him that she would allow herself to love again when roses bloomed in winter around here. Here it was the dead of summer and she was virtually on the edge of falling for Dan. She always knew those words would come back to bite her.

Dan soon appeared from the side of the house as she sat and sipped her tea, lost in thought. She told him to go change and come join her in the pool. His response was why didn't she just come with him and help him change, soon they were in her room making love.

The rest of the day was spent swimming, laughing and doing absolutely nothing. Some of Diane's favorite pastimes lately. After dinner she asked if he had to leave or could spend the night with her as Mike was going to be at a friends in town tonight. She really didn't want to be alone tonight and wasn't looking forward to Dan leaving the next morning as she knew it would be days before she saw him again.

He told her that he had a million things to do and would have to go back to town tonight as his flight was a very early one. They made love again before he had to leave. As he kissed her goodnight and opened the door she hugged him close, looked him straight in the eyes and said "I love you Dan."

"What did you say?" he asked as he stood in the open door. "I said I love you Dan, those are words I never thought I would say again to another man" she said. He pulled her close, kissed her deep and told her that he loved her too. She watched and waved as he backed out of the drive and was soon out of sight.

She poured a glass of wine and sat at the table. "Did I actually say those words out loud just now?" she asked herself out loud. She was in total disbelief that she had allowed her mouth to say the words that her brain had been trying so hard to suppress.

She knew that she had just taken an important and unchangeable step in her and Dan's relationship. And, she couldn't turn back now, not after what she had just allowed herself to say to him. She took her wine into the living room and sat on the sofa.

Legs pulled to her chest, in total darkness and just stared into emptiness. She couldn't believe that she had done that tonight, or to be more accurate, said that tonight. What in the world had possessed her to do such a thing, she had been adamant with Greg that she could not commit.

Now here she sat alone staring off into the night wondering if she had done the right thing or had just made a mistake that she would be sorry for the rest of her life. Her mind was reeling and she felt like she was being pulled in a million directions all at once.

She sat until the wee hours of the morning wrestling with what she had said and decided that she meant it or she never would have said it. With that sorted out for the moment she went up and crawled into bed, she was exhausted so it didn't take long for sleep to overtake her.

She slept in the next day knowing that Mike had spent the night in town and figured that by now Dan was either on his way to Chicago or already there. She showered and dressed and went down to make coffee.

Just like every other morning, except this morning wasn't like any other. She knew that her life in many ways would be changed forever with her little slip of the tongue last night. She also knew that before she said a word about it to either of her children she had to be absolutely certain that what she had said was right for her, and them.

Before she could sort out the mess that her mind was in at the moment the phone rang. It was Mike asking if she would like to join him and his friends for a movie at the mall. Anything that would help get her mind off last night would be a welcome distraction right now and she gladly accepted the offer. She told her son that she would meet them in about an hour, hung up, gathered her things and headed out the door.

She was sure that any movie that Mike and his friends could all agree on would most certainly not be a romance or anything that would remind her of her current situation.

Knowing her son and his friends, it would be either a movie with lots of cars, lots of things blowing up or lots of scantily clad young women. Or a combination of all the above.

She pulled into the parking lot and saw Mike and his friends all gathered around Mike's car. From what she could gather by their actions they were trying their best to be "cool."

Starting to second-guess herself for agreeing to spend an afternoon with her son and his friends, she decided it would be the lesser of two evils. It would be an improvement over sitting alone wondering if she had made a terrible mistake last night.

Before she knew it they were all seated in a dark theater with cars and bridges and buildings blowing up all over the screen. This was a definite distraction she thought and smiled. She offered to get snacks, drinks, popcorn, anything they needed. She quickly took a list and headed for the snack bar. Actually she just wanted to try and restore some of her hearing to normal before her head imploded.

She had been right she thought as she ordered snacks and waited as they were being prepared. The movie had lots of cars, lots of explosions and a lot of scantily clad young women in it, just as she had predicted. She returned to her seat loaded with drinks and things and was soon mobbed by the group of hungry teenagers she was with.

After the movie they all agreed that pizza was definitely on the menu for dinner tonight. She welcomed the thought of not having to cook or clean up afterward and joined them. They went to the local pizza parlor and set about the job of pushing tables together and fighting over who would sit by whom.

It was kind of like watching the three stooges. Except there was a lot more than three and they were all most definitely stooges. Diane soon found herself having fun and what she had said last night was the furthest thing from her mind at the moment. This was a good distraction and she was happy that her son had invited her to join them.

It was almost as if he somehow knew that she was in need of a distraction and would do all he could to give it to her. As they ate and passed different pizza's they had ordered from person to person, Diane's cell phone rang.

Hoping that it wasn't Dan at that moment, she answered it and found Debbie on the other end. "I made it to LA, I'm at the school, I am unpacked and officially moved into my dorm, and I love it mom" was her daughters greeting.

Diane could now put her mind at ease knowing that her daughters' trip had gone well and she was now safe and sound at school. They talked for a while and soon she handed the phone to Mike. He was so excited to hear that she had made it and was settled in.

He too had been worried about his sister and was glad that he could now rest easy knowing that she was there and safe. They talked about the restaurant they went to when they went out during Christmas break last year. Debbie told him she went there for dinner tonight and it was great.

They talked about the beach and how soon her classes would start and about how he just had to come out during Christmas break this year to visit her. It was the perfect ending to a perfect day for Mike and Diane both.

They went home that night feeling much more at ease and happy. Debbie's classes were starting soon and Mike would be starting his junior year in a week. The time was getting away from her.

She could remember when they were little, she thought she would have them forever. Now the reality was sinking in that she would have to let go of her baby sooner than she wanted to. They quickly locked the house and exchanged their nightly hugs, kisses and I love you's and headed to their rooms.

They both were tired and tonight Diane didn't think she would have any difficulty falling fast asleep as soon as she crawled between the covers, she was right.

The next week passed faster than she thought and soon she was back to her morning ritual of getting her son up for school. "Next year will be the last year that I will have to do this" she thought as she went down to make his breakfast. They had talked over the last week and decided a trip to see Debbie over Christmas would do them both good.

Mike was so excited about another trip to California and she had to admit that she too was looking forward to making plans once again to go. She also missed Debbie more than she thought and couldn't wait to see her. She would start making reservations and plans soon.

If this year was anything like last year the time would go by quickly and be upon them before they knew it. She decided not to wait to make all the necessary plans. Dan had returned from Chicago but it was a short-lived stay in town. He was soon on the road again setting up more offices in surrounding areas.

She knew what his job was from the start and knew that traveling extensively was a very big part of it. She also knew that it was very hard to have a solid relationship when one of the people involved was never around.

It was beginning to put a strain on her and how she felt and Dan was well aware of it. He just told her that he would be able to spend more time with her soon and she always let that satisfy her for the moment.

The next few weeks passed quickly, Dan was around sparingly and Mike was getting anxious to leave and see Debbie. It was more than enough to keep Diane busy and her mind occupied. Before she realized, Thanksgiving was here and dinner with her parents and Mike were her agenda.

Dan had been called back to Chicago and would be stuck there until after the Holiday. She couldn't say that she was overly happy about it but she also knew that there wasn't anything she could do about it either.

Thanksgiving passed and soon Mike's winter break was upon them. They would be leaving for LA in just a few days. Mike stayed in town with friends to celebrate Christmas early as he would be with his mom and sister in sunny California this year, again.

He was the envy of all his friends, and some of their parents as well. Leaving the cold, the snow and all the icy conditions behind to spend two weeks in the sun and surf.

Diane used his time in town and the fact that he would not be home to her advantage. She had Dan over so they could spend a little time together before she left. Tonight she had something to ask him and she wasn't about to leave for LA without doing it. She couldn't believe that she was going to do this tonight, but, she was going to ask Dan to move in when she returned from her trip.

She had a romantic candle light dinner ready when he arrived and was dressed in her sexiest lingerie. She met him at the door with a passionate kiss and I love you. He returned her kiss and her sentiment telling her that he too loved her and was taken back by the magnificence of this remarkable woman.

She was breathtaking tonight. They ate dinner and didn't waste any time moving the activities of the night to her bedroom. She wanted him and she was not about to wait a minute longer than she had to.

Tonight was like any other night with Dan, they made love and no matter what she did or he tried, it came up short and not fully satisfying. She resigned herself to the thought that Dan just may not be as good a lover as Greg no matter what he does or how hard he tries.

Her times with Dan were nice but didn't move heaven and earth as she had felt with Greg. Maybe this was as good as it would get and she could live with that, she loved Dan.

As they lay, wrapped in each others arms she decided that now was as good a time as any to bring up the subject and ask him to move in. "Dan, you know that I love you and can't think of my life without you in it" she said. "When I return from seeing Debbie I would like you to move in with me.

I want us to take the next step and start really being together" she went on. Her suggestion was a shock to him as he wasn't prepared for anything like that from her. He told her that when she got back they would go off, just the two of them, and talk it over.

He told her that with her leaving it wasn't the right time to think about making a serious commitment like that. It should be something they discuss and a decision they make together he told her.

Diane could understand his reasoning, it was like her asking him to move in, but in the same breath, saying but wait till I get back from my trip. She told him that she would wait and they would talk about it in more detail when she got back. She was soon fast asleep wrapped in his arms.

When she rose the next morning, she found herself alone in bed. Thinking that Dan may have already gone down to start coffee, she quickly showered, dressed and went to the kitchen. She found herself alone all together as Dan had left before she had woke.

She looked for a note or something telling her where he had gone. There was a note on the fridge saying that they would talk later, he had an early appointment and had to leave before she was up. He signed the note love Dan, that put her mind at ease as she thought that maybe she had drove him away with what she had suggested last night.

They spoke on the phone later that day and he seemed to be genuinely sorry that he had to leave like that without waking her and telling her that he was going. She told him that it was fine it just worried her that she might have upset him with what she had asked. He assured her that her asking him to move in had nothing to do with his leaving. Early appointments where his only reason for leaving her like that.

He asked when she was leaving and she told him they would be leaving the next morning and would be gone for two weeks. He told her that the time had went by so fast that he didn't realize it was already upon them. He told her that he would miss her madly and be counting the days till her return. She said she too would be marking days off on the calendar anticipating her return.

The rest of her day was spent packing last minute things, reaffirming reservations and schedules and waiting for Mike to get home from town. He had made a last minute trip to town to pick up Christmas gifts Diane had bought and would need to take with them.

This trip would be a bit different than their last. They would drive over near the airport tonight, eat and stay at a nearby motel. Diane even had parking arranged for her car while they were gone. Mike returned quickly and they loaded their bags in the car with the packages he had just picked up, locked the house and were on their way.

They arrived at the motel and checked in before going to find a nice place to eat. They even contemplated taking their bags and packages over to the airport tonight and checking them so all they would need tomorrow would be their carry ons.

They found a restaurant close and were soon seated. Waiting for their meal, Mike thought it best to go ahead and take their bags and things over tonight and check them, saving them time in the morning. As they ate Diane agreed that her sons' idea was a good one and said they would take their things over after they ate.

"That would just save us time in the morning mom" he said between bites. "I know, you're right, it would be less to deal with in the morning." She wholeheartedly agreed with her son. They finished their meal, Mike just had to have dessert and she couldn't say no to him, then went back to the room and gathered all their bags and things.

Mike quickly went in and found a cart to load their things on and soon they were at the counter showing their tickets and checking their bags. The lady behind the counter said she would confirm their tickets now, then in the morning they would only have to go straight to the gate to board. "This was one of the best ideas you've had in a long time" she told Mike. "Yeah, I do come up with a good one every now and then mom" he said with a big smile.

With bags and packages checked, seats and tickets confirmed they went to check out the long term parking facilities and see where they felt the car would be safest while they were gone. They were pleased to find that parking was available inside and the car would be kept out of the weather at the very least. With everything done and all their bags checked they went back to the motel to settle in for the evening.

Mike went to the lobby and bought bags of microwave popcorn, found a microwave and was soon knocking on the door with freshly popped bags and drinks in hand. Diane had found a good movie on the television while her son was out scouring the countryside for food. "I see you found something to eat" she said and laughed then helped him before he literally dropped it all on the floor. They soon were lost in the movie and before long were both tired enough to call it a night. They exchanged their familiar nightly hugs, kisses and I love you's and were both soon sound asleep.

Diane was the first to rise, as usual. She showered and changed quickly before rousting her sleepy son. She figured it a safe bet to guess that he would just put on shoes, grab his baseball cap, thus eliminating the need to comb his hair, and stumble to the car.

She gathered their remaining bags and took them to the car before she attempted to wake him. It would be a lost cause if she did so before she was ready to walk out the door as she knew he would only roll over and go back to sleep.

She knew her son all too well and knew that he would sit straight up in bed, say "I'm ready" and as soon as she disappeared through the door would simply fall over and be fast asleep again. She quickly put their bags and things in the car, stopped by the desk and checked out, then went back to lead "sleepy" to the car. She did one last check of the room, making sure she had not overlooked anything and shook her son telling him it was time.

He did exactly what she had guessed. Slipped on his shoes, grabbed his cap and said "I'm ready." "I just knew you would do that" she said as she led her sleepy son to the car and headed for the airport.

Diane found a well-lit spot in the parking garage and felt that the car would be safe for the most part. She quickly parked, shook her son and said they were there and together they grabbed the remaining bags and headed for the terminal.

They quickly found the gate they would board from and sat patiently waiting for the announcement saying they could board. Mike put his big head on his mom's shoulder and was soon asleep. She put her arm around him and hugged him tightly to her waiting for their boarding call to blurt out of the loudspeaker. They didn't have to wait long, they boarded on time and the wait for take off was a short one. They were in the air and on their way before she knew it.

She would guess that Mike would sleep most of the way, so, she decided it would be a good idea to try and get in a nap herself. She was woken by the announcement from the pilot that they would soon be landing, even Mike woke for that. They stretched and yawned, shaking off the stiffness of sleeping in their seats and prepared for landing.

Landing was smooth and uneventful and they soon were looking for their bags and things at the baggage check area. Mike was soon grabbing this and that trying to catch everything on the first pass, he was successful. He quickly went and found a cart and they were soon headed for the loading area in front of the terminal. Debbie was to be waiting and they soon heard "mom, Mike, over here."

They looked around and found Debbie jumping up and down frantically waving her arms calling their names. They loaded her car and were soon on their way to the motel they would call home for the next two weeks. As soon as the last of their bags and things were in the room, Diane and Mike both mobbed Debbie and hugged her so tight she thought they would never let go.

They were so excited to see her and Diane couldn't believe how well her daughter looked, not to mention a little jealous of her fantastic tan. Before long they were lost in conversation, catching up on what was going on back home, what was new and what Debbie had experienced so far. They talked most of the afternoon and soon realized they were more than ready for a late lunch as Diane and Mike had not eaten since last night.

Deciding that pizza would be quick and filling yet not ruin their appetites for dinner later, they walked to the little pizza parlor they had found on their first trip out. They ordered and found a table on the beach and picked up where they had left off on their catching up. Their drinks and meal soon came to the table and it was just like old times, they were once again together.

Debbie told them all about her classes, how much she liked her professors and how she had decorated her dorm and just loved it. "I've got some girls that just can't wait to meet you, they've seen pictures of you in my room and think you're cute" Debbie whispered to her brother. He smiled a smile bigger than he was and Diane knew that something was up, it either had to do with girls, cars or food.

She knew her son all too well and knew that a smile like that could only be from the mention of one of those categories. "I'm not even going to ask" she told them and broke out laughing. It felt so very good to see Debbie and know that she was getting on so well. Diane had worried that all this might be a bit overwhelming to her. They finished their lunch and walked the beach back to their room. It was as beautiful and peaceful as Diane had remembered it from their first trip.

Debbie wanted to take Mike to the campus and introduce him to some of her friends. Diane knew this was code for take him to meet some girls and told them to go have fun as she wanted to unpack and sit on the beach for a while. Mike was now well rested and ready to go.

Diane was a bit weary from the flight and just wanted to relax so this worked out for all of them. "We'll be back in time to go to dinner mom" they told her as they hugged and kissed her and darted out the door. "Yep, just like old times" she said to herself and smiled as she went about unpacking and putting things away.

With things unpacked and put away, clothes hung up that needed to be, she now had time to herself to relax and unwind a bit. Diane quickly put on her tiny little teal bikini, grabbed a towel, took a drink from the refrigerator and headed down to the beach to find a nice quiet place to sit and relax. She found a spot that was just perfect and was soon lost in the soothing sounds of the waves lapping the shore and the distant cries of seagulls.

Now she could get used to living like this she thought as she applied sun screen and spread the towel and sat down. A gentle breeze was blowing in from the ocean. It was warm and welcome and soon she was lost in the moment. It was definitely the kind of day that tourist brochures were made of she thought as she watched surfers riding the waves to the beach.

She would make the most of the sun and beach the next two weeks she thought to herself. After all, Debbie and Mike would probably spend a lot of time together with Debbie's new friends.

She was glad her daughter had settled in so quickly and was fast becoming an accepted permanent addition to the area. She had always found it easy to make friends and could "fit in" in practically any situation.

Debbie had called regularly since leaving home and always kept Diane up to date on new friends, guys she had met and was interested in and all the local gossip. Diane almost felt a part of the area too as completely as her daughter kept her informed.

She looked at her watch and realized it was fast approaching the time she would estimate the kids would return. She got up, picked up her towel and headed back to the room. She quickly showered and changed and watched some televison until they came bounding through the door laughing and teasing each other like they had never been apart.

Mike quickly showered and changed and they were off to dinner. They went to a local eatery that catered to students from the campus, Debbie wanted to introduce her mom to some of her new friends.

The spot was clean and somewhat quaint yet definitely geared toward a student clientele. Diane almost felt a hundred years old as she looked about at all the young people gathered there. She quickly found that she fit right in and was soon having as much fun as the rest of the crowd.

She was suddenly glad that Debbie had brought her here. They ate and played pool, darts and video games until it was getting late and Diane could tell that jet lag was definitely creeping up on her.

Debbie seemed to sense that her mom was getting tired and

suggested they return to the room so she could get some rest, Diane readily agreed. As they returned to the room Debbie told her mom that Mike could stay the night with her as they wanted to return to the club and stay a while longer.

Diane told them to be careful and she would see them both in the morning. They both promised to be there so they could all go to breakfast together and hugged and kissed her goodnight before they left.

Diane went to her room and changed into her pajamas as she could hear the big comfortable bed calling her name. She wanted to call Dan though and at the very least tell him they were there safe and sound. She called and he was happy to hear from her.

He was glad they had arrived safe and happier yet to hear that Debbie was good and doing well. He told her that he missed her and would count the days till she was back. Before they hung up they exchanged I love you's. Now feeling so much better she crawled between the sheets and was fast asleep before she knew it.

The next two weeks seemed to go by quicker than any of them wanted, yet was fulfilling and gratifying to say the least. Debbie and Mike spent almost every minute together and Diane got to spend more than her fair share of time on the beach redefining her fading tan.

All in all they loved the time together and would begin planning a return trip almost as soon as they returned home. Debbie told her mom that she was going to make the trip home during summer break and a friend of hers would probably make the trip with her. That was good news to Diane and Mike both.

They spent their last night together and Debbie took them to the airport the next morning and saw them off. The trip home was quick and without incident. They were fast becoming old pros' at this Diane thought as they prepared to land. Mike gathered their bags and met her at the front of the terminal as she went and retrieved the car from the parking garage.

They soon were on their way home and looking forward to

doing nothing but relaxing for the next day or two. As they pulled into the drive they noticed that once again the drive had been kept clean and clear from what looked like a fresh blanket of white that had fallen while they were gone.

They both suspected Greg and Mike said he would call and thank him after they got everything inside. The next couple of days were definitely casual and restful, they were having a late Christmas again and her parents were joining them for dinner tonight.

Diane made it a point to invite Dan to join them, wanting to start including him in such gatherings. He of course was out of town once again. Stuck in Chicago for yet another holiday and from what Diane could tell he wouldn't be back until after New Years.

She was starting to see a pattern emerge and didn't like the thoughts she had suddenly going through her mind. She was beginning to have serious doubts about any kind of relationship with this man.

After all, she was doing all the work and he was reaping all the benefits as it was now. She knew one thing for certain, she was going to get some answers once and for all and would stop at nothing to get them.

Dinner was pleasant as always with her parents and they were so excited to hear Mike tell about the trip and seeing Debbie. They were so happy to hear that she might come home in the summer, they had missed her immensely. They exchanged gifts and talked into the night, Mike helped his grandparents to their car and saw them off safely.

That night was an early one as her and Mike both were still feeling the aftereffects of their trip, they turned in early. Dan returned from Chicago and once again Diane presented him with the idea of moving in with her.

He seemed to avoid giving her any kind of straight answer and that only made her suspicions worse. She was almost certain now that he was either using her or hiding something and she was more than determined to find out which.

School was once again open and spring was fast approaching. Diane couldn't help but think that Mike would start his senior year in high school this fall, she couldn't believe he was growing up so fast. Dan's trips to Chicago began to become more frequent and seemed to last longer with each trip.

She was going to find out what was going on once and for all. She enlisted Greg to help her do some investigative work. She was more determined than ever to find out what Dan was up to. Greg gladly signed on and said he would help in any way he could and assured her that she would never hear I told you so from him. She was so very glad that she could count on him and could now put her plan into action.

Chapter 14

Getting information on Dan was easier than she thought. Specially around town since she was a local girl and he was an outsider. She quickly found that he kept a studio apartment at the motel. They had rooms they rented on a weekly basis and he took advantage of that.

She also found that his company, not him, was paying the rent and only paid two weeks at a time. Giving him the option of leaving quickly without any kind of long term commitment to worry about. She soon found that an old school friend of hers managed the motel and allowed her access to his room.

She discovered that he traveled light, only the bare necessities and nothing in the way of personal belongings. He took all his clothes with him on every trip to Chicago leaving nothing but a clean, empty room with each departure.

She found this a bit odd, if he were planning on moving to the area. One would think that at the least he would have a few personal things about. A TV, a stereo, extra clothing, pictures of some kind yet the room was virtually empty. Again leaving her to think that he was either using her or hiding something.

Greg was more computer literate than her and soon found that Dan had an address in an upscale suburb of Chicago, if it was the same person. He also found out by calling the corporate office of the company Dan worked for, that he had been with the company for about fifteen years.

He was informed that Dan was a district manager in charge of setting up field offices in new areas they were expanding into. Greg was able to get certain information because of the business he owned. Dan had actually asked Greg for some quotes on printing jobs and it wasn't out of the ordinary for even a small company like Greg's to confirm employment if for no other reason than to insure payment for his work.

Getting any personal information though was pretty much out

of the question and he knew it. So, he kept inquiries about personal things to a minimum. Greg was able to find out one last bit of information that he found damning on Dan's part.

He learned that Dan's stay in their area was about to come to an end as he would soon appoint an area manager locally and come back to Chicago to stay. Greg learned this almost by accident as he told Dan's office that he looked forward to doing business with Dan. That's when they volunteered the information that Dan's stay was nearing an end rapidly. Now Greg was torn, should he go to Diane and tell her what he had found or leave it alone and see if Dan was going to be man enough to tell her himself.

Diane confronted Dan several more times about whether he planned on moving in with her or was content to stay at his studio in town. She was more than persistent hoping it would spur a direct answer to her question, but she was disappointed.

He continued to avoid giving her any kind of concrete answer. Telling her that he didn't want to commit to anything until he was sure his company was going to leave him in one spot for any length of time. He kept telling her that he didn't want to move in and get transferred to another new area and have to leave her all alone once again.

He was doing his best to convince her that he only had her best interests at heart and loved her enough to not want to put her through hell by being ripped away from her like that. He kept assuring her that as soon as he found out how long he was to be in the area, she would get a definite answer once and for all.

She actually started to have second thoughts about what she had been thinking about Dan. Maybe he actually did have her best interest at heart and was trying to not hurt her in the long run. She told him that she stopped by his room one day and found that he had already left for Chicago, covering the fact that she had been let into his room to snoop.

She went on to say that his room seemed so empty and cold with the lack of any personal things about. He covered that nicely too by telling her that he quickly learned to live out of his suitcase when he had first been promoted. He told her that trying to support himself on the road and attempting to keep a normal life in a city, miles away was soon a luxury that he saw pointless.

So, he only owned the things he needed to live from area to area. She was actually buying it, she could see his point of view and he was winning her over to his way of thinking fast.

She was soon becoming ashamed of herself for thinking that he was anything but honorable. Soon she was telling him how very much she loved him and thanking him for taking her feelings into consideration like that. They were soon in her room making love like there would be no tomorrow.

Little did Diane know that her tomorrow's with this man may be very limited. He had for the moment calmed her fears and quieted her suspicions, Dan wasn't sure how much longer he could keep doing this though. She was not dumb and he was more than sure she would soon see right through him.

He could only hope that it wouldn't happen before he was out of the area safe and sound for good. Before they realized it summer was once again upon them. Mike was out of school again and Debbie would be coming home soon as she had confirmed her plans to come back for the summer.

Everyone was so happy that Debbie and her friend would be spending the summer at home. Diane's parents couldn't wait to see their granddaughter, they had missed her so much. Mike was already planning things to do, places to go and all their friends were planning party after party anticipating her return home.

Life for the most part seemed to be good. Her and Dan spent as much time together as his job would allow them. She even suggested to Dan that he could retire and help her manage the remaining parcels of land she had to sell and could oversee the construction process. Reminding him that she had more than enough money to last them a lifetime.

He quickly dismissed her idea telling her that he would feel like a kept man and would eventually wind up hating himself for it. He went on to tell her that he loved his job and couldn't see himself retiring even when he was old enough to.

She knew in her heart that he was right and would never try to keep him from doing something that he loved to do, and it was plain to see that he loved his job.

Dan's trips to Chicago were becoming more frequent and lasting even longer than ever before. What little time he did spend in her area seemed to be taking him away from her more and more. Her suspicions were once again getting the best of her.

Now she was once again second-guessing herself and wondering if she had been taken advantage of by believing his lies. She was now more determined than ever to find out once and for all, she again asked Greg for help.

Greg could see that this was something she had to do. More over, he knew that it was something he couldn't stop her from doing so he agreed to do what he could to help. Debbie wouldn't be home for another week and Dan had announced that he was once again making a trip to Chicago, he was leaving in two days.

She told Greg that she needed him to get Mike off for a few days somehow so she could follow Dan to Chicago. She was going to find out once and for all just what he was hiding there, even if it killed her inside to do so. Greg knew that this was something she would have to do on her own.

He agreed to get Mike off on an unannounced camping trip. He knew that Mike would love the chance to get away and do some fishing. And, wouldn't question being gone for several days, it would be the perfect cover. Greg agreed to stop by later when Mike was home and offer the invitation to go camping. Diane said she couldn't thank him enough for his help.

Mike was just about to sit down to eat when Greg knocked on the backdoor. He quickly asked him to join them and Diane said they had more than enough food if he would care to stay. Greg accepted and soon they were all at the table passing this and that and exchanging small talk. Greg asked Mike if he had any plans for the next few days.

He told him about having some time off and wanting to go camping and fishing and was wondering if he would like to join him. "Besides I figured you could use a break since you're going to be cooped up in this house with three females all summer" he went on.

Mike agreed that although he loved his mom and sister and was looking forward to Debbie being home for the summer, he could use some time fishing and having some guy fun. Greg said he would put the finishing details on things at work in the morning and they could leave tomorrow afternoon if that would work for Mike.

He told Greg that he would be ready and they decided on where to go, as there were several lakes nearby. Some offering cabins and boat rentals. They decided a cabin would be best, just in case the weather didn't want to cooperate and a boat could get them out to some good fishing spots.

Diane was glad that her plan was working out, she could now find out just where she stood with Dan. Even if she didn't like what she found.

After dinner Mike and Greg went to the garage to start gathering gear they would need to take on their trip and she quickly called Dan. She knew that he was leaving day after tomorrow and he had always been honest with her about what time he was leaving and what flight he was taking.

She didn't know if it was stupidity on his part or if he just never thought that she would care. Either way she was fishing tonight, fishing for information. She asked if they might meet in town for breakfast before he left and he told her that he was taking the early flight out.

She found out when he would leave and with a little prodding even discovered what flight he would be on. She was proud of herself, she even discovered that he would be flying coach. That meant that she could be one of the last to board and fly first class, he would never know that she was on the same flight.

First class would also allow her to be off first and be out of sight before he even got off the plane. Greg and Mike were still outside so she took advantage of the situation and booked a seat on the same flight as Dan, first class of course.

The next day she helped Mike pack everything they thought he might need on their trip. She made sure he had enough money for unexpected things that could pop up. She even packed them enough food to feed an army.

She was going to be sure of one thing, if they didn't catch any fish they would still eat well. She knew how important that would be to her son. They had thought of everything and Mike was ready when Greg pulled in the drive to pick him up. As Mike loaded his things into Greg's car, Greg pulled Diane aside and asked if everything was ok.

She told him that it was all working out better than she thought and she should be back before them. "I sure hope you know what you're doing Diane" Greg said as Mike finished putting things in the car and asked if he was ready to go.

"I hope I know what I'm doing too Greg" she said as they made one last check of the car and prepared to leave. "I'll have my cell phone if you need anything" Greg whispered as they started to back out of the drive. "Have a good time you two" she shouted as they pulled off and waved until they were out of sight.

Now to put her plan into action. She would first need a disguise that would be believable yet render her unrecognizable. The last thing she needed was Dan knowing who she was. She called her friend Nancy that owned the beauty salon in town and told her a varied version of what she was doing.

She simply left out a lot of the details. Nancy assured her that she could help and told her to stop by after six tonight as they would be closed and would not be interrupted.

Diane made a mental checklist of everything she needed or needed to do yet. She had her seat booked on his flight, she was taking care of the disguise tonight. She needed to go into town a bit early and stop by the mall. She wanted to pick up a new travel bag, a few new clothes and all essentials that she might need for her fact-finding mission.

She would buy a new bag and clothes so she would be assured that nothing she would be wearing would be familiar to Dan in anyway. The last thing she needed was to go out of her way to do all this only to be recognized and everything would be ruined. She would never find anything out if that were to happen and she had already come too far now for that to happen.

She was bound and determined that she could do this she thought as she pulled into the mall. She went from shop to shop looking for what she needed. Makeup, essentials, and last-minute things that she thought about along the way. Soon she was pulling behind the beauty salon. Feeling like a secret agent or world class spy, she knocked on the back door and Nancy let her in.

As she sat in the chair and Nancy fired suggestions at her, they decided not to do anything that would be in any way permanent. Hair color seemed to be out of the question and cutting her hair had never been an option.

With choices running out fast Nancy went to the back of the shop and brought back a black case and set it on the counter. Diane gasped as Nancy opened the strange looking case. It looked someone's head inside it, but as Nancy withdrew the decapitated victim Diane soon saw it was a wig and plastic head used to hold it.

"Whew, I thought you had an extra head and wanted to do transplant surgery this evening" Diane said and they both laughed. "It probably wouldn't do any good anyway" Nancy teased in return. Soon she was a stunning blonde with short, cutely styled hair.

New makeup gave her a definite new look and when Nancy was done and turned her around to see herself in the mirror Diane saw a total stranger staring back at her. "It's perfect" she said, "even I don't recognize me" Diane went on.

"He won't have a clue as to who you are sweetie" Nancy said

as she marveled at her work and nodded approvingly. "Thank you Nancy" Diane said as she hugged her friend and slipped out the back once again, to her waiting car.

She opened the backdoor and peeked inside, seeing if Mike and Greg may have come back unannounced. If either of them saw her like this they would think she was a burglar or something. She really didn't want to explain to either of them why she looked like this.

The coast was clear and she quickly went about gathering everything she needed that was to be packed in her new bag. Her bag packed, her disguise done, and one that would fool her own parents she might add, she was proud of herself that she had done all this on her own. As she sat and sipped a glass of wine and thought. She could only wonder if she was honestly ready for whatever it might be that she would find in Chicago.

She could only hope she was and could hope that what she finds will be nothing but an overactive imagination on her part. Time would tell and that time would run out soon. The flight was leaving at five in the morning and she would be on it.

She turned in early this evening as she wanted to make sure there would be no possibility of her oversleeping. She rose early, dressed in her new clothes, grabbed a soda out of the fridge as she could get coffee at the airport and headed for her car.

The drive to the airport was becoming a familiar one, she thought she could almost drive it in her sleep now. Soon she was parking in the garage once again. This time she found an out of the way, slightly deserted area and parked.

She was certain that Dan wouldn't notice her car even if he too parked in the garage and drove right past it. She was satisfied that the car was unnoticeable and to a point concealed. She walked mostly in the shadows not wanting to be seen or to draw any sort of attention to herself and entered the terminal.

She was a bit early so she could pick up her ticket and go straight to the gate without waiting in a line or being seen by Dan.

She picked up her ticket and went to the restaurant close to the gate she would board from and quickly ordered coffee. She needed it desperately this morning.

She sat by the windows but more in the back of the room. Again she was nearly invisible to anyone that wasn't purposely looking for her. This way she could keep watch for Dan to arrive and make sure he boarded before her.

She didn't have long to wait, he arrived shortly and waited impatiently at the gate. He almost acted like he couldn't wait to get on that plane. Before long they announced they were boarding and Dan was one of the first on.

She waited until last call to board was announced and quickly found her seat. There would be no turning back now, she was on the plane. He hadn't seen her and probably wouldn't recognize her anyway. She was determined to do this, now all she had to do was keep herself from chickening out and looking for a parachute.

The flight took off nearly on time and before she realized it was preparing to land. "That was a short flight" she thought to herself as she readied herself to be one of the first off. As soon as the door was open and passengers allowed to leave, she was out the door and made her way to the front of the terminal. She was sure that he would have to leave through the front even if he hailed a cab to do so.

Diane soon spotted him coming toward the doors. She watched intently to see if someone was picking him up or if he would catch a taxi, as she thought he might. She didn't have to wait long, a car pulled up almost directly in front of Dan and stopped.

A younger woman got out, ran up and hugged him tightly and helped him put his bags in the trunk. Diane quickly got in a cab a few cars behind them and told the driver, "I know this is going to sound like a stupid line from a cheap movie, but, follow that car."

She pointed out the car she wanted to follow and slumped slightly in the back seat. She was already sorry she had made this trip. "Maybe that was a sister or a close friend, she was a bit younger" she thought to herself trying more to make excuses than face reality.

The ride was rather long and seemed to take them to some sort of suburb of Chicago. She was soon able to see that it was an upscale neighborhood though. The houses lining the streets were huge, manicured lawns, professionally landscaped, they were beautiful.

She couldn't believe that Dan could own a house in this area. So once again she was trying to tell herself that his parents must live here and that must be a sister.

She wasn't at all certain at this point if the excuses she was trying to convince herself of were for her benefit or his. At this point she just felt numb, like someone had hit her right in the middle of her heart and she was hoping that things weren't as they seemed.

Before long the car Dan was in pulled into a drive and Diane told the taxi to stop back far enough not to be noticed. Suddenly the front door of the house opened and two small children appeared.

Diane would have guessed them to be between maybe six and ten years old., one boy, one girl. They ran to Dan and each hugged a leg, he quickly bent down and picked them up, one in each arm.

They hugged and kissed him and it was very plain to see that this was not his parents' house. And, that was not his sister, it was his wife and children.

She could feel her heart breaking into a million pieces right now and only wanted to crawl into a hole and die. She wrote down the address and told the driver to take her to the nearest motel. "I'm so terribly sorry ma'am" he said as they drove off.

A motel was close and it too was upscale with plenty of amenities. She was happy for that as she needed to be somewhere right now that wasn't a dump or in a bad part of town. She knew herself and knew that she would be walking for hours trying to sort out all the confusion in her head as soon as she was checked in.

She quickly checked in, said she would only be there for the night and went straight to her room where she collapsed on the bed sobbing heavily. What little was left of her heart was now breaking because she could feel it. She cried until she cried herself to sleep.

Diane woke and freshened up, knowing that she had to find somewhere to eat soon. She wasn't about to make herself any sicker over all this than she already was. She found the motel had an adjoining restaurant and quickly went inside, found a booth in the back and slid in. A waitress appeared soon and took her order. As she waited for her food to arrive, she tried desperately to sort out the billions of things whirling through her thoughts right now.

How she could have allowed herself to be fooled like that. How she fell for lie after lie from that man. Why she hadn't seen the warning signs sooner, they were there and everyone but her could see them. She was interrupted by the clanking of plates as the waitress sat her meal before her and asked if there would be anything else right now. She assured the young woman that she would be fine and thanked her.

She ate without thought, paid her bill, left a tip and wandered out into the warm evening air. All she could do was stand there as if she were lost. She soon found herself walking, paying as close attention as she could muster to her surroundings.

The last thing she needed right now was to become lost. She walked and thought and thought and walked. Neither seemed to be doing any good tonight so she returned to the motel. She learned they had a lounge and soon was seated ordering a glass of wine. Maybe that would calm her nerves and clear the cobwebs of her mind.

The lounge was empty for the most part, she was glad for that. She didn't need company tonight and the last thing she wanted was some lonely guy hitting on her. She listened to the music softly coming from the speakers and sipped her wine.

She just couldn't believe that she had allowed herself to be taken in like that. Greg and Mike both had done their best to warn her in the most gentle and subtle way they could. She chose to ignore those warnings though. Her sons' words kept echoing in her mind, Mike had told her that he didn't trust Dan.

As she sipped her wine and ordered another, she thought back to how things could have been different. Had she only let herself admit to Greg that she loved him and was just afraid of being hurt again. Instead she allowed herself to fall in love with a man that used her and broke her heart.

How could she let such a thing happen she thought. The hours were passing quickly and after several glasses of wine she decided to give in and go to her room. She changed for bed and crawled between the covers, again she cried herself to sleep.

She showered, changed and checked out early the next morning. Going once again to the restaurant for her much needed coffee and breakfast. With every intention of flying back home as soon as she could get a flight, she soon found herself hailing a taxi and handing him Dan's address.

She had the driver stop short of his home. Again not really wanting to be noticed and asked him to wait. She got out, walked the opposite side of the street, and just as she was passing his house noticed Dan and the children playing in the front yard.

She unmistakably heard "Daddy" repeated several times and knew that if even a shred of doubt remained, it had now been swept away. She noticed the younger woman coming out the door to join them. It was everything in her very being to keep from walking over and confronting them both. Telling her how lousy her husband was in bed and shattering his life as she felt he had done to hers. One thing kept her from doing just that though.

Those innocent children, they had no idea that their daddy was anything but a hero in their eyes and she just couldn't do it to them. She stood there, just watching them all, it was Dan that noticed her across the street. He looked directly at her, she was not wearing the wig nor was she trying to hide her identity any longer. He looked as though he had just seen a ghost. He turned completely white and was undeniably shaken by seeing her standing there.

He covered himself well, something that Diane knew first-hand he was very good at and soon his wife and children disappeared back into the house. He walked toward her and asked what she was doing there. Asked how could she have followed him like that, asked what she intended to do now that she knew.

Diane displayed more self control and respect for herself than most people would have been able to. She merely said "I just had to know for myself Dan, goodbye."

She turned and walked back to the waiting taxi, got in and told the driver to take her to the airport. She didn't even look at him as they passed. She looked straight out the windshield in front of her and acted as though he weren't even there.

How badly she had wanted to walk up to him and slap him right in front of his wife. She wanted desperately to hear his wife ask "who is this Dan?" Just so she could say "yes Dan, tell her who I am" and hear his explanation to all of it.

She wanted to scream to his wife that she was the woman her husband had been sleeping with for over a year back in Iowa. She wanted to see his wife throw his clothes in the street and tell him to get out and never come back. But she couldn't face herself had she done any of that with his children there.

That would make her as low and cowardly as Dan and she wasn't about to give him the satisfaction of thinking anything like that about her. He would remember her as a lady with poise and class. A lady that in the end was much too good for the likes of him. She smiled at the very thought, "imagine that, I found something to smile about in all of this" she thought to herself as the cab wound its way to the airport.

She was pleasantly surprised to find a flight leaving for home within the hour. She bought her ticket and waited in the lounge for the call to board. The faster she got away from both Chicago and Dan, the better she would feel. Soon her flight was boarding and she was home quicker than she realized. The house was still empty and welcome to her right now. She wasn't in the mood for company anyway.

She called her parents and asked if they would like to come by for dinner tonight. She also didn't relish the thought of being alone the entire evening and right now family was about all the company she could handle. They said they would be there around six and she was soon busy straightening up the house and preparing dinner. It was a welcome distraction.

As she went about doing dishes, laundry and just everyday straightening up the phone rang. She was shocked to hear the voice on the other end, it was her ex Steve.

She was relieved as she was sure it would be Dan and right now she had nothing more to say to him. As a matter of fact, she had said it all when she said goodbye. Steve asked how her and the kids where, telling her that he was now living in Florida.

He told her that they lived in Tennessee for a short time before moving on to Florida. She told him of Debbie going off to LA for school, that Mike was about to start his senior year and they were all fine. She told him that Debbie was spending the summer at home this year and would be there in less than a week.

Diane found it strange that she could exchange small talk and pleasantries with her ex so easily. Yet somehow found it helpful and healing at the same time. Maybe she had hated Steve long enough and it was finally time to let the past be exactly where it belonged, in the past. They spoke for a while and before hanging up he gave her his phone number and address. Just in case her or the kids should find a need to contact him.

He surprised her yet again before he hung up the phone, telling her that he was so very sorry for what he had done to her. He told her that what he did was inexcusable and unforgivable and that although she may not believe a word he says anymore, and with good reason.

He still loves her to this day and always would. He told her that she was his first love and a person never really forgets their first. He also told her that leaving her was the biggest mistake of his life but he knew it was a mistake that could never be corrected.

She was taken back with his sudden honesty. He had never before given her an inkling of what happen and how. Today she finally felt some closure and was thankful for that.

She told him to feel free to call anytime he wanted as she would never refuse to talk to him and would never turn him away if he was in need of something. "You're right about something Steve. You too are my first love and you never do forget your first" she told him before she hung up the phone.

Her parents arrived early as they usually did and she was glad. She had had a very trying day today. First with Dan then with Steve calling and it was all she could do to keep her wits about her. She told her mom about her call from Steve, it surprised her mother too. "I didn't honestly think you would ever hear from him again after he moved without telling anyone where he was going" her mom told her.

"I know mom, I never thought I would hear from him again either but I'm glad that I did" Diane told her mom. They ate dinner and her dad went into the living room to watch a baseball game on TV. Diane and her mom sat in the kitchen and had a little girl talk.

It was the perfect end to a day with such a disastrous start Diane thought as she walked her parents to their car. They exchanged hugs, kisses, and I love you's, then she watched and waved until they were safely out of sight.

She locked the door behind her and took one last look around the house before going up to her room. She needed to relax and get a goodnight's sleep so she quickly drew herself a warm bath. She soaked in the luxurious bubbles and let her mind go totally blank for a while.

She didn't want to think about anything or anyone right now except herself and how good it would feel to sleep in her own bed tonight. She soaked until she felt the water becoming rather cool.

She then got out, toweled off, put on her pajamas and slipped between the covers. She tossed a bit, thoughts of the day still entering and leaving her subconscious but was soon fast asleep.

Chapter 15

She rolled and stretched trying to fight through the haze of slumber to find the dawn of yet another day. Thinking that yesterday might have been nothing more than a nightmare. She quickly got up, showered, dressed and headed for the kitchen to start coffee. Almost expecting the phone to ring and it would be Dan. She looked by the back door and saw the new bag she had bought to follow Dan to Chicago with.

Then the reality sunk in and she knew that this had been no dream. No nightmare that she could wake from to find all things well and untouched. It was real and what she had learned by following him was as real as anything could get.

Like a slap in the face, it shook you to your very soul and you knew that it was real. The one thing she was thankful for, if she could find anything about the whole mess to be thankful for, was that Dan had at least had the decency to not move in with her and make her relive everything every time she looked around and saw something of his about.

Maybe he had cared just enough to keep her at arms length and that was why she could never get him to commit to moving in with her. At least that was what she thought and what she wanted to think.

She couldn't bring herself to think that she had never been anything more than a sex partner for that man. He had to have cared for her in some strange way or he would have taken advantage of her in more ways than he had. God knows she gave him the opportunity to.

She had offered him access to her money, her family, her house. Her entire life without restriction and he never took the chances presented to him. That had to mean something she thought.

Maybe in his own strange way it was all Dan could offer her, or anyone for that matter. Diane was even beginning to feel sorry for his wife, it was evident that she loves him and trusts him. She doesn't have a clue what he is doing to her behind her back and that is the really sad thing. To love someone so much that you allow yourself to become so blind that you can't see the things that are right in front of you.

Well as far as Diane was concerned Dan was nothing more than a chapter in her life, and that chapter was now closed. She would go on with her life and she would learn something from all this. She would learn that she is capable of loving someone if she just allows herself to. She learned that it was better to take a chance and have it not work out than to close yourself up and block yourself from the world around you.

She learned that life does go on and just because one relationship didn't work out, doesn't mean that the next one won't. And she learned the most important thing of all. She learned that life is to be shared and all you have to do is open yourself up and allow those around to share it with you. She had become so hard and bitter, calloused and withdrawn. She didn't think she was capable of loving or trusting again and all because Steve had left.

She realized that yesterday after having the chance to really talk to Steve. To listen and not blame or judge, to accept and not look for pity. She learned that she was much stronger than she ever thought herself to be.

She found that she has more class and respect for herself, and those she loves, to let people like Dan turn her inside herself again. As she sat and reflected back on the last year and things she would do differently if given the chance, the phone rang.

She again expected it to be Dan with some off the wall excuse about how he was leaving her but it was so difficult with the children, it was Greg. "Are you ok, I've been worried sick since we left" he told her? She assured him that she was fine but told him what she had learned by following Dan.

"I'm so sorry Diane, I thought you would find out something like that in the end. But, couldn't bring myself to say anything to you about it" Greg went on. "You know that I wouldn't have believed a word from you or anyone else until I found out for sure on my own. You know me better than that" she told him. "I know but it doesn't make it any easier to handle or accept does it?" he asked her.

"Did you feel like that when you suspected your ex-wife of cheating Greg?" she asked. Almost sorry she had allowed the words to escape her lips. "Exactly like that, I wouldn't have listened to anyone either, I had to find out for myself to believe it" he told her. "Guess we have more in common that we ever thought" she told her friend. She then quickly changed the subject asking how her son was doing.

Greg told her that they were having a great time but would probably be back tonight. Telling her it was so crowded there with summer travelers that it was really hard to move without stumbling over someone. She told him she knew that Mike was hating that, he liked his privacy when he went somewhere like that.

They talked a bit and Greg told her that they would see her tonight. She told him that she would have dinner ready when they got home and asked how burgers on the grill sounded. Greg asked Mike and told her they both thought it sounded great. She heard Mike in the background holler "hi mom, love you mom, see you tonight mom."

"Smart aleck kid" she said and laughed. She told Greg she would see them tonight and hung up. She went about straightening up the house and doing the dishes from last night before heading to town to pick up things she would need for dinner tonight.

She knew her son and knew that Mike and Greg both would approve of the menu she would have for them tonight. Burgers on the grill, french fries, corn on the cob, garden-fresh salad, baked beans and fresh watermelon for dessert would be the order of the evening.

She grabbed a shopping cart and started up and down the aisles looking for all the things she knew she would need for dinner tonight. With everything she could think of, and some things she hadn't, in her basket she headed for the checkout. She was going to head straight home but decided that lunch was beginning to sound very good right now. And, she really didn't feel like doing any of the work.

She stopped at the local Dairy Queen, ordered a salad and sandwich and just had to have a root beer float to wash it down with. She found a booth and slid in. Soon the place was full of people she knew and before long she was lost in conversation with old friends.

It was a definite improvement over her last couple of days. She was so very glad she had stopped. She was able to learn the current gossip, happy to hear that she wasn't included in it, and catch up with good friends.

She headed home in a much lighter mood than she had come to town in and felt good about that. She put her groceries away and found she still had plenty of time before Greg and Mike would be home. So, she decided to indulge herself with some "Diane time" at the pool.

She went up and put on her little teal bikini, grabbed her root beer float, turned the radio on, pulled up her chaise lounge and laid back to enjoy the hot and sticky afternoon. "It doesn't get any better than this" she thought to herself as she turned from front to back and back to front to keep from burning.

Her silky skin now hot from the beating sun she decided to cool herself off with a few laps in the pool before starting dinner. She swam and splashed and enjoyed her time to herself.

Soon she was peeling potatoes, making hamburger patties, mixing beans brown sugar and catsup together for her baked beans and cleaning corn. She was about to take things to the grill to start dinner and have it ready when the guys got home when they came through the door.

They were laughing and carrying on and it was apparent that they definitely had a good time. Greg quickly grabbed the gigantic tray Diane was trying to balance and helped her out to the grill.

Mike grabbed everything else and followed close behind. She told Mike to go wash up and get his swimming trunks on then told Greg, "you go wash and change too."

Greg and Mike just looked at each other, neither of them was about to argue with her and did as they were told. Greg said that he would be back soon as he had to go home and change but would be gone for only a few minutes.

Mike went straight upstairs, did as he was told and joined his mother by the pool. "Did you guys have a good time?" she asked when her son reappeared. "Oh yeah mom, it was great, too many people though" he said as he started looking for something to snack on.

She playfully slapped his hand telling him he was going to ruin his dinner. "Like that could ever happen" she said as they both laughed. "I keep telling you that I'm a growing boy mom" he said as he went back to looking for food. They were soon joined by Greg and now she was slapping two boys' hands. They were into everything, just like a couple of two year olds.

"Do you two mind?" she asked but couldn't keep a straight face as she asked it. "No, we don't mind at all, you go right ahead, don't let us stop you" Greg said. Of course he and Mike both were moving in the opposite direction when he said it.

Diane picked up the spatula and waved it at them. A playful warning to leave her alone and let her fix dinner. As she put on the burgers, she heard a huge splash, then another. As she turned and looked at the pool she saw Mike and Greg splashing and trying to dunk each other. She couldn't help but smile. She was glad they had come home early, they were just what she needed right now to keep her mind off Dan.

Dinner done and placed on the patio table she hollered and told the "little boys" to come and get it. Mike was the first to reach the table and that came as no surprise to Diane. Her son could outrun the wind if food was involved. Greg was a close second and that kind of surprised her.

She thought Mike would have his plate and be eating before Greg even got close to food. They talked and laughed and Greg could see that it seemed to be good medicine for Diane. He was glad that she wasn't taking it as hard as he thought she would.

He remembered what it had been like shortly after Steve had left and didn't want to see her go through anything like that again. He would of course be there if she had taken it as bad as he had imagined. Then again, she had been very good at holding it together with the kids and family around when Steve left too.

He fully expected it to sink in and hit her full force once she had time to be alone and think about it. And again, he would be there for her. For now he wanted to enjoy the moment and was glad to see her laugh and enjoy herself.

After dinner she told them that they could help put things away and clear the dishes because she too wanted to enjoy some time in the pool. "Yes mom" Mike said as he pouted and hung his head. Greg made little circles with his foot and pouted with Mike. "That's fine, I'll do it myself but neither of you get watermelon for dessert" she said as she started picking things up and placing them on the tray.

Greg and Mike just looked at each other and smiled. They moved like they had been shot from a gun and before she knew it everything was in the house and the dishes were in the sink. They both looked at her and smiled, picked up clean plates and forks and chanted "we want watermelon" over and over.

It was comical to say the least and all she could manage to do, was serve them dessert. These two had definitely made her day and she saw nothing in sight that could ruin her mood.

They finished their watermelon and pulled up chairs by the pool to tell her all about the last couple of days and the fun they had. It did her heart good to see Mike and Greg get along so well. She had been so worried that Mike would feel like he had missed out on things not having Steve around the last couple of years.

She knew that he would need a man in his life and couldn't be happier that Greg had stepped in to help. Greg and his ex had never had children, he always told her that his ex didn't want children as she feared it would confine her too much.

Diane always thought that Greg would have made a fantastic father. She only wished his ex would have given him the chance to find out. They laughed and talked, talked and laughed, letting dinner settle before anyone even got close to the water.

It was Diane that got it all started, without warning she slipped in the pool and started thrashing around wildly. Splashing water everywhere and soaking both men. "That's it, this is war" Mike said as he jumped in the pool and started toward his mom.

"Remember, I am the one that makes your meals" she said with a sly little smile. Mike stopped dead in his tracks, looked squarely at Greg and said, "you get her, I have to live with her." Greg laughed and said, "yeah pal, but she knows where I live" and joined them in the pool.

"Looks like she's got us both" Mike said and winked at Greg, then they both charged her. They splashed and played and had a great time. Diane was so very glad they had decided to cut their camping trip short and come back. Soon Mike was heading in to change and told her that he was going to town to meet friends but would be home early. That would leave just her and Greg, if he too didn't leave.

Diane and Greg went in as well, it was getting dark and they didn't feel like turning on any lights. That would only attract bugs and drive them out anyway. Greg pulled out a chair at the table as Diane poured them each a glass of wine. She joined him and they were soon lost in conversation. She told him all about her trip, what she discovered and how she had handled the situation when she left.

He was proud of her for not causing a scene. It wouldn't have benefitted anyone anyway and would probably only put her in a worse light with the children present. He told her that he was only a phone call away anytime she found the need to talk, and she definitely knew where he lived if she just needed to take a short walk. She was glad to have a friend like Greg so close and always ready to listen and lend that proverbial shoulder to cry on. It meant more to her than he could ever know.

He told her about what he found out when he called Dan's company, about him not being in the area much longer as it was. "I should have told you about it Diane" he told her. "I wouldn't have listened anyway, you know this stubborn redhead" she told him.

"I know but I should have tried, I should have found a way to make you listen" he told her. "Greg you know good and well that I wouldn't have listened, I would have just suspected you of having some ulterior motive behind your accusations and you know it" she told her friend.

"I guess, I still think there should have been something I could have done to make you listen" he said. "Nothing short of duct taping me to a chair and force feeding me would have worked and we both know it" she told him. They both laughed at the mental image they just got from her comment.

"Hey, I never thought about something like that but thanks for the help should the need arise again" he said and laughed. "I'm hiding all the duct tape" she said and they laughed so hard they were almost falling off their chairs.

It felt good to Greg to see her laugh, she had an infectious laugh and to him it was one of the most beautiful sounds in the world. They talked until night was fast getting away from them. He said he had to be going as he had to open the shop in the morning. She walked him to the door and thanked him again for looking out for her.

He told her again that he was but a phone call away should she feel like talking and said goodnight. She waved till he was out of the drive and went up to get ready for bed. She was beat and didn't think she would have any trouble falling asleep tonight. She was right, she was asleep almost as soon as she crawled between the covers. Mike coming in shortly after she had turned in didn't even wake her and it usually did.

She rose early the next morning, showered, dressed and went to make coffee. The same morning ritual she had been performing for years now. She put the dishes in the dishwasher from last night as she sipped her first cup of coffee and tried to fully wake up.

With nothing in particular to do today she decided it would be as good a day as any to go to town and get grocery shopping done. Debbie and her friend Toni would be there tomorrow and she knew that Mike had about eaten her out of house and home. After all she thought, he was a growing boy.

At least that's the excuse her son always used so why shouldn't she just borrow it for a while. In the back of her mind she feared running into Dan and right now that was the last thing in the world she needed to do. She was coping with all of this rather well and knew if she saw him she would lose it.

She was determined not to let that happen. She did pass the office his company had set up, not knowing if she did it to see if she might see him or to see if he had the nerve to come back here and take the chance of facing her.

Either way she drove past and noticed a well-dressed woman coming out of the office. She was a stranger, Diane got the nerve to stop and roll down her window. "You new in town or just filling in for the guy that is usually here?" she asked with a smile. She was quickly told that Dan had requested to be assigned to another area and they had just turned this area over to her.

"Well, welcome to town, hope you like it here" Diane said as she waved and drove off. "I guess that answers that" she thought as she drove off. Dan would not be coming back to town to face her or anyone else for that matter.

She wasn't sure if that put her more at ease or made her that much more furious. At least she wouldn't have to worry about choking that cheating, lying, two-faced son of a.... "Ok Diane, that's about enough of that" she thought to herself as she continued on to the supermarket.

With a slight spring in her step and unexplainable calmness today she grabbed a cart and started up and down the aisles. She knew they needed almost everything as she had let supplies at home dwindle. It was just her and Mike for the most part and she just didn't stock up like she used to anymore.

She was glad the carts were a bit oversized or she would be trying to steer and push two of them right now. She tried to stay away from frivolous or impulse buying and stick to what she knew they needed. So far she was doing a bang up job. She was proud of herself, any other time she would just grab what looked good and fill a cart.

Today she actually paid attention to what she needed and looked for sale prices and bargains. Debbie would be proud of her, she was always telling Diane that she needed to pay more attention to sales and such. With her cart to the point of spilling over the sides, she headed for the checkout before she was in need of that second cart.

As she pulled into the drive she noticed Mike and one of his friends were there, "good you're home, I need some muscle" she said as she exited the car. Mike and his friend just looked at each other and compared biceps, "I think she needs you" Mike said to his friend and laughed. "If you want to eat, I need you too" his mom quickly told him. That was all it took, mention food and that boy would attempt to move a mountain.

Soon the bags were all carried in, everything was put away and Mike was asking what was for lunch. She knew there would be a price to pay for asking her son to help carry in groceries and put them away, after all, it was food. She told them to go out and play with their cars and she would fix something and bring it out to them.

As she was fixing sandwiches for the horde the phone rang. She caught herself cringing as she still feared a phone call from Dan. Much to her surprise and relief it was Debbie telling her mom that they would be there in time for lunch tomorrow.

Debbie told her mom that her friend Toni and her were sharing the driving and it seemed to be going much smoother and faster than when she had made the trip on her own. Diane quickly hollered out to Mike telling him that his sister was on the phone.

He nearly knocked the door off the hinges as he came crashing through the door reaching for the phone. "Hi sis, how's the trip going?" he asked. They talked as Diane put the finishing touches on lunch and she heard him ask just before they hung up, "so sis, is your friend cute or what?".

Leave it to her son to ask something like that she thought as she placed sandwiches and chips on plates and grabbed sodas from the fridge. He handed his mom the phone and grabbed the plates and drinks. "Thanks mom, you're the best" he said as he headed out to rejoin his friend in the garage.

"You must have had either food or money" Debbie said as Diane got back on the line. "How did you guess?" she asked her daughter. "I just know my brother" she told her mom and they laughed. They said their goodbyes and Debbie said she would see them all tomorrow around lunch. Diane told her to be safe and hurry home.

She was so excited that Debbie would be home for the whole summer. It would almost feel like she had never left and she wondered if that was going to be a good thing or a bad thing, then smiled. Diane quickly started burning up the phone lines, calling everyone she could think of telling them that Debbie would be there around noon the next day. She told everyone to be there early and that she was going to have a big lunch to welcome her daughter home.

Diane's mom and dad said they would be there in the morning to help and couldn't wait to see their granddaughter. Mike and his friend came in and asked if she needed anything as they were going to town to pick up some things they needed for Mike's friends car. She told him of her plans for tomorrow and Mike said they would make some stops in town and make sure her friends knew to be there.

They both even volunteered to help set up tables and chairs and Mike suggested stopping by to see if Greg could do a huge banner for the front of the garage welcoming Debbie home. Diane thought it a fantastic idea and said that she would appreciate all the help she could get. Mike assured his mom that they would return soon with more help than she knew what to do with and disappeared out the door.

By early afternoon Diane had a yard full of people. The drive was full, cars were being parked along the road in front of the house on both sides and streamers and decorations were soon being placed everywhere. The majority of them teenagers, friends of Debbie and Mike's.

Parents started showing up shortly with tables, chairs and offerings of food. Diane was overwhelmed, it was almost as if the entire town was pitching in and she was touched that her daughter meant so much to so many people.

Before evening everything was arranged, food was being brought in the morning or had already been dropped off. Greg had made several banners for the house, garage and yard, he even made signs to line the road leading to the house.

It was more than Diane could have hoped for She was moved by all the people donating things or lending a hand to assure that Debbie's homecoming would be a memorable one. She always knew that her daughter was popular but had no idea until now just how much she meant to so many.

Greg, Mike and his friend were the last to come in. They had been setting up and arranging tables and chairs and making sure everything was perfect. She had a late but hot dinner waiting for them and they all sat and ate. The kitchen abuzz with anticipation of Debbie's return tomorrow. Greg told Mike to make sure he stopped by the shop in the morning around ten. He had a special surprise and it would take him some time to finish it.

Mike and his friend Jeff said they both would stop early and help with the project. Diane asked what they were up to now. Greg explained that while they were setting up for tomorrow several of their friends had an idea and he offered to help.

He would make signs welcoming Debbie home, they just wouldn't be described as ordinary signs. Now they had piqued her curiosity and she had to delve deeper into this plot, "spill it you three" she said.

Greg explained that he once had ordered some material that could be used outdoors. Each piece was huge and the job never materialized, so, he was more or less stuck with this stuff. He would put one letter on each piece, they were practically big enough to cover the side of a car. When he was done and the letters arranged, the message would spell out "welcome home Debbie" and would take seventeen cars to complete.

Diane was in total awe, Mike told her that they had enough cars to make the sign. It would be along the road just before she turned in to come to the house. Jeff told her that they were going to video the process and follow Debbie as she approached the house.

"It's going to be awesome" he said. Diane was amazed and could think of no better way to welcome her daughter back home, it had been nearly a year since she left.

With the details worked out for their project Mike and his friend went to his room as Jeff was staying the night. Diane and Greg talked a bit before he too said he should leave so he could get an early start tomorrow. She told him of Dan requesting to be reassigned to a new area and seeing the woman that replaced him today.

Greg couldn't believe that Dan was being such a coward about all this. "He should be man enough to face you and let you have your say in all this" he fumed.

The thought of what that man did to her drove him wild with anger and he wanted to make a trip of his own to Chicago to tell Dan so. He knew that it wouldn't do any good nor would it change or help anything so why bother. He had made up his mind however that should Dan ever show his face in town again he would have to deal with him before he even got close to Diane.

Diane walked him to the door, thanked him for all his help and said goodnight. Telling him that she expected to see him tomorrow when Debbie arrived. “Just try to stop me” he said with a smile. He assured her that he would be there as soon as they were done with their special project.

She watched until he was out of sight and made a final check around. Making sure the house was secure for the night and headed for her room. She poked her head in Mike’s room and he and Jeff were both sound asleep already, she went to her room and soon joined them in slumber.

Chapter 16

Diane thought she was the first to rise the next morning. She quickly showered and dressed as she still had so very much to do before her daughter arrived. As she entered the kitchen to start her morning coffee she was greeted by a pleasant surprise. Her coffee was already made. She found a note from her son on the table saying they had already left to help Greg and would see her later.

She poured a cup of much needed coffee and went to the backyard to check the condition of the tables and decorations as they had sat out all night. Everything was perfect and she was sure her daughter would be speechless.

"That would be a first" she muttered to herself and smiled. Debbie wasn't usually one to have a loss of words. She quickly went in the house to start putting the finishing touches on some things and to start yet others.

Diane's parents had just pulled in the drive and her dad was carrying in an armload of things. She opened the door and greeted them. "Have you seen all the signs along the road?" her mom asked her. Diane told her that she hadn't had the chance to see any of them yet.

She was glad to have the help and before she knew it the house and yard were once again full of people. Some bringing food, some bringing flowers, some bringing drinks, all bringing smiles and good wishes.

The day was going to be a good one and she welcomed the distraction. It had definitely kept her mind off her love life, or lack of. The morning was slipping away fast and Debbie would soon be there. Mike and Jeff pulled in and said they wanted to show everyone some pictures they had taken of the cars lining the road with the signs on them.

Mike went to the computer and hooked up his digital camera and downloaded the pictures for everyone to view. They couldn't believe the sight and knew that Debbie would be ecstatic.

Mike said they had to get back and wait for her. They even had people in town watching for her and were giving updates by cell phone. He told his mom that the sight in town was about the same. People were lining the streets and signs saying "Welcome Home Debbie" were all over the place.

Diane was beside herself with pride and happiness that her and her children meant so much to so many people. This is exactly why she would never move away. Everyone treated you like family even if they barely knew you.

As they sat food on the tables in preparation of her daughters' arrival, the phone rang. It was Mike telling his mom that she was on her way up the road. "She's coming, she's coming everyone" Diane yelled. It looked like the entire town turned out and most of them were in her yard or lining the road.

Suddenly Diane could hear cheers and whistles and knew that Debbie was home. She went to the drive to watch for her daughters' car to come into sight.

Debbie pulled into the drive, followed by car after honking car, people were everywhere. Debbie got out of the car and ran to her mom and grandparents waiting to welcome her back. There wasn't a dry eye to be found for miles at that moment. Diane felt a gentle hand on her shoulder.

She turned to see who had came up behind her and saw Greg. He stood there smiling and crying at the same time. Debbie practically knocked him over as she grabbed him and hugged him so tight he thought he would pass out.

The rest of the day was a festive one, people coming and going all day. It was perfect and turned out better than anything she could have ever planned on her own. Diane felt as if she hugged, kissed and thanked everyone in town.

She was so hoarse she could barely speak at all. The food and merriment went well into the evening and dark fell before the last people called it a night. Debbie was finally able to settle in for the night and her friend Toni was in total awe of the happenings of the day. It was unlike anything she had ever seen before.

Mike and Debbie were soon huddled in front of the television with a huge bowl of popcorn, lost in one of their favorite movies. Diane and Toni soon joined them and before long they were saying goodnight and turning in one by one. Debbie and Mike the last to give in. Diane slept well that night, it was as if everything were right in the world.

For the moment anyway. Her children were both home, teasing and laughing like they had not been apart for nearly a year. And, she felt good about how things had worked out between her and Dan. Even though it had ended badly and she had been terribly hurt. She was glad that she had found out when she had, before she let him get any more involved in her life.

As she rose the next morning, she heard the distinct clinking and clanging of dishes in the kitchen. She could smell the unmistakable smell of freshly brewed coffee rising up to greet her. It was beckoning her to the kitchen. As she entered the kitchen she found Debbie, Toni and Mike already eating breakfast and a place was set for her. She poured her morning coffee and joined them at the table as Mike got up and fixed her a plate. She wondered what they could be up to now.

They were being much too nice and that could only mean they wanted something. She smiled, just like old times she thought to herself as she sipped her coffee. She soon found out that they planned on spending much of the day in town showing Toni the sights and meeting friends. Now Diane could see why they were getting on her good side. They were going to abandon her and let her fend for herself today.

"Just like old times" she thought to herself and smiled. She assured them she would be fine by herself and told them to have a good time. They told her they were planning on meeting friends for pizza later and asked if she would like to join them.

The idea sounded good and she told them to call and let her know what time she should meet them and she would be happy to.

Soon she had the house to herself again, fully expecting to find a mess that would take a week to clean up waiting for her in the yard.

She was dumbfounded when she stepped out. Everything was clean and picked up, the tables and chairs had been put away and she had nothing to do after all. She had been so busy greeting people and thanking them that she completely lost track of what the yard looked like or who had stayed to help clean up.

She went back to the kitchen expecting to find the mess there as she knew that she hadn't done any dishes last night. She hadn't even thought to look at breakfast as she was just so happy to have her daughter home that she couldn't focus on anything else.

"Oh my God, the cleaning fairies have been here" she said as she stepped into the kitchen. It was spotless and everything was clean and put away. She looked about to make sure she was in the right house.

She couldn't imagine who had done all the work as she thought she remembered a mess that would make a normal woman pull her hair out when she went to bed. Maybe she was dreaming she thought as she pinched her arm. "Ouch," no she wasn't dreaming. The only thing she could think of was the kids. They had to have done all this before she got up this morning.

With the whole day to herself now she decided to take in some sun and relax by the pool. She went up and changed into her bikini and took her usual spot by the pool. The only interruption to her day was the ringing of the phone. It was Debbie telling her that they would meet her for pizza at six this evening. With the time now set she showered and changed for dinner. Her trusty old shorts and tank top were the fashion of the evening.

She drove to town and saw the parking lot of the pizzeria was full to overflowing. She could only imagine that her children and their friends had pretty much taken it over for the evening. As she entered the building she quickly found out that she was right. Debbie met her mom and hugged her. "We have a place saved for you right over here" she said as she guided her mom to their table.

Greg was even there and Diane asked how he got roped into this tonight. He told her that Mike kidnaped him and brought him there.

Tonight was again a night filled with friends and good times and she was glad she hadn't passed and made dinner for one. Something she had thought about doing. They laughed and talked, some paired up into teams and played darts.

Others played pool, still others took over the pinball and video games. Diane felt like she was babysitting a hundred five-year-olds. As their party started to dwindle and people were leaving Diane told Greg that it might be a good time to make their break.

They laughed and he told her that he was right behind her. She told the kids they were leaving and she would see them at home. Greg followed her to her car and told her that he needed a ride back to his shop to pick up his.

"You really did get kidnaped didn't you?" she asked and laughed. "You know your son, he can be very persuasive when he wants to be" Greg told her as she climbed in. "Yes I know my son" she said and they both busted out laughing as she pulled out of the lot and headed for town.

Greg told her that he would follow her back to her house as he got out and shut the door. She told him that if he could keep up, he could follow her, as she pulled off getting a bit of a head start. She was feeling rather victorious as she pulled in the drive, thinking she had left Greg in the dust.

As she was getting out of her car and gathering her things she heard a familiar voice ask what had taken her so long. She turned to see Greg standing there. "How in the world did you beat me here?" she asked. He told her that he knew a shortcut and laughed as they went into the house.

Diane poured them each a glass of wine as they sat and reflected back over the last couple of days. Greg was glad to see her so relaxed and happy. He knew that Debbie coming home for the summer was the best thing to help keep her mind off Dan and what he had done to her. As they talked the phone rang.

It was Debbie telling her that they would be staying in town tonight at a friends and asking if she would be all right alone. She assured her daughter that she would be fine and told them to have fun and she would see them tomorrow.

"Got dumped again huh?" Greg asked as she hung up the phone. She laughed and said she was used to it with those two. Before they knew it, and after several more glasses of wine, they found themselves in her room throwing caution to the wind and not second-guessing why. They made love that night like it was the first time for both of them.

It was so complete, so satisfying, so loving. They made love tonight, not just casual sex or too much wine, they made love. It was clear to them both that this was something much more than casual sex between two people with an agreement to keep feelings and commitments out of it.

Greg took her to heights never reached before. They shared something tonight that could neither be denied nor ignored. It was something that neither of them would soon forget, nor was it anything they wanted to.

Diane woke first and went to start breakfast before waking Greg. She knew he had to be as worn out from the activities of late as she was and didn't have the heart to disturb him just yet. She started coffee, put on bacon, set the patient old toaster out to lend its part in today's meal and went to tell him it was time he showered and came down to eat.

She went back to start eggs and put the finishing touches on everything just as he came in the room looking for coffee more than anything. She had a cup on the table waiting for him and told him to sit down before things got cold. He wasn't about to argue with her or tell her he didn't have time, he knew it would be a lost cause anyway.

Greg spoke first and told her that he was sorry for last night. Trying to blame it on the wine and the excitement of the moment.

She wouldn't hear of it, she told him they both knew that the wine had nothing to do with it. And as for the excitement of the moment, they both were willing participants.

He quickly told her that he didn't want her to feel that last night happened out of pity for what had happened with her and Dan. She assured him that it was the furthest thing from her mind. Diane told him that he knew as well as her that it was something they both wanted and neither of them was going to stop until it happened.

He couldn't argue with her on that point. He had been dreaming of holding her in his arms since the last time they had been together. He also knew that right now was no time to attempt to pursue any kind of relationship given what she had just been through with Dan.

Besides, he was more afraid of being pushed away than to live with things the way they were. He could live with their relationship being one of friendship and good sex if that's all she felt she could handle right now. He had decided when they first started being intimate that he was willing to wait a lifetime if he had to for this woman. She was worth the wait in his mind, and heart.

It was getting late and Greg had to go home and change before heading to the shop. He told her that he would call her later and kissed her goodbye. Neither of them wanting to second-guess nor question last night. They both were content to leave things as they were, for the moment anyway.

The rest of her day was as normal as any other and the kids were home shortly after Greg left. They spent most of the day enjoying the sun and splashing around the pool. Toni could hold her own with Mike, and Diane and Debbie were surprised how quickly she was fitting in. It was almost like she too had grown up there and known all of them her entire life. Diane was glad that her daughter had a friend like Toni.

The summer was passing quickly and it would soon be time for Debbie and Toni to return to California. That was something Diane wasn't looking forward to. Diane had several more dates with Tom and in the end they came to a mutual agreement that they were just not compatible enough to be anything more than friends. She liked spending time with Tom.

There just wasn't any chemistry between them that would warrant either of them trying to avoid the inevitable. He was a very nice guy and had become a good friend during their time together. Tom almost seemed relieved as he too knew that they were going nowhere.

He told Diane that should she ever just need a good friend he would always be there to listen and lend a helping hand. They left things at that and seemed to become closer than ever before. He turned out to be one of the best friends Diane ever had and she was happy that she had not turned him down when asked out. If she had, she would have missed getting to know him. With Debbie and Toni leaving soon she spent all the time she could with them. Greg was around more now than ever and life was good once again.

Before she knew it they were all saying goodbye to her daughter, for a while anyway. Debbie and Toni both agreed to fly back for Christmas. Mike was busily getting ready for his last year in high school and had gone out for the football team this year.

Practice and friends kept him pretty busy and Diane was seeing less and less of him. Something she knew she would have to get accustomed to. He had applied to several colleges but was holding out hope of being accepted into UCLA. He wanted desperately to join his sister in California.

Acceptance letters were trickling in, he and Debbie talked regularly and she was doing what she could to help him join her. It was becoming a busy time going to football games, pep rallies and celebration dinners at the pizzeria. Mike was emerging as a star on the football field. Diane was dating, she had been on several dates and as of yet not found her knight in shining armor.

Of course she really wasn't looking all that hard either. Mike finally got his letter from UCLA and had been accepted and offered a scholarship in football. She couldn't be happier for him. He and

Debbie would soon be together again and that put her mind at ease. She knew they would watch out for one another.

Fall had come and winter wasn't far behind. Diane decided that instead of Debbie and Toni coming home for Christmas, her and Mike would go there and get things finalized as they had two years prior for her. Besides, sandy beaches and never-ending sunsets were fast becoming her idea of an ideal Christmas. She already had the plans made and the trip booked.

Mike couldn't be happier and was counting down the days till they left. Greg was taking them to the airport and picking them up as he had the first trip they had made out. All in all life was good and Diane was happy. Her and Greg spent time together and passion was something that was once again in her life.

The trip to the airport was quick and full of laughs. Mike asked Greg if he wanted another bikini from California, Greg was smart enough to pass this time. The flight was now familiar and went quick and they soon found themselves in the same familiar suite they always got. Well the two times they had been there anyway.

They finished their business at school first, leaving the rest of their trip to sightseeing and having time to spend with Debbie and Toni. Mike signed up for his classes, met the football coach and was assigned his uniform and equipment, and like Debbie got a private dorm.

The next two weeks were filled with fun and togetherness and came to an end much quicker than any of them would have liked. It seemed that they had just arrived and were preparing to leave again, the time passed so quickly.

Soon Mike and Diane were winging their way home once again, looking for Greg as they grabbed their bags and headed for the front door of the terminal. Greg hadn't disappointed them, he was there complete with hugs and I missed you's and soon they were on their way home again.

The time was getting away from Diane and before she knew it or wanted it, she would find herself saying goodbye to her son and watching him drive off to join his sister. She decided that the time had come to buy him a new car as well since he would be driving to California as his sister had before him.

Like Debbie, Mike too would have a new car to make the trip with and transportation problems would be the last of his worries. They went car shopping as spring was in full bloom. Diane really didn't want to buy him a new car in the dead of winter, a useful tip Greg had given her.

Greg had mentioned the unforeseen chance of a winter wreck, even if not Mike's fault, would ruin a new car and the chances of him having trouble with it would be greater. She had to agree as it was sound advice and Mike did have a reliable vehicle to drive right now that would get him through the rest of the bad weather in their area.

Spring would be a much better time to shop for a new car and would give him plenty of time to work out any bugs while still at home. They looked at every dealership in town and she let him pick out the models he liked. Then she compiled a list of the ones she liked.

They compared notes and put together a third list of models they agreed they both liked and narrowed down the choice to one car. Mike respected his moms opinion and they both even asked Greg for help as he also respected and trusted Greg's opinion as well.

Soon he was driving his new car and couldn't be happier. It was practical yet sporty and easy on gas. Graduation was fast approaching and summer would follow close behind, leaving Diane to say goodbye to her baby. She of course had a huge graduation party for him.

Greg once again stepped in to help with anything he could. He was so very proud of both Mike and Debbie and couldn't love them more had they been his own children. Diane was grateful for all he had done for her and the kids. Greg had always been there over the last few years and she didn't know what they would have done without him. She wasn't about to find out either she thought, not now, not ever.

Summer was upon them and once again was proving to be a dry hot summer. Humid and sticky, almost sauna like. The pool got more than a workout that year. Mike always had friends over and Diane and Greg took advantage of it every chance they got.

It was a welcome relief from the one hundred-degree heat of an Iowa summer and they all took advantage of it as often as they could. Mike had his things packed and ready for his upcoming move. Leaving only things he would no longer need or things that could be packed at the last minute.

The days were passing so fast and Diane was beginning to feel the anxiety of being really alone for the first time in her life. It left her feeling empty and hollow and she told Greg that he would have his hands full as soon as Mike's car left the drive. He was prepared for it and told her that he was up to the challenge. He had promised Mike that he would look after her and would make sure she was kept busy.

Mike was a bit anxious about leaving home as well. He knew he would miss his mom immensely but knew how strong she was and that gave him strength as well. The day came sooner than Diane would have liked.

She soon found herself sharing hugs, kisses, goodbyes and I love you's for the last time in a long time with her son. They stood in the drive hugging each other tightly, neither of them really wanting to be the first to let go. They were both in tears and knew the time had come.

It was the hardest thing she had ever done in her life but she had to let her son go. He soon would be with his sister and start a new life, a rewarding life. She told him to be careful, to call every night as Debbie had done and stick to the route mapped out for him.

"No detours mister" she said as she kissed him one last time. "I promise mom, I'll be fine and will call tonight" he said. He hugged Greg and told him to take care of mom for him, Greg assured him he would.

By this time all three were in tears and Diane and Greg smiled and waved until his car was out of sight. “I’m gonna miss the big lug” Greg said as he wiped the tears from his eyes. “Me too Greg, me too” she said as she clung tightly to him and they went into the house.

Her and Greg went to dinner in town as she really didn’t feel like cooking tonight and Greg could understand that. They made it an early dinner as Greg wanted to have her back in plenty of time to get her first call from Mike when he stopped for the night.

They shared a few laughs, well, more like giggles, and he could tell she was going to have a hard time dealing with this for a while. They didn’t have long to wait before Mike called and told his mom that the motel was just as Debbie said it would be.

It was nice, clean and comfortable and he told her he had already ate and was ready to turn in for the night. They talked a while and he told her of the things he had seen along the way and soon they were saying their goodnights. Mike said “I love you mom and thank you for everything” before he hung up.

She could now rest easier tonight knowing he was safe. She went through the very same thing when Debbie left and could remember it as if it were yesterday. Greg offered to stay tonight if she wanted the company. He said he could sleep on the couch if she wanted, although he fully expected her to convince him that she would be fine alone.

She did exactly as he had predicted. She told him she would be fine and had to get used to being alone in the house anyway. He could understand her thinking and respect her wanting to be alone. Sometimes we all just have to deal with situations on our own terms and tonight he knew she would have to deal with this on hers.

He told her that she could call even if it was the middle of the night and he would be right down. He kissed her goodnight and headed for his car. She waved and thanked him for everything and told him that she was going to be fine.

That first night alone was a sleepless one for the most part. She was up and down, tossed and turned and even checked the empty rooms of her children several times. She had picked up the phone what seemed like a thousand times to call Greg but never dialed the number. She knew that she was going to have to get used to this.

She showered and dressed and went to the kitchen almost expecting to find Mike there making coffee for her. She soon realized that was more wishful thinking than anything. She was making coffee when she heard a knock on the door. Greg was standing there with an empty cup.

"Are you asking for donations or want coffee?" she asked as he joined her at the table. "Wow, that's a tough one, how much could I get if I were asking for donations?" he asked and they both laughed. It was good to hear her laugh Greg thought. There would surely be more tears than laughs for a few days anyway he thought.

"I think I could find some lose change around here" she fired back and they laughed even more. She was glad that Greg had stopped this morning, she had needed a good laugh right now. She made them breakfast and Greg patiently waited, not wanting to seem rushed or hurried today. He would spend the whole day with her if she felt she needed it.

"Can I help with anything?" he asked as she pulled out plates from the cupboards. She assured him that she was an old hand at this and would be fine. He took that as a no and sat back and waited. They talked and laughed and before he knew it she was practically pushing him out the door. "You have to work today and I'll be fine" she told him. He told her that he could take a hint and laughed. "What are your dinner plans tonight?" he asked before leaving.

She told him that she had planned a nice quiet dinner for two and he better be there around six or would eat it cold. He saluted and said he would be there on time. They laughed and she kissed him goodbye. "I'll see you tonight you nut" she said and watched until he was out of sight. The forecast for the day was like most any other day, sunny, hot and humid so she decided to take advantage of her newfound privacy and do some skinny dipping at the pool.

She went to her room, undressed, put on her robe and nothing else and headed for the pool. Something she had never really done until now. She somehow found this new freedom a bit exciting and exhilarating.

"I could get used to this" she thought as she let the warm water caress every inch of her body. She was glad that her closest neighbor was Greg and his house was almost a quarter of a mile away. She got out of the water, laid her robe on her chaise and let the hot summer sun dry her from head to toe.

As the morning slipped away and afternoon crept upon her swiftly she decided it a good time to get dressed and start thinking about dinner, as she had invited Greg and had no idea yet what she would make. She went to her room, showered and dressed and went to the kitchen to see if she hadanything she could make that would remotely resemble dinner.

She was still making dinner as Greg arrived, he was early as usual. She told him to pour them a glass of wine and she would have salad ready in a minute. He asked how her day went and she told him of her nude sunbathing by the pool.

She blushed as she told him how good it felt. "Now where was I with my binoculars?" he asked and laughed. She told him that he didn't need binoculars to see her naked and he knew it.

Dinner was done and they sat and ate, talking about his day, her day and waiting for her nightly phone call from Mike. She knew that tonight and tomorrow night would be his last nights in a motel as his trip would come to an end and he would meet Debbie in LA. She would rest easier knowing that he was there safe and sound. She still wouldn't rest until she got used to him being gone, but she would rest easier.

Greg cleared the dishes and helped put them in the dishwasher, as Diane poured them another glass of wine. They were about to go into the living room when the phone rang. Greg could see her face light up, he just knew it was Mike. He could tell by the first few sentences that he was right. It was Mike checking in for another night. Mike told his mom that the room was nice, restaurants were close and that he had already ate.

They talked and laughed about all the sights he was seeing and how beautiful everything was. He was as excited as a kid on Christmas morning. They talked for quite a while and she told Mike that Greg was there, he asked to speak to him. "Hey there stranger" Greg said as he picked up the phone. "How's the trip going so far?" he asked. Mike told him all about the things he had seen and told him that he was having the time of his life. The only drawback was being alone on the trip.

He then asked Greg how his mom was handling things so far. "Is she a total basket case and driving you out of your mind yet?" Mike asked. Greg assured him that she was handling it far better than he had thought she would and that they all should be very proud of her. "She's a remarkable lady buddy" Greg told him. He quickly agreed and said that he had known that for a long time.

Greg told him that he missed him and to have a safe trip and handed the phone back to Diane. They talked a while and she could hear in her sons voice that he was getting tired. She told him to get a goodnight's sleep and call her tomorrow night from the last motel.

He promised her that he would and they exchanged goodnights and I love you's and hung up. Again tonight she seemed to be a little more at ease since hearing from her son and knowing that he was once again safe for the night. Greg was proud of how well she seemed to be handling this. They sat, talked and sipped their wine until they both could hardly stay awake. He told her that he really should be going but reminded her that he was still only a phone call away.

She walked him to the door and kissed him goodnight. She

again thanked him for helping her get through another day and said she would talk to him in the morning. "Are you stopping by with that old empty cup of yours again in the morning?" she asked as he headed for his car. "I guess you'll find out in the morning" he said and waved as he backed out of the drive.

Chapter 17

Diane woke the next morning feeling much more relaxed and rested. Not knowing if it was because she had slept well or because she had been so exhausted from lack of sleep, she just couldn't decide.

She showered and dressed and headed for the kitchen to make coffee just in case Greg stopped again this morning. She was determined to be ready for him this time. She was sitting at the table with her first cup when he entered the door. "Help yourself" she said and pointed to the coffeepot.

"I see you were ready for me this morning, you are good, aren't you?" he asked then they both laughed. "Why yes I am good aren't I?" she asked in return teasing him for a comeback. He looked like a deer caught in headlights.

"I got nothing this morning" he said as he joined her at the table. They laughed and talked and she was again glad he had stopped. She was always glad to see Greg though. He asked how she slept, "remarkably well believe it or not" she said. She explained that she wasn't sure if she was getting used to the idea of both kids being gone or if it was more exhaustion as she hadn't slept hardly any the night before.

"Either way I got a decent nights sleep and feel pretty good this morning" she said as she went for another cup of coffee. Greg told her that he really should be going and said that he would stop and say hi tonight after he closed the shop. She said she would be looking forward to it and walked him to the door.

She went about straightening up the house and decided that today was grocery shopping day as she discovered just how low she had let things get when she tried to piece together a dinner for her and Greg last night.

She again needed about everything and had to get used to shopping for one now that the kids were gone. Well maybe for two if Greg kept stopping by. She gathered her things and headed for town.

She spent the whole day in town wandering from store to store seeing if anything in particular caught her eye. The supermarket would be her last stop as she didn't want groceries sitting in the car on a hot summer day like today, it would ruin everything she thought.

She found some things in a local craft store that she found appealing and decided to try her hand at a few crafts. Maybe it would keep her mind and hands both busy for a while she thought as she picked up a few things.

With her shopping done for the most part she headed for the supermarket and grabbed a cart. Moving up one aisle then down another until she had everything she thought she needed. She loaded her things in the car and pointed it toward home.

She was carrying in bags when she heard the car pull up, it was Greg. He hurriedly started grabbing bags to help. Once they had everything inside, he looked about the kitchen and asked if she had bought out the entire town. "It kind of looks like it doesn't it?" she asked with a smile. "It sure does" he said and just shook his head and laughed.

She asked if he would like to stop by again for dinner now that she actually had things to make. He said he would see her in about an hour and left. Diane was glad that her and Greg were spending more time together. He was a good friend and a bigger help to her sanity than he could ever know.

She busied herself putting things away and before she realized it an hour had passed and Greg was at the door once again. They decided on something on the grill. The evening was gorgeous and the pool was so inviting on a warm night like tonight. Greg started the grill and helped with dinner.

Soon they were sitting down to eat and waiting for the phone to ring again. Diane had brought the cordless phone out with them so they wouldn't have to make any mad dashes for the house and take the chance of missing a call from Mike. They cleared the dishes and finished cleaning up just as Mike's call came in. They both were excited to talk to him and see how his day had went on the road.

He told them he was at his last stop and would be in LA around noon tomorrow as he was going to get an early start. He told Diane that he had already talked to Debbie and she was expecting him. She was going to meet him at the edge of town and he would follow her back to campus.

Diane was glad to hear that Debbie was meeting him. She knew her way around and could assure that he didn't get lost. Now she felt much better. They talked for a while and soon were saying their goodbyes and I love you's one more time. She seemed much calmer and relaxed after tonight's call Greg thought.

Maybe because she knew his trip was almost at an end and he soon would be with Debbie. Whatever the reason he was glad for it. As they sat by the pool talking about nothing in particular Diane stood up and asked Greg if he would like to take a swim with her. He quickly told her that he would have to run home and change but could be back in just a few minutes.

She took him completely by surprise as she stood up, took off all her clothes and jumped in the pool. She swam to the side and looked at him, "you don't need to go home and change" she said. He wasn't about to argue with her. He took of his clothes and joined her in the pool, but they weren't doing much swimming.

Their swim was a short one and soon they were in her room making love. The old clique of seeing fireworks was underestimated that night. She saw much more than fireworks. The entire heavens opened up and swallowed them both. They rode wave after wave of passion and bliss, hoping this night would never end. They made love well into the night. They collapsed into each others arms and soon fell fast asleep.

Diane was the first to rise, she showered, dressed and went downstairs to the kitchen like she did every morning to start coffee. As she set about the task of making breakfast for Greg, something she was doing regularly lately, she heard the shower upstairs and knew that Greg was up.

He joined her shortly and she already had that much needed cup of coffee waiting for him as he pulled out a chair and joined her at the table. They talked about where they thought Mike might be on his westward trek as he had told them both that he was going to get an early start this morning.

Diane knew that her son was more than excited about finally joining his sister today and knew that he was up at dawn and on the road again. She was glad this would be his last day. Driving a distance like that is a drain on anyone and doing it alone only seems to make it worse. Greg asked her if she was going to join them in California for Christmas this year or were the kids coming home. She told him that she really hadn't given it any thought yet.

"I guess that's something that I really should talk to them about though" she said as she sipped her coffee. "If I'm going there I should start making plans soon" she went on. "Although it would be kind of nice to have them here this year too, I really don't know Greg, but thanks for bringing it up."

Greg knew that she was not the type to wait till the last minute to do anything. If she was going to join the kids out there, she would soon be making plans, booking tickets and reserving her room for the trip.

He noticed the time and said that he really should be going. He still had to run home and change before heading to town to open the shop. He told her to call him at the shop when she heard from Mike and Debbie. "I want to know that he's there and everything went well" he told her as he headed for the door. She promised that she would call as soon as she knew he was there and kissed him goodbye as he headed out the door.

She watched and waved as he backed out of the drive and went about straightening up from last night. It would be a day like all her other days with the exception of the call she was expecting from her children. She looked at the clock and figured the time difference.

California was two hours behind them and if Mike planned on being there by noon, it would be two o'clock her time. She had plenty of time to straighten up the house, do dishes and laundry and run to town for lunch.

As she showered this morning, she decided she would surprise Greg and take him to lunch. After all he had done for her and the kids and all the times he had been there for them all, she had never done anything for him. Not even something as trivial as taking him to lunch. Today that would change. Besides, it would get her out of the house as she knew that she would only sit and watch the clock trying to will the phone to ring.

With laundry and dishes done and both put away, house clean and things out for dinner, she changed and gathered her things for her unannounced lunch date in town. She listened to the radio as she drove to town marveling in the splendor of a late summer morning.

It was an absolutely gorgeous morning and she was in a light and cheerful mood this morning for some reason. She was almost certain that the activities of last night played a big part in the airiness of her mood this morning and smiled.

It seemed that her and Greg were drawing closer and she still wasn't sure that was an avenue she wanted to go down at this point. She also knew that she wasn't about to shut him out like she had done when she had started dating Dan.

She knew in her heart that she practically lost Greg forever over that and wasn't about to do anything as foolishly as that again. As she pulled in front of Greg's shop and parked the clock in the town square was chiming twelve. As she entered the shop she found Greg at the front counter boxing up a job he had just finished.

"I'll be right with you ma'am" he said without looking up. She laughed and told him to never call her that again. She took him totally by surprise, Diane had only been to his shop a handful of times in all the time he had known her.

Worried that something was wrong he quickly asked if

everything was ok. She told him everything was fine, she just wanted to take him to lunch. He practically jumped over the counter in his enthusiasm. He told his assistant that he would be back soon and opened the door for her.

They went to the diner down the street from his shop. They had the best food and it was the gathering spot for most of the town. She was sure she would know almost everyone there. As they walked through the door they were greeted by waves and hello's and she soon found that she was right, she knew everyone.

She hadn't been to the diner in such a long time and it felt good to reconnect with old friends and people she had grown up with. They found a booth and slid in. Their waitress met them at the table with glasses of water and menus and told them she would give them a few minutes to look it over.

They quickly decided on lunch and gave her their order. They talked and laughed while waiting for their meal to arrive. People coming and going, hello's, goodbyes and waves exchanged. "Nice to see you Diane's" and "stop in more often's" they soon had their selections placed in front of them. They ate and talked some more, small talk mostly, nothing in depth or decisions of world importance.

They finished their lunch and walked back to the shop. Greg told her what a pleasant surprise it had been and thanked her for making his day. She told him that it had been her pleasure but needed to get back so she didn't miss her call from the kids.

He understood and told her not to forget to call him after she heard from them. She assured him she wouldn't and waved as she drove off. The drive home seemed shorter and quicker than usual, maybe because she was so anxious to get the call saying Mike was there and his trip was over.

She practically sprinted into the house expecting to hear the phone ring the minute she opened the door, it didn't. Her wait wasn't a long one, the phone soon rang and it was Mike. He told her that he was there. Debbie had met him and they stopped for lunch. Debbie and Toni were helping him move into his room and were taking him to dinner tonight to introduce him to their friends. He was so excited and Diane was glad his trip was finally over.

They talked a while then Debbie got on the phone telling her mom not to worry. He made it safe and sound and her and Toni were going to show him around and watch out for him until he was familiar with his new surroundings.

That definitely made Diane feel better. That was one of the advantages she saw in having Mike join Debbie out there. They had always watched out for each other and she knew that this would be no different. They were together again and that was important.

Diane brought up the point that Greg had made this morning about whether they would come home this year for Christmas or would she be joining them out there. After a short debate and a vote was taken. It seemed that they would come home and Toni would join them if she didn't mind.

Diane told them that Toni was more than welcome to come back with them. "Then it's settled, you'll have three more for Christmas mom" Debbie said. Diane was happy they chose to come home this year.

They talked a bit longer and soon goodbyes and I love you's were exchanged. They told her they would continue their weekly calls and would talk to her soon. Diane felt so much better now that she had heard from them. Mike was there, Debbie was helping him blend and fit in and she would hear from them in about a week, life was good.

As she was about to go up to her room and change into her robe, and nothing else, to spend the rest of the afternoon by the pool she remembered that she had promised to call Greg after they called. She had nearly forgotten and knew he would be crushed if she didn't call.

He loved those two like they were his own. She quickly called and told him that they had called. Debbie and Toni were helping him get settled and would take him under their wing until he was familiar with the area.

He was happy to hear that Mike had made it without incident and was going to have someone there to help him. He knew that Mike was a strong kid but also knew that he would be more than a little overwhelmed if he had to face this alone. It would be intimidating to anyone to be in a new place like that. Specially if you were an eighteen-year-old away from home and on your own for the first time in your life.

She told Greg that she was going out by the pool for the afternoon but would have the phone close by should he need her. "Maybe I'll sneak up and get a peek of you in that little bikini of yours" he told her. "I'm not wearing one Greg" she said. "Goodbye Greg" she laughed as she hung up the phone and went about gathering the phone, her drink and headed out toward the pool.

She was fast becoming accustomed to her newfound freedom and privacy and was making the most of every minute of it. She turned on the radio, placed it on the table beside her chaise with the phone and her iced tea. Dropped her robe in a heap on the chaise and dove into the water.

The water was warm yet had a cooling effect on her body and the feeling was one that she loved. She swam a few laps before getting out and spreading her robe over her chaise and letting the hot sun dry her as she moved from front to back as not to burn.

Almost expecting Greg to pop around the corner and watch her unnoticed for a while she caught herself looking about for him. She soon was lost in thought and wouldn't have noticed if someone had walked up and was standing right in front of her. A million thoughts whirling around in her mind. Tickets for the kids and Toni to come home for Christmas, Greg and last night, her feelings for Greg and the wonder if they were becoming more than friendship, soon things were just a blur.

She could tell the afternoon was getting away from her and

knew that the blistering sun would soon kiss the horizon setting the sky ablaze with brilliant hues of red and orange. She gathered her things and went to her room to shower and get dressed knowing she would have to start dinner soon.

Soon days were turning into weeks and Diane found herself with more time on her hands than she knew what to do with. She again found herself dating. The several men she had been out with were good company but nothing more.

She still couldn't see herself getting serious about anyone. Yet, there was a definite void and emptiness in her life that she just couldn't fill. The times she felt most complete were the times she spent with Greg and she still couldn't bring herself to look at him as anything more than a good friend and lover.

She knew that Greg was getting mixed signals from her. She was well aware that she was sending them. But, she couldn't bring herself to think of them as a serious couple. She didn't want to push him away or take the chance of losing him.

He was much too important a part of her life to let that happen and she knew it. She could only hope that Greg wouldn't give up on her once and for all and tell her to have a happy life alone, that could kill her inside.

The trip home for the kids and Toni were all arranged and they would be home a week before Christmas. She was more than excited about that. She spent her days doing anything that could take her mind off being alone and her nights with either Greg or going on another pointless date.

Not her idea of what her life would be like when the kids were grown and on their own. Her thoughts recently kept returning to Greg, trying desperately to sort them out and not leave him hanging in the balance.

She knew that the way things were now the only person it was fair to or beneficial to was her. She knew it wasn't fair to him, she also knew that every passion filled night they spent together only confirmed his feelings for her and confused hers for him even more.

She was an emotional mess and needed to sort through all of it before she ended up alone, truly alone, and that was something she did not want.

Greg was the perfect man. He was supportive, loving, caring, loved her kids. Was always there for her and the kids, was everything any woman could possibly want in a man. Then why couldn't she bring herself to open up to him completely and give him the chance he so desperately yearned for. The chance to make her happy.

Maybe it was a fear in the back of her mind that had been there since Steve had left. She thought she found the perfect man in him and look at what happened. Maybe she feared that if she let Greg get that close to her the same thing would wind up happening.

How could she even think such a thing. Greg was nothing like Steve or any other men she had met and dated for that matter. Maybe she should let her guard down and stop holding him at bay. Maybe she should give in to her inner most feelings and finally admit to him, and herself, just how important he was to her.

She knew it was the right thing to do. Even her parents thought the world of Greg and her mom on several occasions had told her what a catch he would be. She would have to sort it out later, she had a date tonight and had to finish getting ready.

Fall was soon upon them and the lush greens were soon giving way to breathtaking shades of golds, reds and oranges. The morning air was crisp and clean and had a distinct chill to it. Winter would soon make its bitter, icy appearance and blanket everything in white. Evenings would find her sitting by the fireplace with Greg sipping a glass of finely chilled wine or making passionate love in front of the crackling warm fire.

These were the times she felt most complete and didn't want them to ever end. Greg had asked her more than once when she would stop fighting the inevitable and let herself fall in love again. She still had no definitive answer for him. All her dates left her hopelessly bored and empty and she soon resigned herself to the idea that she wasn't going to find what she was looking for until she opened her eyes and looked right in front of her.

She could tell that Greg had been on the verge of breaking their cardinal rule and admitting his love for her more than once. She could see it was tearing him apart inside. She herself had fought back the words "I love you Greg" more than once but bit her tongue before the words actually escaped her lips.

She knew in her heart that she loved this man. She knew that he was the one man that she could be truly happy with the remainder of her days. Yet she couldn't bring herself to tell him the words he so longed to hear. She was an emotional coward and knew it.

She hated herself for it but didn't know what to do about it either. Should she give in and finally open the flood gates to her emotions and let Greg share in her secret. Or, hope things would last forever as they were, she was torn.

For now all she could do was hope that Greg would bear with her a little longer and let her sort all this out on her own. She also knew it had to be soon.

Winter was fast approaching and before she knew it the kids would be home for Christmas. She was becoming so excited at the thought of the house coming to life with them running in and out and their playful fights she missed so much.

They called weekly just as promised and things were going remarkably well for them. Mike had quickly become a standout on the football field and had a promising career ahead of him should he chose to take it.

Debbie told her that she had overheard the coaches talking to scouts from the NFL and they were predicting Mike to be a first round draft pick. Greg too had news, he told her of an upcoming trip he had to make to meet with suppliers. Something he usually handled by phone but felt it important enough to do in person this time.

She offered to take him to the airport if he needed and he told her that he would be driving as it wasn't very far away. He told her that he would be gone for a week or more and said that he did have a favor to ask of her if she didn't mind.

He asked if she would mind keeping an eye on the shop for him. Maybe check in once and a while to make sure things were running smoothly. She assured him she would love to. He told her he would call nightly just in case something unexpected came up.

Soon he was packing his things into his car, kissing her goodbye, telling her he would call nightly and would see her in a week or so. She told him that his car hadn't even left the drive and she already missed him more than he could know. He slowly backed out and drove down the road.

It was at that very moment something became painfully clear. More clear than anything had been in her life in a very long time. She knew that she loved him. She loved Greg, she loved him so much she wanted to shout it as loud as she could but it was too late. He had already driven out of sight.

The trip to the airport went quickly and Greg was feeling guilty for deceiving Diane like he had. He wasn't making a trip to meet with suppliers, he was on his way to California to meet with Mike and Debbie.

He had been at the house the last time they called and while he was speaking to them had asked them to call him at the shop where he could talk openly with them about something.

They called a couple of days later due to class schedules and football not allowing them the time to call before then. Right away they asked if everything was ok with their mom.

Fearing the worst he quickly put their fears to rest telling them that he wanted to know if they could pick him up from the airport should he make a secret trip out to see them. He told them that he didn't want their mom to know about the trip. What he wanted to discuss with them would have to stay between them for now.

They agreed and were sworn to secrecy and told him that Mike would meet him at the airport when he arrived. The details were worked out and he was soon on his way. The flight was much quicker than he had imagined and he soon found himself in sunny California.

He grabbed his bags and found his way to the front of the terminal where he found Mike eagerly waiting for him. "Hey buddy" Greg said as he hugged Mike. "I sure have missed you" Mike said as they loaded his bags in the car and headed for the motel.

They talked along the way, more catching up on what was happening back home than anything. Soon they were pulling into the motel. He hadn't booked a suite but nonetheless his room was big, very luxurious and comfortable.

As he stepped out onto the balcony and looked out over the beach he could see right away why they all had fell in love with this place so easily. They sat and talked as they waited for Debbie to join them. Mike had called and told her they were at the motel.

She arrived soon and before long they were huddled together like top secret spies going over a classified mission of world altering proportions. Greg assured them first and foremost that everything was fine at home and their mom was well.

He didn't want them thinking that he was here to covertly deliver some heartbreaking news. Then they settled in for some serious discussion of why he was really there. He started by telling them they both knew that he loved them as though they were his own.

They assured him that they had always known that and loved him too. Greg drew a deep breath and let it rip, his motive for being there. He told them how he felt about their mom and that he was going to stop at nothing to get her to come to her senses once and for all and let him make her happy. Debbie and Mike both were elated. They had always secretly hoped that him and their mom might get together but didn't want to say anything about it.

They weren't sure how he or their mom felt about all of it. They had pretty much just thought of them as good friends. They talked well into the night. Telling each other of their secret feelings and hopes for the future and how happy it would make them to see him and their mom finally be together. Greg was relieved to hear that and knew now that any reservations he and Diane might have had regarding their feelings could be put to rest.

"I'm all for you and mom getting together and will support you and help you in any way I can under one condition" Mike said before they left for the night. "Anything buddy, you know you can say or ask anything of me" he told them both.

"We get to call you dad if you guys get together, ok?" Mike asked as he walked over and gave Greg a hug. "Ditto" was all Debbie could get to come out as she too went over and hugged him.

With tears in his eyes he looked squarely at both of them and said, "it would be the greatest honor I could ever achieve to have both of you call me dad."

The next week was spent touring the campus and meeting their friends. Greg even got to watch Mike at a couple of his practices. They spent every minute they could together and Greg told them of his plan to take their mom in his arms when he got back and tell her once and for all how very much he loved her. Mike and Debbie both said that if that didn't do any good they would lock her in her room until she came to her senses when they came home.

They all laughed and Greg was glad that he had handled things this way. He wanted them to be a big part of his decision to pursue their mother and wouldn't have felt right if he had done this any other way.

They both saw him off at the airport and said they would see him in just a few weeks when they came home for Christmas. They all agreed that this trip would be their little secret, for now anyway. He knew in his heart that he would tell Diane about it at some point but now was not the time.

He could hardly wait to see her as he had missed her with all his heart and didn't feel complete until he was with her. It was as if a part of him was missing. He had called her nightly as promised and told her that he would call when he was close to town. Thinking they might meet for lunch if time allowed.

She said she could hardly wait and would have a table reserved and waiting at the diner if he got in early enough. He called the house and got no answer, thinking she might be in town or on her way he called her cell only to get her voice mail.

Now he was beginning to get a bit worried, it wasn't like her to not answer either phone. Then he thought to call his shop as maybe she was checking in there. He called his shop expecting his assistant to answer, instead he was greeted by Diane. "Is there something wrong?" he asked thinking she wouldn't be answering the phone unless there had been a problem.

She told him they had been short handed this morning at the shop so she came in to do what she could to help. That was one of the things he loved so much about her. Her willingness to help a friend in need even if she found herself in over her head and completely in the dark.

She always did her best to help in any way she could and was always putting others needs before her own. She told him that she figured at the very least she could answer the phone, take messages and run the cash register in an attempt to help in some way. He told her that he would be there soon as he was only minutes from town and would come straight to the shop. She said she would see him soon and hung up.

He entered the shop fully expecting to find total chaos. Instead he found everything under control and Diane taking an order on the phone. His assistant told him what a huge help she had been this morning and that he didn't know what he would have done without her. Greg was so very proud of her for jumping in with both feet and hoping for the best. As she was finishing on the phone he asked his assistant if things were now under control enough to steal her away for lunch.

He was assured things would be fine while they were gone and told them to have a nice lunch. As soon as they were out the door and standing beside Greg's car Diane did something that Greg never thought he would live long enough to see.

She wrapped her arms around him, kissed him deeply, looked him in the eyes and said "I realized something the minute I saw you pulling away a week ago. It wasn't until I saw you drive off that it hit me."

"What is it, is everything ok?" he asked thinking the worst but hoping for the best. "I realized that I love you silly" she said. Greg literally dropped to the pavement, sitting there looking up at her in total disbelief.

She knelt down beside him and kissed him again, "did you hear what I said Greg? I love you, with all my heart I love you" she said. He was in a state of shock and could only shake his head. He almost looked like a bobble head figure as he sat there bobbing his head up and down indicating that he had heard her.

He finally got his wits about him and stood up. Taking her in his arms he told her that he loved her too and kissed her. As they walked to the diner he told her of his plan to come back, find her, take her in his arms and tell her just how much he loved her.

"Looks like I beat you to the punch this time" she told him and they both laughed until their sides hurt. Everyone in the diner waved and said hello as they went to find a booth. It was as if everyone in the place knew what had just happened between them. Everyone was smiling and nodding as if in approval of their decision to finally admit their love for each other. They both knew better but the thought made them smile.

They ordered and ate, made their way to the door waving and saying goodbye along the way and went back to the shop. He told her that he would see her after he finished tonight. She told him that he was coming over for dinner and would stay for breakfast. She kissed him again and told him one more time that she loved him. She liked the way that sounded and didn't think she could ever get tired of saying it or hearing him say it to her.

The drive home was quick and she practically floated to the house. She loved the way she felt and had no regrets for telling Greg what she had. The only regret that she did have was in not telling him sooner. The only thing she could think of was all the wasted time she had spent by not facing her feelings sooner.

She wanted to call her parents, she wanted to call Mike and Debbie. She wanted to climb on her roof and shout it to the entire world. She loved Greg and was going to do everything she could to make him as happy as he had made her.

She instead settled for going to her room, soaking in a nice warm bath and laying out the sexiest thing she could find to wear tonight. Or more correctly, the sexiest thing not to wear tonight. For the time being she simply put on her robe and went to the kitchen to start planning dinner and taking things out to fix. Greg was in store for a night neither of them would soon forget.

Tonight would not be casual sex with a good friend but giving her heart, mind, soul and body to the man she loves completely and totally. Tonight would be the melding of two hearts becoming one, two souls forever joined, two people devoting themselves to each other forever. Tonight would be the beginning of forever and always for them both.

Chapter 18

Diane and Greg spent every moment possible together. She even started helping at the shop. Answering phones, taking messages and ringing up customers sales. Helping not only gave her the chance to be close to Greg but kept her mind occupied and kept her out of that empty house. Debbie, Mike and Toni would be home in less than a week and she was ready. The tree was up, decorations everywhere and Greg had helped with the outside lights.

It looked like Santa's winter wonderland and Diane was like a kid in a toy store with a blank check. Greg couldn't be happier and was anxious as well to see the kids. He and Diane had become closer than ever over the last few weeks since the return from his secret trip.

Debbie and Mike had been kept up to date in the latest developments and couldn't be happier for them. Greg even secretly told them about his plans to give their mom a Christmas she would not soon forget. He told them he was going to propose.

They were out of their minds with sheer delight. They loved Greg like a father and could only hope their mom would accept and find happiness finally. She deserved some happiness in her life after the last few years of disappointment and heartbreak at the hands of their dad and Dan. Greg laid out the plan to them and they told him they would help in every way possible. Anything from getting her out of the house to duct taping her to a chair and locking her in a closet.

The latter was Mike's idea Debbie told him. He said he didn't think they would need to resort to such drastic measures but Mike wanted him to know he was up for it should he be needed. Everything was going as planned, he had the ring bought and had it custom designed just for Diane. He even had his little surprise that no one but him knew about waiting in the wings so to speak. He had never shared this with anyone, but, on their first trip to

California to get Debbie enrolled in school, Greg had ordered a special breed of rose that in fact blooms in the winter. Winter roses.

He had secretly planted them out behind the garage where he knew no one ever looked and had watered and nurtured and cared for them for nearly two years now. This year they were very hearty and full of beautiful blooms. He couldn't wait to show Diane that roses do bloom in the winter around here.

Remembering what she had said the first time he ever asked her when she would allow herself to love again. He was going to show her that this was the time to allow herself to love. He could hardly wait to see the look on her face when she saw them.

The next week passed quickly and everything was ready for the kids to arrive. Diane had gone to the supermarket and stocked enough food to feed a platoon for the entire winter and Greg made three huge snowmen. Each holding a sign welcoming the kids home. Diane was pleased as Greg had taught her how to make the signs and let her help with them. She couldn't wait to see their faces when they were greeted by the large snowy welcoming party.

Diane and Greg rented a minivan to pick them up from the airport. There would after all be three kids and all their bags. They knew that neither of their cars would be big enough and couldn't see the sense in taking both. It was much easier to rent a van and make one trip, one vehicle. Greg parked in front of the terminal and Diane went in. She wanted to be the first person they saw as they got off the plane. She couldn't wait a minute longer to see her children, especially Mike.

He was her baby and had been the last to leave. She felt like it had already been a year since she had seen him even though it had only been a few months. She practically knocked them over as she grabbed and hugged them. "I have to breathe mom" Mike said as she relaxed her grip on him. Mike found a cart while Debbie, Toni and Diane collected their bags. They talked and laughed as they made their way to the front of the terminal where Greg had been patiently waiting for his turn to welcome them home.

They quickly exchanged hugs, loaded the bags, loaded the weary travelers and headed for home. They talked along the way, catching up on everything from local gossip to who was seeing whom now. As they pulled in the drive the kids saw the frosty welcome wagon waiting to greet them and welcome them home.

They piled out of the van and Mike quickly armed himself with snowballs. Debbie, Mike and Toni were soon in a fierce snowball battle as Diane and Greg unloaded bags and dodged stray snowballs.

Once inside Diane told them to get out of their wet clothes, pile them in the laundry and join her and Greg in the kitchen for hot cocoa. They quickly did as they were told. Now it felt like Christmas to Diane. The house was alive again with the children home, her and Greg were a couple finally, and her parents were coming for Christmas dinner.

It couldn't get any better she thought. Little did she know of Greg's plans to make it better but that would come a bit later. They spent the day catching up and Greg and Mike wandered off somewhere by themselves. Leaving Diane and the girls to some girl talk.

Over the next few days Greg secretly put the final touches on his plans. Not even Mike and Debbie knew what he was doing or what would happen and when. They only knew that he was going to ask their mom to marry him and hoped and prayed that she would say yes.

Diane had the funny feeling that something special was going to happen but couldn't unearth anything that would indicate just what it might be. So, she like the kids, waited rather impatiently to see just what was in store for them all this Christmas.

Diane took the kids and Toni Christmas shopping and before they knew it the tree was surrounded by brilliantly colored packages with gold and silver ribbons and bows. It was a sight that couldn't be described with words. Mike and Debbie had taken

Toni to town and met old friends for welcome home parties and gatherings and Diane and Greg made the best of their time alone.

Christmas Eve was soon upon them and still nothing spectacular had happened. Mike and Debbie grilled Greg for particulars but he wasn't talking. Christmas Eve that year was picture perfect. It looked like a postcard had come to life right before their eyes.

There was a fresh blanket of white that fell the night before. Two inches of fresh new snow greeted them Christmas Eve morning. The trees, fences, lifeless bushes and brush were all painted in a fresh coat of white frost, it was absolutely breathtaking. Everything was covered in white and had an almost angelic appearance. It was perfect for what Greg had planned for this evenings activities, even if he was the only one at the moment that knew about them.

The day started like any other. Diane rose and showered, dressed and made her way to the kitchen to start coffee and breakfast. Greg came by early to clear the freshly fallen snow from the walks and drive and soon Mike was helping him. Debbie and Toni helped Diane with breakfast and soon they were all seated around the table eating.

Together, like a real family again, Diane thought to herself and smiled. It was the perfect start to a day that she didn't think could get better. Her parents would be there around four to help with dinner and see their grandchildren. They had missed them so much.

The day passed quickly and soon the house was packed with people, presents, and food and snacks everywhere. Diane had gone all out this year cooking and baking for two weeks prior. They ate dinner, cleared the dishes and everyone went to the living room to gather around the tree.

There was a warm crackling fire in the fireplace and the tree was aglow with tiny white lights. Illuminating the colorful decorations placed about it, it was beautiful. As they sat and talked someone noticed that Greg wasn't in the room with them. Diane went to the kitchen to see if he might be in there, he wasn't anywhere to be found.

As Diane reentered the living room to join everyone the phone rang, it was Greg. He told her to have everyone get their coats on, bundle warmly and meet him in front of the house in five minutes. "Who was that mom?" Debbie asked as Diane stood there with a confused and bewildered look on her face. "It was Greg, he said that we all need to put on our coats, bundle warmly and meet him in front of the house in five minutes" she told them.

"Ok someone spill it, what in the world is going on here?" Diane asked with a huge smile. Everyone looked at each other then her and swore that none of them had any idea what was going on. They all did as Greg had asked and bundled as warm as possible.

Diane and the kids even grabbed some warm blankets from the hall closet and headed out the front door. They all stood and waited looking about to see if anyone could spot Greg or see anything out of the ordinary, they didn't.

Soon they heard the distinct sound of bells. They were getting closer and were coming from the direction of Greg's house. "What in the world" was all Diane got out before the source of the sound came into sight. It was a horse drawn sleigh, beautifully decorated with garland and red bows and tiny white lights everywhere.

As it pulled up to them and stopped they all let out a gasp. It was the most beautiful sight that any of them had ever seen. Greg stepped out of the sleigh and helped everyone in one by one. Telling them to use the blankets for additional warmth as the ride would be slow but cold.

Diane was the last to get in and looked at him in awe. "How in the world did you do all this without any of us knowing?" she asked. He joined them in the sleigh, told the driver to go and snuggled under a blanket with Diane, telling her this was only the beginning.

The ride wasn't a long one but very enjoyable. It was one that none of them would soon forget. There were containers with fresh, hot apple cider, cinnamon sticks and cups to help keep them warm during the ride, it was unbelievable.

Not really paying any attention to where they were going, they talked and laughed and soon came to a stop. Diane looked and noticed they were behind her garage in the backyard.

"What in the world are we doing here?" she asked as Greg helped her out of the sleigh. "You'll find out soon" was all he would tell her. He strategically planned the ride so the sleigh would block anyone from viewing his final and biggest surprise. His bed of freshly blooming roses.

Soon everyone was unloaded and standing about wondering what exactly would happen next. They didn't have long to wait as Greg was well aware that it was cold out. Besides he couldn't keep this to himself a moment longer. "Some of you are already aware of this, some it may come as a surprise to you" he started. He took Diane's hand in his and went on.

"I have loved this woman for a very long time now. I was merely waiting for her to come to her senses and love me in return" he said. "That finally happened a few short weeks ago and she made me the happiest man in the world, well almost the happiest" he continued. Diane's parents looked at each other and hugged each other tight. They had been hoping that their daughter would again find love and happiness and thought the world of Greg.

Greg now turned to look Diane in the eyes and went on. "Diane I asked you one time when you would ever allow yourself to love again. Do you remember what you told me?" "I told you that I would allow myself to love when roses bloom in the winter around her" she answered him.

"But Greg, we know that doesn't happen here and I love you anyway" she said. At that moment Greg nodded and the driver pulled the sleigh forward revealing the secret Greg had been protecting for two years. A large bed of freshly blooming roses, everyone gasped.

Then Greg did something that no one expected. He took Diane

by the hand and led her to the blooming plants and knelt before her. "These are special roses" he told her. "As a matter of fact one of them has a tiny secret to reveal to you. It's the one with the red ribbon tied to it" he said as she bent down to take the delicate bloom in her hand.

"Open it carefully" he told her as she almost surgically parted the petals of the tiny bud. She gasped and put her hands over her mouth. "Go ahead, take it out" he told her as she again opened the bud and daintily reached inside. She withdrew the most beautiful diamond ring she had ever seen.

"Now I would like to ask you to make me the happiest man in the world Diane. I love you with every ounce of my very being and you know that" he said as tears formed in his eyes. "I want to share my life with you in every way and show you that happiness is ours if we take the chance to face it together" he went on.

"Diane, will you please marry me and spend your life with me?" he asked on bended knee in front of those beautiful blooming roses. Everyone there that night was in tears, not tears of sorrow but tears of joy. "Say yes mom" Mike said and nudged her. She turned to look at her children and parents, everyone was nodding yes. "Yes Greg, yes, yes, yes, I'll marry you" she said as she pulled him to her and kissed him.

He carefully took off her glove and slid the ring on her finger. "I love you Diane, I think I always have and know I always will" he said as he thanked the driver. The sleigh pulled out of sight and they all returned to the house. Soon they were all once again gathered in the living room in front of the fire.

Diane was showing everyone her ring and it was soon clear that this would indeed be a Christmas that none of them would soon forget. Debbie and Mike ran to Greg and literally knocked him over as they hugged him. The three wound up in a huddled heap on the living room floor.

Now Diane knew that nothing in this world could make this Christmas better than it was right now at that very moment. She had once again found love and knew in her heart that it was a love that would last a lifetime. Her children loved Greg as much as he loved them and they couldn't be happier for them.

Even her parents agreed that this was the greatest present they could have ever hoped for. The house was once again filled with love and togetherness. It was once again a family home.

Mike and Debbie made the best of the time they had left on this trip by spending as much time as they could with their mom and Greg. Toni soon realized that she was a part of this family. They included her in everything they did and she couldn't be happier for her friends or Diane and Greg had they actually been family.

Greg finally told Diane of his trip to see them in LA. Debbie and Mike told her they agreed to them being a couple under one condition. Diane couldn't wait to hear what that condition might be.

They told her what they had told Greg and she couldn't be happier. Their own father had cut himself out of their lives and she knew that they too had a void that needed to be filled. She was glad they chose Greg to fill it.

She was ecstatic that they wanted to call Greg dad. Greg was even happier and felt like he finally had a family of his own. Soon Diane and Greg were taking them to the airport and seeing them off until the summer.

Diane and Greg had set a date while they were home and decided to wait till summer so the kids could be in the wedding. Debbie would be Diane's maid of honor and Mike would be Greg's best man.

They were all so excited and couldn't wait to help them make all the plans. Even Toni would be in the wedding and help them with the plans. "Bye mom, bye dad" they hollered in unison and waved as they boarded their flight home.

"That sure sounds good to hear that" Greg told her as he wrapped his arm around her and they walked to the car. The drive home was one Diane actually looked forward to now. Before all she had to look forward to was an empty house, Greg had changed all that.

She knew they had so very much to discuss and work out yet. But, she also knew they would make it happen. Greg put his house up for sale and moved in with Diane shortly after the kids went back.

He was spending all the time he could with Diane and neither of them saw the benefit of having separate homes any longer. They decided to put off shopping for wedding dress and major details until Mike and Debbie were home for the summer and could help.

It was Greg's idea for Diane to let Debbie help her pick out her wedding dress. He knew that anything they agreed on would be breathtaking. Greg would wait for Mike to help him pick out tuxes and things. Summer would be upon them before they knew it he told her.

The weekly calls from the kids were now ended with mom and dad instead of mom and Greg and they only got happier and closer with time. The kids had even asked them to come out for spring break and they could make an early vacation of it. Diane and Greg quickly accepted the offer. Spring came quick and Diane and Greg soon found themselves lounging on the beach with the kids marveling at the spectacular sunsets.

Summer was soon upon them and they were once again making the familiar trip to the airport to pick up the kids. Soon they would all be busy picking out this and that. Dresses, tuxes and making all the final arrangements.

They decided that Greg's shop would do the invitations and printed things they needed. After all, that was what he did for a living. The arrangements were finally made.

Flowers, cake, church, everything was ready and the reception would be held at the house. It would be a wedding the entire town would turn out for and a day full of celebration and new beginnings.

Debbie, Mike and Toni enlisted the help and generosity of everyone they knew and soon tables, chairs, tablecloths, decorations and everything that could be imagined were set up and waiting for the "I do's" to be completed. The big day was now upon them and it was proving to be a day they would never forget. Diane's dad would give her away and Mike, Debbie and Toni would stand up with them.

The ceremony was beautiful and everything they expected. Everyone had tears streaming and people lined the streets to greet them as they emerged from the church as man and wife. Greg had arranged for their trip to the house to be in a pure white horse drawn carriage pulled by two white horses, it too was gorgeous.

The reception proved to be as big and extravagant as they expected. Everyone from town was there to celebrate the beginning of their new life together. Their honeymoon was the whole summer and spent with the kids, it was the best time they had ever had.

Before they knew it, time had crept up on them and it was once again time for the drive to the airport to see the kids off. That summer they all decided that Mike and Debbie would spend summers in LA and Christmas at home.

Christmas had taken on a new and special meaning now and none of them could imagine not spending it together at home. With hugs, kisses, goodbye mom and dad's out of the way they soon disappeared through the door to board their flight.

The trip home was now one Diane looked forward to. She knew that she would no longer return to an empty house and loneliness but to a home with her husband. What a difference a year had made in her life. It had made a difference in all of their lives.

Greg and Diane were inseparable, they spent every moment they could together. They did everything together and life couldn't be better. They even started sharing a chore that had been born out of love.

They now took care of their winter rose garden together, nurturing and loving them. The love they shared together soon took root in their special roses. Each winter seemed to bring more blooms than the last, heartier and more beautiful with each passing year.

Christmas at their house found a new tradition also. Each year Greg arranged for the family sleigh ride complete with apple cider and cinnamon sticks ending at their garden of winter roses. They made the trip to California to see Debbie graduate with her bachelors' degree. Debbie decided to go on with her education and try to get her doctorate.

Mike was making quite a name for himself in the world of sports and had contracts lining up as soon as he completed his senior year. There was no doubt that Diane and Greg would soon be watching their son play football every Sunday on television.

Diane's parents bought Greg's house and moved into it the summer they were married. Greg thought it best to have them closer to them as they got older. He loved her parents and by them being close they could lend a hand as often as they needed it.

Each year that passed brought the two of them closer than the last. They soon realized that love never fades but grows and blossoms if shared and nurtured, like their roses. Diane never heard from her ex Steve again.

It was unclear if he had stayed in Florida or moved on to parts unknown. What started out as a favor to someone Greg thought to be a friend, one more out of pity and feeling sorry for Diane and the kids, had grown into a love that neither of them knew possible.

One thing was certain though. They both knew in their hearts that this was a love that would and could stand the tests of time and would rise above all obstacles. They proved that each and every day. To themselves, their family and friends and more importantly to each other.